To Christin... ... ... You were a little more than two when you toddled into my day care, and almost thirteen now. With your black hair, flashing brown eyes, and affectionate nature, it isn't hard to imagine the woman you'll become and the hearts you'll break along the way. Miss Sherrie loves you.

Sherrie Eddington

For my three lovely nieces, Jennifer Selvidge, Lesley Selvidge, and Jessica Selvidge, and the brothers who gave them to me, Les and Mike.

Donna Smith

Prologue

"Mini, that cat has been staring at me for an hour."

Her husband's fearful whisper jarred Mini out of a light doze. She lifted her head and blinked, following his line of vision to a cage built into the wall of the transport truck. Huddled in a corner of the cage crouched a tiny black-and-white kitten, its eyes a marvelous emerald green. The poor thing looked terrified.

"It's just a kitten, Reuben."

"But look at the way she's staring at me!" Reuben persisted. "I get the distinct impression she'd like to eat me."

Mini couldn't resist teasing him. "Well, we *are* birds, darling. You know how the food chain goes." After two hundred years of marriage, Mini still couldn't understand his unreasonable fear of animals, especially cats. She suspected she was the only witch alive who didn't own at least one cat.

Reuben blinked his beady eyes, offended by his wife's amusement. "It's not funny. I still haven't forgiven you for turning me into a bird, and I'm especially displeased about this latest stunt you've pulled." He flapped his wings to emphasize his point. "You should have discussed it with me first."

"You would have said no."

"Precisely!" Reuben cried.

"Which is why I didn't consult you, bird brain!" Mini could feel her patience running out. "You were driving me crazy—I had to do something."

"So you agreed to this assignment without a thought for my feelings."

"On the contrary, I was thinking of *you*," Mini argued. "If we succeed in getting Justine and Zachary together, the Peacemaker agreed to reduce our sentence. I, for one, will be glad to get out of these feathers and back into my witch's robe."

Reuben began to pace on the perch, his fear of the cat forgotten for the moment. "I'll be glad to return to my witch status as well, but I want you to promise me you'll never do this again." He slanted her a warning look, ruffling his feathers in an effort to look imposing. "The next time you lose your temper, point that witchy finger of yours elsewhere. The Peacemaker warned us that she won't tolerate another embarrassing display. We're setting a bad example with our domestic squabbles."

"I've apologized a hundred times," Mini said stiffly. "How many more will it take to convince you that it won't happen again? I don't like being a bird any more than you do."

Slightly mollified, Reuben ceased his agitated pacing and ambled closer to his wife. "Which brings me back to our present predicament. Our powers are limited, and from what I saw in your crystal ball, it will take more than a little magic to get these two star-crossed lovers back together."

"I don't agree. Justine and Zachary belong together. You saw for yourself how perfectly matched they were when they met on the cruise ship."

"That was over a year ago. People change, Mini."

Ignoring his pessimistic outlook, Mini lifted her foot and studied her claws, idly wondering if the mortals would notice if she zapped on a light coat of paint.

Sadly aware that Reuben wouldn't recognize romance if

it slapped him on his beak, she pointed out, "They're both still single. That should tell you something, darling. After a year of trying to forget each other, at least one of them should have had a serious relationship. Instead, Justine spent her free time cleaning cages and feeding fish at her pet shop, and until Zack came to his senses, he had immersed himself in his father's business."

Reuben tried to wiggle his eyebrows before he remembered that he didn't have any. "Yes, but when he *does* date—wow! I have to admit that his taste in women—"

"Reuben!" Mini bristled, glaring accusingly at her husband. "Have you been using my crystal ball when I'm not around?"

"Uh, no, dear. . . ."

The transport truck hit a pothole, sending the cages clanging against each other. Mini and Reuben were momentarily distracted as they scrambled for a foothold on the perch. The entire trip had been bumpy, further agitating their frayed tempers.

"I don't believe you!" Mini screeched, startling the kitten. It hissed and spit, batting at the bars of the cage as if to counter an attack.

Reuben stared at the frightened cat in horror. Slowly he crumpled to the cage floor.

Her beak open in shock, Mini hopped down to where her husband lay. "Why, the silly warlock's fainted," she muttered. "What in the world will he do if he sees the snakes?"

One

꩜

"Won't you at least consider it? Christopher can manage the store for a week, can't he? He's been working here long enough to know the business."

Up to her elbows in fishy water, Justine Diamond tried to ignore her badgering sister-in-law and concentrate on catching the elusive *Betta splenden*. Finally she trapped the slippery fish against the glass and scooped him into the net.

The patchy area marring the deep red of his skin confirmed her worst fears. "It's ick all right," Justine announced grimly. She brought the tiny net closer to the light hanging above the aquarium. The *Betta splenden*, a Siamese fighting fish well known for its aggressive behavior, squirmed helplessly in the net. "There's a slim chance the others aren't contaminated since he's had his own little corner of the aquarium." If she could only get so lucky. The last time she had lost an entire tank of expensive tropical fish to the dreaded affliction.

Beatrice Diamond folded her arms and refused to budge as Justine attempted to pass her in the narrow aisle. "Ignoring me won't make me go away," she warned. "You need this vacation, and so do I! Clay can't go because of that silly trial coming up, so that leaves you. It's been over a year since your last vacation, Justine. I know how hard you work, and it just isn't healthy for a woman your age."

Justine cupped her hand under the dripping net. She faced Bea with a calm, serene expression that she knew drove her sister-in-law nuts. Hopefully Bea wouldn't guess how much she was trembling inside at the mere mention of a cruise ship. "He won't last much longer out of water, Bea. I have to put him in the quarantine tank."

With an explosive, exasperated sigh, Beatrice moved aside. But Justine knew her well enough to know she wasn't about to admit defeat. With Bea on her heels, she made for a small isolation tank and carefully lowered the Betta into the water.

She turned to find Bea glaring at her. When anger didn't work, Bea would plead, which would be harder to ignore. Justine hesitated. She could end the entire discussion by telling Bea why she would never go on another cruise, but even after a year she couldn't bring herself to confide in Bea. The memory of her stupidity still made her cringe.

"This is a *free* vacation, Justine. They drew Clay's name at the Christmas party last year. A *free* seven-day cruise to the Bahamas, meals included."

"I know." In fact, Justine could recite the entire vacation package by heart, thanks to Bea.

"I'll handle the extras, so you won't be out a single penny."

"I can't."

"I'll buy you a new wardrobe, too," Bea promised recklessly.

"No, thanks." Mildly amused, Justine wondered if her brother had suffered the same relentless attack before he convinced her he couldn't go. "Why don't you take Jennifer?" Jennifer was Bea's best friend. She was single, childless, and operated a beauty shop down the street. In Justine's eyes, she would be the obvious choice.

Bea grimaced. "She doesn't trust any of the girls to watch the shop."

"I don't blame her," Justine retorted. She wiped her hands on a towel and threw it aside, waving her hand in the direction of the north wall where a long row of aquariums were shelved. "I took *one* day off to have my teeth cleaned, and look what happened—the fish have ick. I could lose the entire stock."

"They're just fish!"

Justine placed her hands on her hips. "Those fish are part of my bread and butter." She also sold birds, dogs, cats, and had recently added an exotic animals section to her inventory, much to the delight of her three nephews, but the majority of her income came from selling a wide variety of tropical fish.

"Won't you even consider it?" Bea pleaded.

This was the part that Justine dreaded most. She loved her sister-in-law—considered Bea the sister she never had—and found it nearly impossible to resist her when she pleaded.

But going on another cruise was out of the question; she'd never survive the memories it would evoke.

"No, I won't consider it, Bea. I can't go." Justine gentled her voice before adding, "The simple truth is, I don't *want* to go."

"But why? You've said yourself that you had the time of your life on your last cruise." When Justine blanched visibly, Bea's gaze narrowed with suspicion. "You *did* have a good time, didn't you, Justine? You didn't leave anything out?"

Not for the first time, Justine was tempted to blurt out the whole ugly story. But not all of it was ugly, she amended silently, and that was the part she couldn't talk about.

Unfortunately she couldn't forget it, either—or Zachary Wayne, hunk extraordinaire. In the rare moments when she allowed herself to remember, she wondered where he was and if he was still laughing at how easily she'd fallen into his arms.

In the end, she wisely changed the subject. "What about the boys?" She knew her brother put in a lot of hours at the firm and very few at home.

"Jordan and Drew are old enough to stay by themselves, and they've already agreed to keep an eye on their brother."

It seemed Bea had everything worked out, Justine thought, searching her mind for another obstacle. "And Jordan's football games? You're willing to miss those?" Her sixteen-year-old nephew was an avid player, and Bea his most fanatic fan. Justine knew that her sister-in-law taped every game Jordan played.

Bea's pleading expression suddenly underwent a startling change. She bristled, her blue eyes darkening to a stormy gray. "I haven't had an opportunity to tell you, have I?"

Bewildered, Justine shook her head. "Tell me what?"

"That Jordan's been kicked off the team!"

Justine's shock was genuine. She knew what football meant to Jordan, and what his playing meant to her brother. "Are you serious? Why—who—"

"That new coach, that's who!" Bea snarled, effectively distracted from her mission. "Jordan made one lousy C−, and the coach gave him the boot. Says he won't allow *idiots* on the team."

"He actually called Jordan an *idiot?*"

"Something like that. I mean, I know the rule book says the boys have to maintain a certain average, and I agree, but this call wasn't fair. Jordan got the flu and missed an oral test."

"Didn't his teacher give him a chance to make it up later?"

"That later was *after* report cards. There was a mix-up or something, but this new coach refused to budge. Jordan said that *he* said he could come back when he brought the grade up to par."

In the room adjacent to the main shop, a puppy began to whine and bark. Others soon followed his cue. A parrot began to call out in a nasal, whiny voice, "Hello! Hello! Hello!" His repetitive greeting, interspersed with nerve-wracking screeches, never failed to incite a riot among the other birds.

Justine hated to leave Bea so clearly upset, but it was feeding time. Soon they wouldn't be able to hear each other anyway. "There has to be something we can do," she said, raising her voice above the din, "but right now I'm being paged."

Covering her ears with her hands, Bea shouted back, "Come by for coffee after you close! I don't intend to let Coach Wayne get away with this!"

Long after she'd gone, Justine stood frozen by the counter, trying to convince herself she'd heard Bea wrong. Surely there were a thousand Waynes in the world. A million. She shook her head, firmly, then again for good measure. No, of course it wasn't the same man who had left her on a cruise ship without a word of explanation after the most memorable four days of her life.

It couldn't be, because if it was, there wouldn't be enough room in this town for the both of them.

"Hello! Hello! Hello!"

"You'd better shut him up, Mini, or I'll—"

"Okay, Okay!" Mini assured her irate husband hastily. Thank the stars Justine had taken them directly to the room housing the birds before Reuben recovered from his fainting spell! He remained blissfully oblivious to the fact that only a few yards away in another small room lounged a variety of reptiles from snakes to harmless little turtles.

She didn't think it would matter to Reuben that the reptiles were safely ensconced in aquariums.

Facing the parrot, she folded her pretty green feathers and mumbled a quick spell. "There, that should do it. He won't be saying hello for a long while."

"Good-bye! Good-bye! Good-bye!" the African gray parroted.

Reuben cast Mini a look filled with disgust. "That's what I get for sending a witch to do a warlock's job!" he sneered.

Mini lowered her beak, ready to flog the sneer from his face. "You'd better watch your mouth, buster!"

"I would if I *had* a mouth," Reuben retorted. "Thanks to you, I have a beak sharp enough to slice bread!" Suddenly, his eyes widened on the doorway leading into the main store. "Shh! Justine's coming this way!"

Mini's anger deflated instantly. She took one look at Justine's pale, tension-filled face and whispered pityingly, "Bless her heart. Bea gave her quite a scare, didn't she?"

"She'll be a lot worse when she finds out the new coach *is* Zachary Wayne," Reuben mumbled.

Sidling close to him, Mini resumed her role of a lovebird and pressed her bright yellow chest against his in a loving caress. "Hopefully she'll give him a chance to explain why he left without telling her good-bye," she whispered in his ear.

"You mean, you hope he gets the chance *before* she throws something at him?" Reuben's own low whisper grew husky as Mini continued to stroke his feathers. She lifted her foot and rubbed it up and down his wrinkled leg. "Mini, if you don't stop that, we're going to give Justine a shocking lesson about the birds and the bees."

"Probably nothing she hasn't seen before," Mini purred throatily.

Relaxed by Mini's seductive voice and familiar touch, Reuben nearly fell from his perch as the parrot began to squawk again at the sight of Justine.

"Good-bye! Good-bye! Good-bye!" The abrasive screech that followed was a rude assault to the ears.

"That does it," Reuben muttered darkly. He stretched a green-feathered wing to its full glory, pointing it with ominous intent at the unfortunate parrot.

"No! Reuben . . ." Mini hid her beak in her wing, unable to watch. She was so thankful his warlock powers had diminished with his size!

"Good . . ."

Justine paused with her hand on the cage door housing the canaries. The parrot had stopped abruptly, as if someone had clamped a hand over his beak. "Ridiculous," Justine scoffed out loud. Ignoring the odd shiver that rippled along her spine, she finished feeding and watering the canaries and closed the cage doors before approaching the *African gray*.

The parrot hopped anxiously from perch to perch, flapping his wings, but remaining oddly silent. Frowning, Justine came closer and peered into the cage. She gasped and drew back.

There was something circling the parrot's beak!

She opened the door and reached slowly inside, removing the strange contraption from the parrot's beak. Her gaze went wide as she held it up to the light. She rubbed her eyes and looked again. Made entirely of leather, it resembled a muzzle used to keep dogs from barking.

Justine clutched the miniature muzzle and turned around, her gaze running rapidly around the room. This had to be some kind of practical joke, she reasoned, fully expecting to find one of her nephews lurking behind a cage.

She saw nothing out of the ordinary; monk parakeets, with their brilliantly hued colors of green, gray, and blue; canaries, in bright yellow and olive green; finches; cockatoos; and a pair of adorable masked lovebirds that had arrived on last week's truck. A black mask covered their faces, a bib of yellow circled their necks, and olive green colored their wings and tail. It was difficult to distinguish the sex of lovebirds, but in this particular pair, the female was marked by a gold band circling her leg.

Birds. The room was full of colorful birds, certainly none of which were capable of muzzling an irritating *African gray* parrot. Justine chewed her bottom lip, her gaze returning to the lovebirds. Her interest sharpened. The female lovebird appeared to be flogging the male, battering him with her wing in an act of uncharacteristic violence. She knew the species to be loyal and loving to their mates, not hostile!

Silently Justine approached the cage. The moment the female bird caught the movement, she instantly stopped flogging the male and became as still as a statue. The male lovebird seemed to glare at his mate before he calmly began smoothing his feathers into place.

"What's up with you two, huh?" Justine murmured softly. Maybe Bea was right and she *was* spending too much time here, because the look the male had given his mate had seemed almost . . . human. With a sheepish grin, she shook her head and turned away.

Someone whispered behind her. She couldn't make out the words exactly, but it sounded something like, "Complete idiot," followed by a grunting sound. Justine stopped in her tracks. The hair on the back of her neck prickled to attention. Slowly she turned around and faced the lovebirds again.

They stood balanced on the perch, and this time they were huddled together as if they couldn't get enough of one another.

Justine relaxed, smiling at her own foolishness.

Just a pair of lovebirds, nothing sinister or human about them. Still : . . she couldn't forget the abuse she'd witnessed. She tapped a finger against her jaw as she studied the two lovebirds. Just to be on the safe side, maybe she should bring them to the front of the store. There she could keep a sharp eye on them and also give customers an opportunity to see them when they walked in.

By the time Justine finished feeding the rest of her critters, cleared the end of the long counter near the front door, and settled the cage securely on the worn countertop, it was five o'clock. She dusted her hands and shook a stern finger at the lovebirds. "If I catch you two fighting again, I'll have to separate you."

It was an uncanny coincidence, Justine told herself, that the female chose that moment to settle her wing over the male's feathered back. But darned if it didn't look as if she were trying to reassure her!

Pushing the silly thought away, Justine clipped the water bowl back onto the cage wires and closed the door. "I guess I need to call you something," she mused aloud. "How about Luke and Laura? Of course, this is just temporary. Your new owners will probably rename you."

"Do they really understand what you're saying?"

The voice, deeply sexy and achingly familiar, caused Justine's heart to do a triple somersault. Her back went rigid; her fingers turned white where they gripped the counter. When her vision grayed alarmingly, she focused her dilated gaze on the lovebirds.

They seemed to be watching her intently. Not the newcomer behind her, but *her*, as if gauging her reaction. She grabbed the insane thought like a lifeline. If she could imagine such an improbable phenomenon, then perhaps she had also imagined the voice—

"It's a small world, isn't it . . . Justine?"

She slowly relaxed her grip on the counter. Her back had begun to ache, so she concentrated on relaxing that, too.

It appeared she hadn't imagined the unforgettable voice of Zachary Wayne after all.

Two

Zack forced himself to stay by the door, watching the rigid line of her back and fighting the urge to rush across the room and pull her into his arms. Behind him on the street, snow continued to drift lazily to the ground, mingling with the inch or so that had accumulated throughout the day.

She'd lost weight, he decided. Or maybe it was the over-sized sweater and loose-fitting jeans that made her appear smaller, more fragile than he remembered. Her dark-brown hair was longer, too, the braid ending just below her shoulder blades with a provocative little curl.

When she finally released the counter and turned, Zack realized not much had changed about her face. His hungry gaze skimmed her heart-shaped face, lingering with a pang of remembrance on the fullness of her lips and finally settling on her eyes. *Tiger eyes,* he'd called them, and she had squirmed in his arms and laughed her husky little laugh that haunted his dreams.

Light brown, almost golden in color, and framed by thick dark lashes, those unforgettable eyes regarded him now with unveiled hostility. Her reaction surprised him. He'd been ex-pecting shock and perhaps embarrassment at seeing him after the way she had led him on aboard the cruise ship, then heartlessly forgot about him.

But he hadn't forgotten—would never forget the magic of those four days with Justine. When she hadn't called, an ache had begun to settle into his heart. It had grown bigger with each day that passed when he didn't hear from her.

Breaking free of her gaze, he brushed the snow from his coat and stamped his feet on the rug, giving himself time to control his emotions. Finally he looked at her again.

Her expression hadn't changed.

"How have you been?" he asked, sticking his frozen hands inside his coat pockets.

Her chin tilted just a tad, her tone that of a distant, wary stranger facing a possible threat. "I'm fine. Great. Really busy," she added pointedly. "I was just about to close the shop."

Something told him she wasn't hinting for an invitation, but Zack hadn't turned his life upside-down just to give up at the first sign of resistance. "How about coffee? We can talk—"

"No, thanks. I have other plans." She reached for her coat and struggled into it, then yanked her gloves on.

"When—"

"Never, okay?" Her movements jerky and abrupt, she hit a button on the cash register drawer and removed a set of heavy keys. She slammed it shut. "We have nothing to talk about. Besides, I'm involved with someone."

Zack caught her shoulders as she tried to reach the door, panic making him careless. Her comment had sliced into him like a knife. "I don't know what happened to us, but it's not over."

A fine brow arched in disbelief, but Zack sensed her reaction wasn't all that it appeared to be. Maybe it was the way she trembled that convinced him she wasn't as unmoved as she pretended.

"You don't know? Then I'll tell you what happened to us. We had a fun time and then we went our separate ways." He felt her shrug beneath his hands. "It happens on cruises all the time."

"A fun time," Zack echoed, not believing it. His grip tightened, holding her in place as he closed his mouth over hers in a kiss meant to remind her that it wasn't nice to lie.

Surprised by the unexpected move, Justine responded to the mastery of his mouth with her heart instead of her brain, but only for an instant. The barriers she had taken care to build in the long, lonely months after their affair shook, but held strong.

Why was he doing this to her? Why, after thirteen months of heartache, was Zack back in her life? She broke free with a gasp, struggling against his hold with a growing urgency. She had known if she saw him again—"Please let me go!"

"Can you tell me you didn't feel that?" Zack challenged softly.

Instead of answering, she turned her face away from his heart-stopping, hazel eyes. She pushed open the door. Cold air swirled around them, mixed with big, wet flakes of snow. Justine welcomed the cold to her flushed cheeks. She had thought her heart was safe, that she would never see him again to know otherwise. "I told you, I'm involved with someone. Now, get the hell out of my shop."

"Justine . . . look at me."

She whipped her head around and fixed him with a bright stare. The pain-filled words were out before she could stop them. "Why are you here?" Then, before he could answer, she shook her head so vehemently her braid flew back and forth. "Never mind. I don't really want to know." And she didn't, because she knew she wouldn't believe him. Or maybe she was afraid she *would*.

"I think you already *know*."

Zack brushed by her and stepped out into the snow. Justine flipped the light switch just inside the door and followed him. She fumbled with the lock. Damn, her hands were shaking so badly she could hardly hold the key! And to think she had to drive to her brother's house.

"Let me."

He didn't leave her much choice, taking the key and turning the lock before she could form a protest. Her grudgingly voiced "Thanks" died to a whisper as he wordlessly placed the keys into her gloved hands and tromped through the snow to a Ford Explorer parked behind her compact van.

Her throat ached with unshed tears. Everything she'd tried to forget came rushing back; the laughs and the lovemaking, the hushed giggles and the romantic dinners, the plans they'd made for their future, the special way he'd made her feel, as if she were the only woman in the world for him.

All a crock of bird droppings.

She swallowed hard as his taillights disappeared into the curtain of snow. Why was he here? Was he participating in some sick ritual where he had to see how badly he'd wounded his victim? Justine tossed her snow-covered head, rapidly blinking her eyes as tears threatened. Whatever his reasons for being in her town and invading *her* space, she was determined that he would never know how much he'd hurt her.

She wouldn't give him the satisfaction, she vowed. If they happened to bump into each other again—and Cannon Bay wasn't that big a town—then she would be better prepared. She could do it. She could be cool and polite, distant and unaffected.

On the outside, anyway.

Inside the darkened store, Reuben waved his wing and chanted a quick spell to produce a tiny glowing lamp and a table to support it.

Mini fretted about the light. "Someone walking by will see the light through the window. What will they think?"

Her warlock husband shrugged. "Unless it's Justine, I don't think it will matter. They'll assume it's a reflection from the aquarium lights." He shuddered dramatically. "I refuse to sit here in the dark with all these . . . these *creatures* roaming around."

"They're not roaming, Reuben dear," Mini pointed out patiently. "They're all caged like we are. So, what did you think?"

"About what?"

Mini narrowed her beady eyes, drawing each word out slowly so that it would have sufficient time to soak into his arrogant brain. "About . . . Zack . . . and . . . Justine . . . *kissing.*"

"Hmm. From what I could see, it was *Zack* doing the kissing." Reuben hopped to the bottom of the cage and closed his eyes, mumbling a chant beneath his breath.

"She wasn't exactly fighting him. What are you doing now?"

"I'm hungry." He spread his wing. There was a popping sound, then a puff of smoke.

Curious, Mini leaned forward as the air cleared, revealing a miniature table groaning with food. A whole roasted chicken, baked ham, crusty bread, and wine. People food. She shook her head and sighed. "Reuben, birds do not eat meat, nor do they drink wine. It'll make you sick."

He snorted and spent several moments balancing his stocky bird body on the chair. His tail kept getting in the way. "I refuse to eat birdseed. It's disgusting!"

Mini recognized that stubborn look beneath his black mask. "Have it your way, but don't expect any sympathy from me when you're puking your guts out later."

"Please, Mini!" Reuben protested. "I'm trying to *eat* here."

"Sorry." The smell of real food made her stomach growl. She hopped to the feeder and began pecking at the variety of seeds, hoping to influence her husband. Actually the sesame seeds were quite good, she decided, searching for more of the same. She paused to look at her husband, grinning as he tried to fit his beak into the goblet of wine. "Reuben, what do you think their chances are, really?"

"Whose chances?" He muttered a quick chant beneath his breath, and the goblet became a bowl. With a satisfied sigh, he buried his beak in the red brew and sipped noisily.

Mini's temper flared. She opened her wing and removed her tiny crystal ball, seriously considering throwing it at his head. But, no, she decided. She might accidentally hurt him and she didn't fancy explaining *that* to the Peacemaker.

Taking a deep breath, she tried again. "I'm talking about Justine and Zack, *darling*. Do you think she'll forgive him?"

This time Reuben proved that he wasn't as absentminded as he pretended to be. He dropped a half-eaten chicken leg and propped his wing on the table. "*Her* forgive him?" he squeaked. "What about *him* forgiving *her?*"

"I don't understand."

"She threw him out of the store!" He sounded outraged on Zack's behalf. "A man has his pride, you know."

"Pride?" Mini stomped over to him, her feathers standing on end. "Pride, you say? Well, what about a woman's heart? I believe that's more important than a man's pride." She whirled away from him, her long, feathered tail catching the bowl of wine. It went spinning to the cage floor. Mini twitched her wing tip and made it vanish before a single drop of wine managed to soak the newsprint that served as their carpet.

She thought about doing the same to her heartless husband.

Seeing how furious she was, Reuben hastily backtracked. "Mini, you know that Zack didn't mean to break her heart. It was that blundering fool of a steward who's to blame. He forgot to give her the message."

"Yes, but *Justine* doesn't know that!"

"Neither does Zack," Reuben exclaimed triumphantly. When Mini turned to glare at him, he quickly wiped the smug expression from his face. "They're either both at fault, or both innocent. Pick one."

Mini's feathers settled dejectedly. "What are we going to do?"

At the sight of his wife's misery, Reuben's heart softened. He could handle her anger—sometimes shamefully reveling in it—but he could never tolerate the love of his life to suffer sadness. With a few mumbled words, he cleared the table of its clutter. "Wife of mine, come here and share a drink with me."

Mini glanced up, her eyes widening at the sight of the candles and delicate crystal goblets now gracing the table. She tipped her head and peered suspiciously at the liquid.

"It's only water," Reuben assured her. "Come, have a seat. And don't worry, we'll think of something."

Sweeping her tail feathers aside, Mini sank down on the velvet-lined chair opposite her husband's. Her eyes watered. How long had it been since she'd last seen Reuben look so tenderly at her? Fifty years? Seventy-five?

Too long, was her dismal thought.

Twenty minutes after leaving Justine at the door of the shop, Zack stepped out of the shower and reached for a towel, his mood darker than ever. Once again the water had been more than a few degrees below the comfortable stage, something he'd been meaning to mention to the landlord. He suspected he not only shared the second story with his neighbor across the hall, but a water heater as well. A *small* water heater. Either that or his neighbor took abnormally long showers.

Shivering, he belted his robe around his waist and padded barefoot to the living room. Made of gleaming hardwood, Zack suspected it would be cool in the summer, but right now it was damned cold. If he intended to live here for any length of time, he would have to buy a rug. Or several.

The red button on his answering machine flashed urgently, so he hit the button and continued on to the kitchen with the intention of making himself a pot of coffee. Maybe the hot liquid would warm him up. He grimaced; it was for certain that *Justine* wasn't going to anytime soon.

His younger brother's voice booming from the answering machine stopped him in his tracks.

"Zack, this is Thomas. Haven't heard from you in a couple of weeks so I thought I would see what's up. Have you found her yet? Talked to her? I'm going crazy here, so keep me posted, okay? And don't you dare get married without inviting me and Miranda. She'd never speak—"

Zack smiled when he realized Thomas had run out of time on the tape. His smile faded as he dialed Thomas's number. Miranda, Thomas's wife, picked up the phone. "Mandy, it's Zack. Is Thomas around?"

"Zack!" She sounded pleased and excited to hear from him. "How are you? How's . . . everything?"

His sister-in-law tried hard to be subtle and usually failed. Like now. "I'm fine. Everything is fine." Zack was relieved when Thomas snatched the phone from his wife. He wasn't ready to talk about his disastrous encounter with Justine.

"Get my message?" Thomas demanded.

"All fifteen minutes of it," Zack joked. "How's the weather there?"

With a hint of snugness, Thomas said, "Oh, about eighty degrees and sunny. How about there?"

Zack frowned, glancing at the window to confirm that it was still snowing. "Cold. How's business?"

"Great. Don't worry, we've got everything under control."

Zack closed his eyes and pinched the bridge of his nose in frustration, wondering if his brother would ever feel comfortable with his decision. "I'm not worried. The business belongs to you now."

"You might change your—"

"I won't change my mind," Zack interrupted. If he couldn't play football, he would teach it. Thomas had always possessed a head for business and was the perfect choice to run the chain of hardware stores. In fact, he still hadn't figured out why his father had left *him* head of the business and Thomas the house, instead of the other way around. Thomas was married and had a house of his own, while Zack had still lived at home when his father became ill. Not that he'd stayed there much after his career got off the ground.

Zack heard Miranda whisper something in the background, then Thomas covered the receiver for a moment. Despite himself, Zack's lips twitched. He suspected his sister-in-law was about to burst with curiosity.

Too bad he would have to disappoint her.

Thomas finally came back on the line, sounding apologetic. "Miranda is dying to know, Zack. I told her you probably would have said something if you had anything to say—"

"Nothing happening yet." It wasn't exactly a lie, and he wasn't the kiss-and-tell type anyway. "Tell her I'll let her know before the wedding bells toll." If Zack had to guess, he'd say Miranda had plenty of time to find a new dress for the occasion.

"I will. So, how's it feel to coach a football team?"

Once onto a safer subject, Zack relaxed and filled his brother in on the joys and headaches of coaching a team of rowdy, hormonally charged teenagers. It was a temporary job that he thoroughly enjoyed, and once football season ended, he knew he would miss the team.

Thirty minutes later, after reassuring Miranda he was staying warm and well fed, Zack hung up, poured a mug of coffee, and went to stand by the window. He had arrived in Cannon Bay in late September; it had snowed three times in the month he'd been here, and it was snowing now. After living in the warm, sunny climate of Florida, he supposed it would take him a while to get used to the colder climate of Nebraska.

He looked down at the pretty, snow-covered street below and thought about his unsatisfactory reunion with Justine.

His gut tightened as he remembered the kiss. For a fleeting moment, she'd responded, and in that moment Zack was reminded of the long, lonely months of self-imposed abstinence after meeting Justine and falling in love. Why hadn't she called? She must have realized that he didn't have her number or her address.

The only clue he had was that she lived in a little town in Nebraska called Cannon Bay, and *that* wasn't even on the map.

Justine Diamond wasn't listed, and he didn't know the name of the small business she'd mentioned briefly during their four-day acquaintance. It had been a vacation, and he supposed they both avoided the subject of work and careers for obvious reasons. Time for that later. Zack's fingers tightened around the warm mug.

There hadn't *been* a later.

He'd fallen head-over-heels in love with a woman for the first time in his life, yet he'd left the ship without getting a phone number. How careless and stupid could he be? A hastily scribbled explanation with his phone number, given to a passing steward, obviously hadn't been a good idea. He should have taken the time to search the ship and explain his leaving face-to-face. But he had panicked, spurred by the urgency of the message from his brother and reminded by the captain that the boat taking him to shore would not wait.

As the weeks turned into months without a call, he began to suspect that Justine had played him for a fool, and that perhaps not giving him her phone number hadn't been an accident on her part, but a deliberate omission.

When he finally accepted this fact, his pride suffered a hard blow. He'd thrown himself into running his father's business until his father recovered from his stroke. Working hadn't been a sacrifice, since his own career had been compromised by a knee injury.

Zack foolishly thought that as the months rolled by she might fade from his memory, but it didn't happen. Instead, the ache in his heart grew until he thought he would go mad if he didn't hear from her own lips that it had all been a joke, or a fling, or temporary insanity. Even then, he wasn't sure that he would believe her. It had been too *real*.

Tonight proved it. Oh, she'd almost convinced him that she felt nothing—until he kissed her. The fire between them hadn't waned, but had grown to an awesome degree. His instincts hadn't failed him; Justine *was* his soul mate. Zack sipped his coffee and watched the snow fall as he contemplated his next move.

This time Justine wouldn't find it so easy to dismiss him from her mind.

Three

Coffee with Bea was never a dull affair, Justine mused, relieved to see that her hands had stopped shaking. She accepted a steaming mug of decaf as her youngest nephew Colby, a tall, gangly twelve-year-old, dribbled a basketball around on the tiled kitchen floor.

Fourteen-year-old Drew dodged his brother and took a seat at the kitchen table. Blond and blue-eyed, Drew was the only one of her nephews who resembled his mother. He was a quiet, serious teenager, preferring computers to sports, much to the scorn of his brothers. Their taunting didn't seem to bother him.

"Hey, Aunt Justine! Watch this." Colby dribbled the basketball around him in a circle without missing a beat, passing the ball from hand to hand until the ball was nothing but a blur.

Justine was suitably impressed. "You're a natural, Colby."

Drew made a face and propped his chin on his hands along the top of the chair. "Anybody can do that," he scoffed before focusing his intent gaze on her. "Have you given any more thought to getting a computer for the store, Aunt Justine?"

"Well, I . . . " She paused as the basketball smacked into the middle of the table. With a sheepish grin, Colby retrieved the ball just seconds before it rolled into her mug.

"Get that thing out of my kitchen," Bea ordered, taking a seat at the table. She added cream and sugar to her coffee, staring pointedly at her middle son.

Justine smiled at Drew's wide-eyed, innocent look.

"What? Why are you staring at me? What did I do?" He smacked his hands against his chest. "I'm just sitting here trying to have a conversation with my favorite aunt."

Bea continued to glare at him until Drew let out a disgusted sigh and got up from his chair. "Okay, okay. I'll go. I don't think it's fair, though, that you're always hogging Aunt Justine to yourself."

"Don't get smart, and it's your turn to clean the upstairs bathroom. If it isn't done by tomorrow, you can kiss your allowance good-bye."

With a groan, Drew shuffled from the room.

"Where's Jordan?" Justine asked when they were finally alone.

Bea sighed. "He said he was going out with his friends."

"You sound worried."

"I am." Bea bit her lip, stirring her coffee aimlessly. "Since Coach Wayne kicked him off the team, he's been so angry, and these days when a teenager gets angry, there's no telling *how* he'll express it."

"Jordan's always been very responsible for his age," Justine reminded her gently. "And any kid would be angry."

Bea slapped her hand onto the table in a frustrated gesture, her eyes sparkling. "That man had no right to do that to Jordan! Wayne's just a substitute. You just wait until Coach Abernathy gets back—"

"He's . . . he's a substitute?" Well, what had she expected? That Zachary Wayne had moved permanently to Cannon Bay just to be near *her?* Justine suppressed a bitter laugh. His presence in town was probably just a wild coincidence.

"Yes, a substitute. He shouldn't be making such a drastic

decision, in my opinion. Coach Abernathy would have understood."

"What happened to Coach Abernathy?"

"His mother is very ill. Dying, I think. He took a sabbatical, and rumor has it he won't be back until after the new year."

"Has Jordan's teacher tried to explain to the . . . new coach about the mix-up with the test?" No matter what had happened between them, Justine couldn't imagine Zachary reacting so harshly toward a child. But then, his defection from the ship had proven that she hadn't truly known him.

Bea snorted. "Everyone has him on a pedestal because he used to play pro football. And Mrs. Shands, well . . . she's rather timid. I can't imagine her approaching him. She's scared of her own shadow," Bea added under her breath.

"Then why don't *you* explain it to him?"

"Because Jordan won't let me." Bea shot her a wry look. "He's afraid I'll lose my temper and make things worse."

Knowing Bea's fierce, protective nature, Justine silently agreed with Jordan. "Maybe Clay can give him a call," she began, but Bea was shaking her head before she finished.

"Nope. Jordan's adamant about both of us staying out of it." Suddenly her eyes narrowed in sly speculation.

Justine recognized that look and groaned inwardly. She held up her hand, palm out. "No, no way." Bea couldn't begin to know what she was asking. "I can't talk to the man. He's—he's—"

"Arrogant, I know." Bea began to plead. "But you're better at keeping your temper, Justine! I've seen you in action with a customer. You can be as cool as a cucumber even when other people are shouting at you."

Knowing there was no way out, Justine took a deep breath and spilled the beans. "I can't be cool with Zachary Wayne, Bea. I know him."

"Of course you know him. Jordan's probably mentioned his name before. When he played for the Miami Sharks, Jordan idolized him." Bea clucked her tongue, oblivious to Justine's meaning. "Poor baby got a rude awakening when he met Zachary Wayne in person."

Justine thought about taking the coward's way out and letting it pass, but knew that she couldn't. Bea might hear it from someone else, and then she'd be unnecessarily hurt. "I don't just know *of* him, I know him . . . personally."

Bea's jaw dropped. "You . . . you *know* him?" she screeched, making Justine wince. "He's from Florida! How could *you* possibly know him?"

"I met him on the cruise." There. It was out. Surprisingly, she felt better. Bea was one of her best friends as well as her sister-in-law, and there had been several times since the cruise that she had wanted to confide in her. However, she had foolishly believed that keeping it to herself would help her forget.

Shocked into silence, Bea rose and poured more coffee into their mugs while Justine braced herself for a long walk down memory lane. She wasn't looking forward to it, especially after that sizzling kiss she and Zack shared earlier.

"Is he the reason why you don't want to go on another cruise?" Bea asked, her quiet voice filled with sympathy.

"Yes." Justine blinked her eyes to clear her vision of unwanted tears. He wasn't worth crying over. Hadn't she learned that the hard way? And just because she had seen him again didn't mean that she was going to turn stupid. In fact, she was more determined than ever to forget about him. Yes, he was drop-dead gorgeous; yes, he was an excellent lover; and yes, he was a great liar. The best.

"What happened?"

The question she dreaded. Justine swallowed a lump that had no business being there and forced herself to speak dispassionately. "I met him the first day, and for the next four days we were inseparable."

"You fell in love?"

Justine nodded. "At least, *I* did." Her lips curved in a self-derisive smile. "You'd think that after Barry I would have been more cautious of men spouting bullcrap, huh?"

"Shoot, even *I* was fooled by Barry. I was just as shocked as you were to find out he was nothing but a two-timing jerk. Is he still pestering you to get back with him?"

Justine nodded absently. She hadn't really loved Barry; she realized it the moment she saw Zachary standing alone at the railing, his pensive gaze staring out across the ocean.

Finding Barry with another woman had hurt her pride; finding Zack missing from the ship without a word of explanation had crushed her heart.

"I should have known better, Bea."

"You went on that cruise to get over Barry," Bea reminded her gently. "And you know what they say: The best way to get over being burned is to dance right back into the fire."

"Well," Justine drawled with a little laugh, "I certainly did that." In a big way.

Bea began to turn her wedding ring around and around, staring at it thoughtfully. "So, you were inseparable for four days, and then he just dumped you? Did he say why?"

"No, he didn't. He just left the ship."

"Without even saying good-bye?" Bea sounded surprised. "That was rather cowardly of him."

Justine had thought the same thing—when the pain eased enough to allow her brain to function again.

"Now he's in town," Bea mused as if to herself. "Do you think he wants you back? I mean, the odds of him coming to Cannon Bay, of all places. . . ."

"It's been over a year since the cruise, Bea. Even if his being here isn't a coincidence—which I think it is—I'm not about to pick up where *he* left off." Not in a million years. Not in *ten* million. In fact, the notion was almost laughable.

"He really did hurt you, didn't he?"

For pride's sake, Justine started to deny it, but realized she didn't have to lie to Bea. "Yes, he did, but he won't get a second shot at it," she promised. "He'll have to find some other gullible fool willing to play his games."

"Justine . . . it just occurred to me that he probably knew Jordan was your nephew. Same last names."

Justine sat up straight, adrenaline jolting her heart into overdrive. When she had learned that he played pro football, she had proudly told him about her nephew's aspirations.

So he knew about Jordan.

The bastard wouldn't stoop so low, would he? She voiced the ugly thought out loud. "You think he might have thrown Jordan off the team because of me?"

Bea shrugged, frowning. "You know him better than I do. Do you think he would pull a stunt like that if he thought it would lure you to him?"

The possibility made Justine so furious it was a full moment before she could speak. When she did, her voice vibrated with anger. "There's one way to find out, isn't there?"

"You're going to talk to him?"

"Damned right I am," Justine snarled. "Zachary Wayne's in for a rude awakening if he thinks I'm the same stupid fool he met on the ship."

"I wouldn't just barge in and start accusing him," Bea cautioned. "It might make things worse for Jordan."

She was right, Justine realized. Her gaze narrowed. Maybe blasting him wasn't the smartest way to go. Maybe it would be safer to beat him at his own game. *But can you?* a taunting voice asked. *Can you play his game without crumbling at his feet the moment he touches you?*

She could! She must. For Jordan's sake and her own.

To her sister-in-law, she said, "I'll be as sweet as sugar, I promise. In fact, I think I'll call him right now and tell him I changed my mind about that coffee he offered me earlier."

No time like the present, Justine decided. Besides, if she did it now, she wouldn't have time to chicken out later.

With a gasp, Mini tucked the tiny crystal ball inside her wing and hopped over to where Reuben lay snoring on a bed of pillows. She leaned over him, then drew back with a grimace of disgust when she caught a whiff of his wine-laden breath.

"Reuben, wake up! I've been watching Justine in the crystal ball, and you'll never believe what she thinks Zack has done!"

Reuben grunted, then continued snoring.

Mini shook him. "She thinks he kicked Jordan off the team just to get her attention!"

"Hmm?" Reuben mumbled sleepily. He opened one bleary eye, then quickly closed it again. He moaned. "What time is it?"

Mini heaved an impatient sigh. "It's not even seven o'clock. You drank too much wine, remember? How do you feel?"

"Terrible, but I'd feel better if you'd let me sleep."

"We don't have time for you to sleep." She began to pace in front of him, her sharp claws shredding the newspaper. "What are we going to do? What will Zack think when Justine accuses him of something so unethical? We had a chance when Justine was the only one angry, but now . . ." She clucked her tongue and shook her head. "This could be bad, Reuben."

Reuben wasn't listening; he snored softly on the pillows.

"You worthless warlock," she whispered. But her gaze was loving as she flicked her wing tip and made a warm blanket appear over her husband.

She would just have to figure something out alone. Absently she brought her wing to her lips and without thought began to nibble as she sometimes did when thinking.

With a disgusted gasp, she spit a feather out. What she wouldn't give for a good nail to chew on right about now. Wisely she folded her wings behind her and tapped her foot instead, concentrating hard. She couldn't use magic on Justine or Zack—the witch's counsel had been very specific about that rule—but she could work magic *around* them.

Justine needed a distraction, Mini mused. Something that might remind her of why she fell in love with Zack in the first place, a chivalrous act on Zack's part that might make Justine hesitate to voice her unjust accusations until she had more time to think about it. Mini felt confident that once

Justine had time to calm down, she would realize that only a monster would use a child in the way she and Bea suggested.

Zack might be a heartbreaker—in Justine's eyes—but he was not a monster.

Mini's thoughtful gaze strayed around the shadowed room, lingering on the long row of aquariums against the wall. Their muted lighting revealed the indistinguishable shapes moving in the water below, and it gave her an idea. She grinned and rubbed her wings together. Yes, it might just work, and as long as she was careful, not a single fish would have to be sacrificed.

Closing her eyes, she began to prepare for Justine's return.

Justine's apartment over the store was accessible only from the exterior stairway located on the left side of the building, and Justine liked it that way. It made her feel as if she were actually leaving the store and going home, when in fact she had only to walk to the end of the building, turn right, and climb the stairs to her front door.

Several years ago when she purchased the building, she'd promptly moved into the quaint living area above the shop despite her parents' protest that it was too small. She loved it—*and* the easy access to her business. If she grew worried in the middle of the night about a sick critter, she was a stone's throw away.

Parking a few car lengths from the storefront, Justine opened the car door and stepped cautiously onto the snow-packed road. A bitterly cold wind snatched at her coat and whistled into every opening it could find, chilling her to the bone. Snow stung her cheeks and clung to her eyelashes; where throughout the day it had fallen in a gentle curtain, it now lashed about with the force of a snowstorm. Even with the gloves, her hands were frozen by the time she got the van locked.

The moment she reached her apartment, she planned to run a hot bath. While the tub was filling she'd feed her hungry misfit family and heat a bowl of soup for herself. A huge mug of hot chocolate topped with marshmallows sounded good, too.

Maybe after she'd warmed her body and her belly she would be better prepared to face Zachary again.

He had answered her call on the second ring, agreeing to meet her at eight; it was now seven o'clock. To give him credit, he hadn't asked why she'd changed her mind, though she sensed he wanted to.

Justine shook her head, suddenly realizing she'd been standing in the cold thinking about Zack when she could have been inside her warm apartment by now. She bowed her head and braved the stinging snow until she reached the sidewalk. The awning over the shop afforded little shelter from the biting wind, but kept the snow out of her eyes. Above her head, the sign reading LITTLE SHOP OF CRITTERS swung back and forth with an eery squall.

Out of habit, she glanced into the big storefront window gracing her shop. She did a double take and nearly lost her balance as she came to a sudden stop on the slick sidewalk.

It was dark inside. Really dark, which could only mean the aquarium lights were out. Justine frowned, drawing closer, praying she was mistaken.

She wasn't, and not only did it look as if the electricity was out, but it appeared the back-up generator wasn't functioning, either.

Not good.

Dammit! Justine slapped the glass in frustration. Just last month she'd had the stubborn thing inspected and serviced! Nebraska winters were generally very cold, and Justine knew her critters, whether they be fish or fowl, would not live long with temperatures plunging into the single digits as the weatherman had predicted they would tonight. As it was, she had to maintain a balmy eighty degrees inside the store.

If she didn't fix the problem she stood to lose her entire inventory of tropical fish, which in turn would eat a sizable chunk into her savings. The reptiles would possibly make it through the night, and the birds she could transfer upstairs to her apartment, along with the puppies and kittens. The transfer alone would take half the night.

But she could not move the fish—her main source of income.

"Just what I needed," Justine mumbled as she unlocked the shop door and quickly stepped inside, shutting the door behind her. Without thinking, she reached to her left and flipped on the light switch. She blinked in surprise when fluorescent lighting flooded the room.

The lights worked . . . but the aquarium lights *didn't?* It would explain why the generator hadn't kicked on, she thought, frowning as she investigated the first aquarium. Lights, air, everything—dead, as if no electricity reached them. The fish still moved energetically in the water, which told her that the power hadn't been off long.

A thrown switch.

Justine let out a sigh of relief as the solution came to her. Of course! Something must have triggered the breaker feeding electricity to this part of the room. A simple problem to fix. She'd just flip the breaker, and the electricity would be restored.

Retrieving a flashlight from her office, Justine passed the caged lovebirds on her way to the storeroom, making a mental note to drop the cage cover before leaving. She should have remembered how the wind gusted in when someone came through the door; it wasn't healthy for the birds to suffer drastic temperature changes.

If she hadn't been so flustered by Zack's arrival . . .

In the storeroom, she tried the light switch with no results. She flipped on the flashlight and opened the panel door of the breaker box, studying the switches. With a slight frown she checked them again, slowly.

Nothing looked out of order; no red buttons popped out to alert her.

With a shrug, she flipped each one off and on anyway,

stuck her head around the storeroom door, and saw that she hadn't fixed the problem.

She tried it again and peeked hopefully around the corner. No lights, no humming sound of the oxygen pumps, no bubbling of the water. Holding her breath, she pulled down on the main power switch. The store was plunged into darkness. She pushed it up again and listened.

Nothing.

Tapping her nails against the door facing, she contemplated her next move. She didn't have many choices. Calling an electrician after hours would cost her a fortune, *if* she could persuade one to come out on a night like this.

Her only alternative would be to run extension cords from the aquariums to the outlets on the opposite wall. Those outlets seemed to be working, thankfully. To get enough extension cords, however, she would have to call Joe, who owned the hardware store down the street. She didn't think he would mind opening the store for her in an emergency situation. He lived in town, so he wouldn't have far to travel.

Justine clicked off the flashlight and went to her office to call Joe. She hated to ask him, but she didn't have much choice. Along the way she paused at the birdcage and released the fancy tassels holding the cage covering aside, her fingers lingering on the gauzy purple fabric. Odd—she could have sworn the material was something thicker, like satin. In fact, she remembered thinking the previous owners must have possessed lavish tastes to fashion a birdcage covering made out of such expensive material.

Now the material was so sheer she could see the female lovebird—Laura—watching her. The male was asleep, his head tucked deeply into his wing. As Justine peered at him, he swayed on the perch.

She fancied she could hear him snoring.

But to her knowledge, birds didn't snore.

Shaking her head at her fanciful thoughts, she dropped the cover and proceeded to her office. She found the number for Joe's hardware in the local directory and dialed. She dialed four times in all, and all four times she got a wrong number.

Four *different* wrong numbers.

Puzzled and more than a little exasperated, Justine checked the number again and was just about to give it another shot when she heard someone knocking on the door of the store. Great. The last thing she needed was a customer thinking she was open for business. She should have turned off the lights.

"I'm closed!" she shouted.

The pounding continued as if she hadn't spoken.

Blowing out an exasperated breath, Justine replaced the receiver and poked her head around the office door to yell again. She froze at the sight of Zack standing outside in the snow. Had she really thought she'd be prepared? Just looking at his six-foot-two muscled frame evoked an instant, knee-wobbling flashback of his hands clutching her hips as he thrust into her, his hot mouth consuming hers in a kiss so deep, so meaningful, she had convulsed around him within moments of penetration.

Sex with Zack would have been fantastic on its own; the fact that she loved him had taken the act to exhilarating heights.

Justine's mouth went dry with fear. She couldn't let him consume her again, *could not* let herself remember what they'd had.

What Zachary Wayne had convinced her they'd had.

Four

~

She doesn't look happy to see me, Zack thought, waiting for
her to unlock the door. He clenched his teeth together to keep
them from chattering. Well, what had he expected? That she
would welcome him with open arms? The previous meeting
should have disabused him of *that* notion. He'd heard it said
it was a woman's prerogative to change her mind, but he
doubted she had in such a short amount of time without a
reason.

So what did she want? To taunt him? Tease him? Play
more games? Zack's lips tightened. He loved her so much it
hurt, but he wouldn't allow himself to be used again by the
lovely Justine Diamond. She either loved him or she didn't,
and he was not leaving Cannon Bay until he had a straight
answer. He'd lived in limbo for the past thirteen months,
wondering where she was, what she was doing, and whether
she yearned for him as he yearned for her. She was like a
stubborn virus in his bloodstream, slowly killing him.

"Hello. You're early."

With those cryptic words, she stepped aside and waved
him in. She shut and locked the door, but didn't look at him.
In fact, Zack thought she was going to a lot of trouble to

avoid his gaze. He decided it was a positive sign.

"I thought you were a customer," she said.

Zack's gaze swept over her tense face, recalling a time when laughter had softened her features, and the soft glow of love had shone from her eyes. *Love for him.* "I tried your apartment, but didn't get an answer. As I was leaving I saw a light on. . . ." While he spoke, Justine's gaze dwelled for an electrifying instant on his mouth before she looked abruptly away. The betraying move made Zack catch a hopeful breath.

"I was on my way home when I noticed the aquarium lights were off, so I came in to check."

"Everything all right?"

"No. Something's wrong with the electricity on the northwest wall. Look, I'm going to have to—"

"Mind if I have a look?" Zack interrupted quickly, sensing he was about to be sent on his way. He didn't want to miss the chance to talk about why they were acting like strangers.

She smiled faintly, as if amused. "Go for it. I'll get you a flashlight." She paused at the door to what appeared to be a small office and added, "The breaker box is in the back."

When Justine returned, Zack followed her to the breaker box, already suspecting from her satirical tone that he would find everything as it should be. He would look not only arrogant, but also like a foolish ass.

Banishing this dismal thought, Zack nearly crowed his triumph when he noticed the fourth red button popped out. He pressed his thumb against it. The lights came on over the aquariums, and the dozen or so pumps hummed to life. Air tubes feeding oxygen to the water began to bubble merrily.

His gaze locked with Justine's. She looked so bewildered he couldn't restrain a chuckle. He sobered quickly when her eyes narrowed. "Sometimes it's hard to tell when the button is out," he said.

"Don't patronize me, Zack."

Now her eyes were bright with temper—a side of Justine

he'd never had the glory of seeing in the four short days they were together.

"I'm not blind, nor am I stupid. All of the buttons were pushed in when I checked." She snatched the flashlight from his hands. "There's something fishy going on around here, and I'm beginning to think you're the shark in charge."

Zack's jaw dropped. She thought *he* had something to do with the electricity not working? Before he could defend himself, she continued.

"It would explain why you were lurking around the front door."

"*You* invited me, or have you forgotten?" Zack countered, stung by her unjustified attack. When she stalked back into the main room, he followed, his anger rising. He was just about sick and tired of her attitude! *She* was the one who had dumped him. *She* was the one who conveniently forgot to give him her number. *She* was the one who hadn't called him. Obviously, her whispered words of undying love were all a part of some twisted, cruel game she enjoyed playing.

If anyone should have an attitude, it should be him!

She swung around to face him in the narrow aisle between the aquariums and the shelves of birdseed. "It was you earlier, too, wasn't it? Just before you came in the front door you sneaked in the back way and put something around the parrot's beak, some type of harness. I guess it was your idea of a sick joke, huh?"

Zack sputtered in the face of her absurd accusation. Put a *harness* on a parrot? Hell, he wasn't sure if he'd recognize a parrot if someone shoved one in his face! She was beginning to worry him with her weird talk. "Will you calm down? Next you'll be accusing me of—" He gasped as a sudden burst of cold water rained upon his head, saturating him in seconds.

"The sprinkler system!" Justine cried, trying to shield her head from the downpour with her arms.

"I guess you think I did this, too?" Zack's caustic remark went unchecked as they ran for her office. He watched as she jerked open a panel in the wall and flipped a switch. The sprinklers sputtered to a stop.

Dazed, Justine glanced around her. What in the *hell* was going on? She spotted the soggy mess of papers on her desk and groaned. "Those were my inventory papers! I'll have to redo them all."

"Has this ever happened before?" Zack asked as he slicked his wet hair from his face. He brushed ineffectively at the wet sheep's wool collar of his coat.

She shook her head, staring helplessly at his wet jeans visible below his short leather coat. They were plastered to his thighs, outlining the rounded muscles and the bulge at his crotch. "You . . . you'll . . . ." She swallowed hard, willing her voice to stop shaking. "We'll have to dry your clothes before you go home." As for the store, she suspected that most of the water would evaporate by morning. Christopher, her assistant, could take care of the rest.

Zack jerked his head in the direction of the door, indicating the wintery weather. "At least we don't have to go back out there to get to your apartment," he stated with obvious relief. "We'd freeze in an instant."

"Guess we'll just have to freeze, then." Justine started to smirk at his dismayed expression until she remembered her plan. Until she found out about Jordan, she had to can the hostile act. "The only way to my apartment is outside, around the corner, and upstairs. This used to be a bakery, but the owners rented the room out. They didn't want the tenant to have access to the store."

To Zack's credit, he took the news like a man. But then, Justine thought with an inward gulp, there had never been any doubt in her mind about Zack's gender. . . .

The moment the lights went out and the door clicked shut on the two mortals, Mini breathed an audible sigh of relief. She wiped her forehead with her wing. Whew! That had been close! She was certain Zack had been about to mention the newest bone of contention between them: Justine's nephew

Jordan. Mini had a bad feeling that if Zack brought up the subject first, Justine would never be convinced she had nothing to do with it.

Luckily she'd thought of the sprinkler system in the nick of time. Doused that subject quick! Mini chuckled at her own joke, glancing sideways at Reuben asleep on the perch. Invisible ropes held him upright, otherwise he would have toppled over in his drunken stupor long before now. Sly warlock! While she had been sipping water, he had carried on with wine in his goblet, zapped of its color!

Mini sniffed, thinking he'd be sorry enough for deceiving his poor wife when he awoke with a hangover. Putting her useless husband from her mind, she opened her wing and plucked her crystal ball from its hiding place. She suspended the glowing orb in front of her, adjusting it to a comfortable eye level. Almost immediately, an image of Justine and Zack appeared. Mini clucked in sympathy at their shivering, bedraggled appearance.

She hoped they didn't catch cold.

"Y-y-you f-f-first," Justine managed to get out as she stumbled across the threshold into the blessed warmth of her apartment. She had beat her own record of two minutes from door to door, but it hadn't been quick enough; her teeth were chattering so badly it made her jaw ache. "I-I-I'll m-m-make u-u-us s-s-something w-w-warm t-t-to d-d-drink."

"No, ladies first," Zack argued. "Look at you—your teeth are chattering!"

Despite knowing better, Justine was warmed by his concern. She hugged her arms around her middle and tried to offer a brave smile as she pointed out, "Y-y-your l-l-lips a-a-are b-b-blue."

"So are yours." Zack reached out and firmly unfolded her arms, tugging on her coat sleeves. "Show me where your thermostat is and tell me what you want to drink. I'll fix it while you soak in a tub of hot water."

Justine automatically turned as he pulled her frozen coat

from her shoulders. "W-w-what a-a-about y-y-you?" Damn!
She couldn't stop her teeth from chattering! She turned back
around in time to see his teeth flash in a wicked smile.

"I'll get warm just thinking about you in the bathtub."

Her heart did a crazy, unruly somersault. Later she and
her wayward heart would have to have a good ole heart-to-
heart talk. She had three things to tell it—it was great, it was
fabulous, it was *over*.

With this stern reminder foremost in her mind, she pretended not to hear the intimate note in his voice, or notice
the way his gaze slid over her with ever-increasing heat. As
for his remark, she ignored that altogether. "I'll j-j-just go
take a b-b-bath, then." *And you can burst into flames for all
I care,* she added silently, daring her heart to misbehave
again. "Hot ch-ch-chocolate sounds g-good."

To show she wasn't completely heartless, she grabbed a
clean towel from a shelf built into the wall next to the bathroom and pitched it to him—football style. "Might be a g-
good idea to d-dry your hair," she stammered just before she
slammed the bathroom door.

Zack caught the towel, grinning at the closed door. When
he heard the click of the lock, he chuckled. So, Justine hadn't
forgotten his habit of joining her in the shower. Good.

Wisely pushing the steamy memory from his mind for the
moment, Zack laid the towel aside and took off his coat,
running shoes, damp socks, and, after a slight hesitation, his
wet jeans. After all, Justine had seen him in less, hadn't she?
Surely she didn't expect him to remain in his wet clothes
until she got out of the bathroom. Clad in boxer briefs and
his shirt, Zack scooped up his wet pants and went in search
of a dryer.

The living room and kitchen were one large room, separated by a breakfast bar. Zack found a compact washer and
dryer tucked behind a curtain adjacent to the kitchen. He
threw his jeans in the dryer and turned it on. He took two
steps away, paused, and swung around to punch the button,
marked *low heat*. With a satisfied smile, he headed to a

closed door next to the bathroom, hoping to find something to put on over his briefs. He might be sly, but he wasn't stupid; Justine would probably shriek if she emerged from the bathroom to find him nearly naked.

Just as he suspected, he discovered a bedroom when he turned on the light. He stood on the threshold, his interested gaze taking in the antique-looking decor. An old-fashioned four-poster bed was situated catty-corner in the room; a dark, gleaming highboy stood next to the bed, and a matching dresser dominated the east wall. His gaze lingered on the thick, downy comforter patterned with pretty roses. The furniture, along with the matching pillow shams and curtains, reminded him of a cozy bed-and-breakfast he'd stayed in during a layover in Atlanta.

He looked at the bed again, easily imagining Justine burrowed beneath the covers fast asleep, or stretching her naked body like a sleepy cat upon awakening. The thought intensified the ache in his groin to an almost painful degree. To distract himself, he moved into the room and looked behind the door.

No robe conveniently hanging on a hook.

Unwilling to give up, Zack opened a closet door and gingerly glanced through the row of clothing. He found a faded green terrycloth robe and slipped it on, inhaling the faint scent of Justine's perfume, a light, flowery fragrance that seemed uniquely her. The robe barely reached his knees, and the belt was too short for tying, but it would have to do. At least it wasn't flowered.

Turning out the light, he shut the door and padded to the kitchen, stopping briefly in the living room to edge the thermostat up a few notches. He filled the teakettle and set it to heating before he rummaged through the cabinets in search of hot chocolate. If she didn't have instant, she was out of luck.

Finally he found the packages next to a box of cat food. Did Justine have a cat? he wondered. He'd seen no signs of a pet, yet the cat food indicated she had one. *Of course she'd have a pet, you dope. She owns a pet shop.*

Frowning, he nudged the cat-food box aside, his brows climbing. *Iguana* food? What the hell was a—

Something nibbled on his toes.

Something sharp and hungry.

Slowly Zack glanced down at his bare feet, fully expecting to find a nice kitty having a little fun.

He froze.

It wasn't a kitty; it was a huge green lizard. No, it was a baby dinosaur, complete with thorny-looking ridges from head to toe. It had to be at least three feet long, if he counted its long, wicked-looking tail, and since it was as ugly as the rest of him, Zack was inclined to.

Whatever it was, Zack wasn't about to let it make a meal of his toes. He slammed the box of cocoa mix onto the counter and scampered backwards.

The iguana—and by this time he realized the identity of his new friend—followed. It bent its thorny head and opened its mouth, reaching for his toes.

Zack cursed softly and moved out of reach again, not really frightened but definitely concerned for his toes. He racked his brain, trying to remember what little he knew about iguanas. Where they meat eaters? More importantly, was *this* one? Or did he just have a thing for toes?

"Easy, boy," Zack said. He watched the iguana crawl across the tiled floor. It didn't move fast, but it was relentless, its black beady eyes locked on Zack's feet as if it envisioned a feast.

Inspiration struck Zack. Stepping quickly around the iguana, he snatched the box of iguana food from the cabinet and poured a generous portion on the floor in the iguana's path. He stood back. Way back.

The iguana turned its fat body and crawled over the pile of pellets as if they were invisible—and kept on coming.

Zack was tired of dancing with the damned thing. The teakettle was whistling, and any moment now Justine would emerge from the bathroom to find him penned against the wall like a coward. "Look, you ugly—"

"Thor. His name is Thor," Justine informed him, her voice shaking with laughter. "Here, put these on."

Instinctively Zack caught the pair of socks. He was torn between a manly urge to scorn her rescue and the urge to save his toes from this T-rex wannabe. Did she really think socks would stop this relentless monster?

Meanwhile, Thor was stretching his neck in an effort to reach his toes again. Zack lifted his foot and balanced himself on one leg. The iguana shifted his thick body and aimed for his other set.

"Put them on, and he'll leave you alone."

"Okay, okay," Zack snarled with silent exasperation. He danced around, nearly toppling over as he drew the socks over his feet. They were a tight fit, but he managed. Cautiously he planted both feet on the floor in front of the waiting iguana.

Thor sniffed, then turned aside, lumbering in the direction of the living room. He long tail swished slowly back and forth as he moved.

"If he's dangerous, why do you keep him?" Zack demanded, his embarrassment surfacing as anger. He wasn't normally afraid of critters, but this *thing* hadn't been normal.

Justine shrugged, looking incredibly sexy with her face scrubbed free of makeup and her damp hair loose around her shoulders. The blue robe she wore looked new, and, to Zack's disappointment, it was firmly belted at the waist.

"Because nobody else wants him. After the third customer brought him back with the same complaint, I adopted him." Her eyes danced with suppressed laughter. "He's harmless as long as I keep my toes covered."

"You could have warned me," Zack growled in a low voice. Maybe if he stayed angry he wouldn't leap on her like he wanted to do.

She cocked her hip against the kitchen counter and crossed her ankles. The robe parted, revealing a length of smooth,

curvy leg. Zack's mouth watered. He firmly forced his gaze
to return to her face. Of course she wasn't teasing him. She
probably had no idea the robe had come open. . . .

"Now, where would the fun be in that?" She looked him
up and down with those gold tiger eyes of hers, fanning the
blaze in his gut. "Besides, if you had waited for your turn
in the bathroom instead of stripping in my living room, then
Thor wouldn't have fallen in love with your toes." Her twinkling gaze dipped to his feet. "Although I don't know what
Thor sees in them."

She'd gone too far. Zack caught her gaze, satisfied when
her eyes widened in recognition of his intent. So, she hadn't
forgotten the little games they'd played. He reached over and
turned off the burner beneath the whistling teakettle, then
began to move slowly in her direction.

What had she been thinking, to tease him this way as if
nothing had changed between them? Justine stumbled back
as he came forward. With a half laugh, half scream, she
turned and headed for the safety of her room at a dead run.

Dear God, if he touched her, she would ignite!

He caught her before she could get the door closed, pushing it open with little effort. Strong arms circled her waist
and lifted her against him; she gasped as she felt the rough
hair from his thighs prickle her bare skin. Her nervous giggle
died away as shock waves of need, long suppressed but not
forgotten, slammed into her. *Zack,* her body cried out in joy-
ful recognition. Her arms went around his neck of their own
accord; her mouth turned unerringly to his the exact moment
he sought her lips.

It was heaven and hell.

They fell onto the bed, the full weight of his arousal finding its haven as easily as his mouth had found hers. Justine
swallowed a whimper. She hated herself for being weak, but
she had missed him so badly. Perhaps they could recapture
the physical glory of their relationship without cluttering it
up with the pain of love. . . .

Zack suddenly stiffened, arching his back. He eased his

mouth from hers, his hazel eyes wide with surprise. His rock-hard arousal deflated like a balloon.

As Justine watched his face, she stifled a disappointed sigh. Another moment and she would have joined him!

Moving only his lips, Zack spoke in a painful whisper. "Please tell me that's not Thor on my back."

Five

Justine lifted her head and peered over Zack's shoulder. She
let her head fall back against the bed, biting her lip against
a betraying giggle. "That's not Thor on your back," she said
in a choked whisper. Poor Zack. He had a cat on his back,
and she had thought he'd . . . he'd . . . Her breath hitched.
She didn't dare look at him.

"Then would you mind telling me who—or what—it is?"
he gritted out, apparently not amused in the least.

His biceps bulged from the strain of holding himself still
above her. Justine resisted the urge to reacquaint herself with
those hard muscles and swallowed a sigh of regret, knowing
her moment of weakness had passed. She was glad, wasn't
she? Yes and no. Her aching body wasn't, that was for
damned sure.

But at least her heart was still intact. Hopefully.

"It's Rogue. He's my cat." She no longer felt like laughing.

"A cat. There's a cat on my back. Any idea why?"

Justine shrugged. "I don't have a clue. He *never* shows
himself when strangers are around." It was true. Maybe
Rogue sensed she was about to do something she was certain

to regret. Animals sometimes possessed an uncanny instinct concerning people, Justine knew. If this happened to be the case, she owed him one.

"Obviously he's gotten over his shyness," Zack muttered. "What do I do?"

"Hold still, and I'll try to sweet talk him into getting down." In the loving voice she used with all her critters, she began to croon to the big tom. "Rogue, come here kitty, kitty! I've got a snack for you. Yes, he's mama's pretty kitty . . ." Her words trailed into silence as she felt Zack's deflated arousal stir in response. She swallowed hard and tried to ignore the instant flash of desire that reheated her body. She was trying to woo the cat, not arouse Zack! Her body still taut with need, she feared she wasn't strong enough to withstand a second assault on her starved senses.

To her relief, Rogue's black, whiskered face came into view at the top of Zack's shoulder. "Don't move."

"I don't intend to."

"That's a good boy, Rogue. Yes, keep coming, darling. That's my sweety."

Rogue was responding—and so was Zack. Sweat beaded his upper lip. Through the thin cotton of his briefs, he could feel her quivering against him. He pressed forward very slowly, so sensitive he could feel her petals parting. How incredibly wonderful she felt. Just as he remembered. No other woman compared, had ever come close to satisfying him physically and emotionally the way Justine had. She had ruined him for all women, and there had been plenty.

But now there was only one.

"You can get off me now. He's gone."

The abrupt change in her voice confused Zack. He knew she wanted him as he wanted her. Her breathing was as labored as his own, and he could *feel* her quivering. Nipples, wonderfully hard, strained against his chest. Her lips said no, but her body said yes.

"Zack . . ."

This time there was no mistaking the order.

With a groan of frustration, he rolled away from her and lay on his back. The ceiling became his focus as he willed his body to cool down. What had changed her mind? He was certain—before the cat—that she'd been just as eager as he to make love. He turned his head slightly to look at her.

She was lying on her back with her arm flung over her face. To hide her expression? he wondered. Well, she could hide the truth from him, and she could verbally deny it, but her body wasn't going along with her plans.

"Why did you come here?"

"You invited—"

"Not tonight," she interrupted impatiently. "To Cannon Bay. Why did you come to Cannon Bay?"

Zack had been prepared to tell her the truth, but after tonight he wasn't sure she was ready to hear it. He didn't relish getting slapped with a stalking charge. His lips curved in a humorless smile as he realized that from what he'd read and watched on television, he certainly fit the MO of a stalker.

"My career is pretty much over, from what the doctors tell me." The knowledge still held the power to hurt. Zack shook his head; he hated self-pity. "I saw an opportunity to teach, so I took it."

He hadn't lied at all, he realized. He'd just omitted the most important part—that he'd come to Cannon Bay to be near her, and the job opening and subsequent offer had been a sheer coincidence. He heard the rustling of the comforter as she turned her head to look at him.

"I'm sorry to hear about your career," she said softly and with obvious sincerity. "Now that we've . . . talked, will you let Jordan back on the team? He has nothing to do with you and me, Zack. It isn't fair to make him a pawn in your games."

Zack thought he'd fallen asleep. Surely he hadn't heard her right? He sat up, searching her face for a sign that told him she was pulling his leg.

She stared back at him, her chin tilted defensively, her golden eyes fixed on him with determination and just a hint of lingering desire. He suddenly found the latter hard to swallow. It was the height of humiliation to think her response had been fiegned, but it would explain her sudden shift from cold indifference to inviting him over for coffee.

"I can't put Jordan back on the team yet," Zack stated, hiding the hurt behind a stony face. He could have explained everything to her and eased her mind about his motives for taking Jordan temporarily from the team, but his pride forbade it. That she would think he would actually stoop so low wounded him to the core. "My jeans should be dry by now."

He slid from the bed and started for the door.

"Zack?"

The plea in her tone stopped him.

"Maybe I was wrong about your motives."

Maybe? Zack gave a brief, bitter laugh before shaking his head and continuing on. Her voice stopped him again, and this time she sounded astonishingly angry.

"But you were wrong about Jordan. He was sick with the flu and missed an oral test. The teacher let him make it up, but failed to get the grade recorded in time."

Zack felt the tension ease out of him. The story Justine told wasn't anything remotely similar to what happened, but it explained her hostility. He was still annoyed enough, however, to keep his mouth shut. Justine would eventually learn that he didn't jump to conclusions, not without all the facts, and especially not with his students.

But she wouldn't hear it from him. Some lessons were best learned the hard way.

"Good night, Justine. Sweet dreams." He glanced over his shoulder just in time to see something slither back beneath her bed. He didn't think it was the cat or Thor.

She followed him into the kitchen.

"Wait just a damned minute, Zack! Did you hear what I said?"

Zack pulled his jeans from the dryer and straightened. He shot her a chiding look. "How could I *not* hear you? You're shouting. By the way, when were you planning to tell me about the snake under your bed?" He'd been hoping to catch her off guard with the question, but he had to admit her startled look seemed genuine.

"I'd forgotten about Squeeze. Don't worry, she's harmless."

"I'm not afraid of snakes, but I like to know when I'm in the room with one—especially one that big."

"She's only three feet long."

"So is Thor, but he eats toes," Zack retorted.

Justine folded her arms, her lips pressed in a mutinous line. "She wouldn't have hurt you. And I really did forget about her—I'm babysitting her for a friend."

Zack believed her. Incredibly, he did. After Thor . . . He balanced himself against the dryer and pulled on his jeans, then headed to the door where he'd left his coat and shoes. Getting out of here before he pulled her into his arms again was his top priority; two rejections in one night might be more than his pride could handle.

"You know, you men are all alike."

He asked because it was expected. "How's that?"

"All brawn and bluster, but when it comes to harmless little critters, you turn into cowards."

Jerking on his shoes, Zack stood and faced her. He should have been angry at the slur against his manhood, but he couldn't be; one look at her and his anger vanished like smoke in the wind. Did she have any idea how beautiful she looked to him? Her hair had dried and now lay like a soft, dark cloud around her face and shoulders; her golden eyes glittered with temper, and beneath the robe her breasts heaved temptingly.

God, he loved her.

"I'll bet you've never even *had* a pet," she taunted.

She was spoiling for a fight, and usually Zack would have welcomed the challenge. But tonight he wasn't entirely certain he could control his more basic urges long enough to give her what she wanted.

Knowing he shouldn't, Zack gave in to one small temptation. He leaned over and kissed her, catching her lips parted as she started to speak. It was a warm, yet explosive kiss, and her instant, eager response went a long way in soothing his bruised heart. Justine felt something for him. Just exactly what would be determined in time.

Wrenching himself from her mouth, he grabbed his coat and curled his ungloved fingers around the doorknob. It was icy cold against his palm.

"Call me when you get home safely," Justine said, her voice satisfyingly husky. She spoiled the effect by adding, "I'd worry about a polar bear in this weather."

With a wry smile, Zack opened the door. A sharp wind hurled snow and ice into his face as if it had been lying in wait. He could hardly see the stairs. "I'll call!" he shouted as he dashed onto the landing.

Mini's loud, uncontrollable laughter woke the entire animal kingdom inside the pet shop. The parrot began to recite his monotonous litany; kittens meowed, and puppies barked in response; and the bird population chirped, sang, and whistled in an offbeat symphony that sent Mini into fresh peals of laughter. Lizards, snakes, and iguanas stirred restlessly in their aquariums. Even the fish seemed to swim faster.

She sat up from where she'd collasped on the cage floor, wiping her streaming eyes and chuckling. "Oh, oh! That was priceless!"

"What, pray tell, is the cause of this fit you're having?" Reuben grumbled in a sleepy voice.

"You—you should have seen Zack with that overgrown iguana!" Mini rocked backwards, her feathers shaking with mirth. "Then—then the cat jumped on his back just as he was about to make love to Justine—"

"They made love?" His attention caught, Reuben sat up on the pillows. The sudden movement caused his head to spin. Mini's image wavered before him. "Does this mean we've succeeded in getting those two irritating mortals together?" he asked hopefully.

Mini sobered, using her feathers to dry her face. It was just like the arrogant warlock to take credit for something he had *not* done! *"We?* The only thing you've done, my darling husband, is grumble, complain, and get drunk!"

Reuben drew himself up to his full height of five inches. He thrust his feathered chest out. "I did not get drunk," he denied with an indignant sniff. "As for my helping you with those mortal fools, you have only to ask."

"Ask you *when?*" Mini wanted to know. She strutted over to him and poked him in the chest with her wing tip. "When you're lying in a drunken stupor?"

"I was not—"

"I nearly had a crisis on my hands, but where was my darling husband?"

"You could have—"

"I *did* try to wake you!" Mini cried hotly. Oh, he could get her feathers in an uproar without even trying! "You woke up long enough to question the time, then went right back to sleep."

"Need I remind you that I didn't agree to this absurd assignment in the first place?"

"So you wish us to remain lovebirds for the remainder of our sentence?" Mini countered in a silky-soft voice. She was angry. Very angry. Angry enough to threaten. "Or would you prefer to return without me? I could explain to the Peacemaker how I tricked you into coming here. I'm sure she'd understand."

Reuben's tiny bird eyes narrowed. "You wouldn't."

"I would." Mini thrust her beak up, hoping he'd mistaken the brightness of her eyes for something other than tears. She nearly had to choke the words out. "Maybe we need a separation."

In the two hundred years they'd been married, they had never spent a single night apart. Just thinking about it made her heart twist painfully. She held her breath as she waited for his reaction.

"I don't want to leave you," Reuben said.

Mini slowly let out a sigh of relief. She'd been so afraid he'd jump at the opportunity. Maybe there was hope for them yet. "Then will you help me with the mortals so that we can get back to our normal lives?"

"I will if I must, although I think we're wasting our time. Mortals are a hardheaded lot."

"Justine and Zachary are special. They truly are soul mates." Mini paused, her eyes growing soft as she gazed at her handsome husband. "Like you and me."

Reuben drew her gently into his embrace. "That we are, my love. I'll never forget how you made me see the wickedness of my ways as a warlock. If not for you, I'd still be causing havoc and mischief the world over."

She lifted her head from his breast to gaze at him. "No regrets?"

He shook his head, touching his beak to hers in a tender caress. "None. Now, can you replay the scene that made you crow with laughter? If I'm going to do my part, I guess I need to become familiar with these silly mortals."

Feeling more hopeful than she had in years, Mini withdrew her crystal ball and prepared a spell that would temporarily turn back the clock. Within moments, Reuben was howling with laughter at the sight of the iguana's determination to feast on Zack's toes.

Mini smiled.

"He's just taking his time because he knows I'm worried. I wouldn't be surprised if he was sitting by the phone right now, tapping his fingers and debating how long he's going to make me suffer."

Justine's audience remained frustratingly silent as she paced the living room and waited for Zack to call. "I mean, surely he's had *some* experience driving on icy roads? And if he hasn't, that should make him more cautious, right?"

Rogue blinked at her from his cozy position on the back of the couch; Thor, who had laboriously climbed *onto* the couch after he'd lost interest in Zack's toes, stared at her with deadpan eyes. Squeeze, a beautiful rainbow boa, had slithered from under the bed and now lay coiled in the corner, her head raised and pointed in Justine's direction as if she listened to every word.

"Even if he *did* get into trouble, he'd know what to do, wouldn't he?" Justine looked from one silent creature to the other, then shook her head at her silliness. "He's perfectly all right. Anyone with half a brain would know better than to walk in this type of dangerous weather. Just because he's from Florida doesn't make him stupid."

She pivoted, then began pacing again. "Maybe I should have insisted he stay, at least until the storm eased."

The phone rang. Tripping in her haste to reach it, Justine snatched the reciever from the hook. "Zack?" she squeaked breathlessly, rubbing her bruised knee.

"Who in the hell is Zack?" a familiar—and unwelcome—voice demanded.

Justine slumped against the wall, her heart pounding. Barry Fowler. Not Zack, reassuring her that he'd reached his apartment safely, but her ex-boyfriend. The reason she'd gone on that fateful cruise to begin with.

"Barry." Justine didn't bother hiding her annoyance. "What do you want?" As if she needed to ask. It was Friday, and like clockwork, Barry always called on Fridays to ask her out on Saturday. In all of the excitement, she'd forgotten.

"Who's Zack?" Barry persisted.

Justine tapped her fingers on the bar, considering her options. She could continue to ignore him, or use Zack's presence in Cannon Bay to get rid of Barry once and for— She sucked in a sharp breath as she remembered that she had told *Zack* she was involved with someone. It had been a desperate lie, of course, but if Zack pressed her to tell him *who* she was involved with, then she would have to come up with someone fast.

Barry was convenient, and not overly bright. She could go out with him a couple of times—just long enough to show Zack that she meant what she said—and then tell Barry she changed her mind again. It wouldn't be anything less than Barry deserved after what he'd put her through.

"That was an old friend of my brother's," Justine lied with crossed fingers. "Now, what were you going to ask me?" The sudden, shocked silence made her smile. Barry was more accustomed to her sharp tongue and instant refusal.

"Well, I thought we might go out tomorrow night," he suggested cautiously. "Try that new steakhouse that opened up last week over on Independence Street."

"Eight o'clock?" Another dead silence followed. Justine prompted, "Barry? Is eight o'clock all right?" If she could be seen with Barry a few times, maybe Zack would realize he was wasting his time. Maybe then he'd leave Cannon Bay when Coach Abernathy returned. She desperately *needed* him to leave . . . because tonight had proven she wasn't as immune to his charms as she'd believed herself to be.

But then, she hadn't planned on running into him again.

"Eight is fine," Barry said, interrupting her thoughts. He sounded disgustingly smug. "I'll pick you up at your place."

The moment Justine returned the phone to its hook, it rang again. She picked it up and automatically said hello. Zack's deep, sexy voice jump-started her pulse.

"Are you still naked?"

Justine's fingers tightened around the receiver. She willed her foolish heart to stop its clamoring. "I wasn't *naked* before," she said cooly. "I see you made it home safe and sound."

He chuckled, telling her without words that he noticed her quick subject change and knew the reason for it. "It was a little hairy, but yes, I made it. By the way, I had fun tonight."

"Fun?" Justine couldn't believe she'd heard him right. "You were chased by a giant lizard and attacked by a fifteen-pound cat! That's not most people's idea of fun."

"Seeing you again . . . being with you made it all worthwhile," he assured her huskily. "How about dinner tomorrow night?"

Justine slid slowly down the wall and closed her eyes

against the incredible urge to do something stupid, like say yes, yes, yes, she'd love to. Why hadn't he just stayed out of her life? she wailed silently. She took a deep breath, knowing there was no turning back once she said the words. "I've got a date tomorrow night." *With someone I hate. I'd much rather be with you, but that would be totally irresponsible of me, and I know—*

"Cancel it."

It wasn't a suggestion, it was an order. A growled, possessive-sounding order. The strength went out of her knees, but she managed to keep her voice strong. "I can't. I told you, Zack, I'm already involved with someone. He's—he's very special to me."

Long after she'd hung up the phone, Justine sat on the floor with her back to the wall, aching for the one man who could fill her soul with light and incredible joy.

Or plunge her world into darkness.

Six

"*He's very special to me.*"

Zack slowly replaced the receiver. He ground his teeth at the thought of Justine responding to another man as she had responded to him tonight. Could he be so totally blind to the truth? Was he imagining her response because he wanted it so badly?

He ran an agitated hand through his hair, forcing himself to consider that coming to Cannon Bay might have been a little extreme on his part. But then, hadn't he wanted to know the truth no matter *what* that truth turned out to be? And he still didn't know. Every time he thought about broaching the subject, of asking her what had happened to them, something distracted him. Hell, when he was around Justine he was lucky to remember his own name!

The phone rang. With a frown, Zack glanced at the Caller ID. His brows climbed when he saw the name of Justine's pet store scroll across the digital box. Surely she hadn't gone back out in this weather?

He lifted the receiver on the third ring. "Hello?"

"Zack, I've changed my mind. I'd love to have dinner with you."

It was Justine, but she sounded . . . different. Still stung by her rejection moments ago, Zack asked, "What about your date?"

"I said I've changed my mind. Meet me at the new steak-house on Independence at eight-thirty."

Zack winced as the phone on the opposite end crashed in his ear. The dial tone that followed confirmed that she'd hung up without saying good-bye. Pondering the strange call, Zack finally shrugged and went to take a shower. Maybe he'd get lucky and grab the hot water before his neighbor across the hall beat him to it.

It was hot, he discovered, but the pressure left a lot to be desired. He was just rinsing the shampoo from his hair when someone pounded on his front door. With a muffled curse, Zack grabbed his robe and shrugged into it.

His neighbor stood in the hall outside his door, dressed in a burgundy satin robe that made Zack's plain terry cloth robe look like something from a thrift shop. Despite Zack's instant dislike of the man, he attempted to break the ice by introducing himself. "Zachary Wayne. I'm your new neighbor."

"Are you aware that we get our hot water from the same source?" the man demanded, rudely ignoring Zack's proffered hand.

Zack didn't care for his attitude, and when he thought of the dozen or so cold showers he'd taken since moving in, he had to bite his tongue to still a sarcastic retort. He was, however, a civilized adult. Or tried to be, which was more than he could say for this man. "I came to that conclusion the day after I moved in and I had to take a lukewarm shower." The first of many.

"Well, I was in the shower just this moment when suddenly the water turned freezing."

"That might be because *I* was also taking a shower," Zack drawled in a sarcastic tone that made the other man bristle.

"The landlord will hear about this!"

Zack was amazed he was having such a ridiculous conversation with his neighbor. He was wet and cold and didn't give a damn *who* the fool told. Immature jerk.

"I've got an idea," Zack said as inspiration struck. "You wait right here while I turn the shower off and we'll go together. Maybe we can convince the landlord to install a bigger water heater."

The other man looked slightly mollified. "Shouldn't we dress first?"

"Yes, by all means. Let's get dressed first. I'll meet you back here in ten minutes." Zack gave him a pleasant smile and closed the door.

He whistled the victory charge as he made his way back to the bathroom to finish his hot shower. He grinned, imagining the look on his neighbor's face when he realized how cleverly he'd been had.

Watching Zack in the crystal ball, Reuben whistled his admiration when he realized what the mortal had done. Maybe *this* mortal wasn't so bad after all, he mused. His wife, however, wasn't impressed.

"I can't believe he did that! Leaving the poor man standing outside in the hall . . . freezing to death while *he* enjoyed a leisurely hot shower." Mini *tsk-tsked*. "Perhaps he *isn't* the right man for Justine."

"I'm sure he had his reasons, muffin," Reuben said, his voice soothing. "That mortal neighbor of his is a pompous ass."

Despite herself, Mini giggled. "He *did* look funny, didn't he? Dressed in a king's robe and acting like royalty. I wonder who he is?"

Reuben shrugged. "Don't we have enough on our hands with Zack and Justine without getting involved with another mortal? A useless one, at that."

"I suppose you're right," Mini murmured. "Reuben, do you think we did the right thing by calling Zack and pretending to be Justine? What if our plan backfires?"

"I don't think it will." Reuben sounded supremely confident. "When Zack sees Justine with that Barry mortal, he'll realize it was all a hoax. Didn't you see for yourself what a strain it was for her to be nice to Barry over the phone?"

"Yes, I did." Mini frowned. "But won't Zack be furious when he sees her with someone else after Jus—we—called and told him she'd changed her mind?"

"Fighting's good for them. They need to clear the air." Reuben closed his wing over Mini and pulled her close, lowering his voice to a husky whisper. "You haven't forgotten what happens after *our* fights, have you?"

Mini melted against him. "No, I haven't, husband. Is that why we fight so much? So we can make up afterwards?" The possibility had never occurred to her before.

Reuben chuckled, nuzzling her beak with his. "You've got a wild imagination, darling. Whoever heard of someone fighting just to add passion and excitement to their lives?"

"Silly, isn't it?" But Mini couldn't get the notion out of her head. It would explain so much about their volatile relationship. Could it be that her tamed warlock subconsciously yearned for that wild part of his personality he had willingly forsaken for love?

A memory, long buried, surfaced in her mind. Long ago her mother had warned her of the consequences of wedding a warlock, but Mini had been so in love she had scoffed at what she believed were the paranoid rumblings of an overprotective mother.

Warlocks *could* be tamed; she had proven that. Other than his grumbling disposition and occasional—all right, *frequent*—bursts of bad temper, Reuben was a gentle, loyal husband.

But at what price?

"What in the heck happened here?" Christopher asked the moment Justine entered the shop the next morning. Christopher was a college student who worked for her part time on weekends and a few afternoons through the week when he didn't have classes.

"The sprinklers went haywire," Justine explained. After a

sleepless night, she felt edgy and tired this morning. The perfect red rose she'd found nestled in a snowdrift outside her door hadn't improved her mood, either. The card attached to the long stem said, *I'm glad you changed your mind.*

Justine frowned as she readied the coffee machine in her office. The only time she'd gotten roses from Barry had been the day after she'd caught him with his hand up that bimbo's skirt. It wasn't that he couldn't be romantic when he put his mind to it, but she knew Barry considered flowers a frivolous waste of money. Candy was his choice of gifts. It hadn't taken Justine long to figure out why; Barry had a sweet tooth.

Back then she'd considered his self-absorbed acts a charming part of his personality. Justine winced to think how gullible she'd been. And then Zack . . .

Her back stiffened. She firmly reminded herself that she wasn't the same silly fool any longer. She was tougher and smarter. Now she *looked* for flaws in men instead of *overlooking* them. No surprises, and no feeling foolish. She jumped as Christopher stuck his head around the office door.

"You might want to take a look at your lovebirds. I think Reuben's feeling a little under the weather."

Justine turned to look at him in surprise. "Reuben? I've been calling them Luke and Laura."

Christopher shrugged. "I'm just going by the name plates on the front of the cage. I figured that's their names."

Intrigued, Justine followed him to the cage on the counter. Christopher had pulled the satin covering aside and tied it with the purple tassels. She rubbed the silky material between her fingers. *Satin.* Her jaw dropped in astonishment. Last night the covering had been made of filmy gauze, although she had thought it was satin before.

Now it was satin again. Was she losing her mind? Shaking her head, she peered where Christopher pointed. Two small name plates, made of some type of beaten metal, were nailed to the bottom front of the cage. How had she missed not seeing them?

"Mini and Reuben," she read aloud. She straightened and

put a hand to her head, dazed. "I can't believe I missed this, and last night I was *sure* this material was . . ." She trailed off when she realized Christopher was giving her an odd look, as if he doubted her sanity. "Never mind. Mini and Reuben it is. Now, what seems to be the problem?"

"See for yourself," Christopher said, indicating the male lovebird.

Justine looked, her brow furrowing with concern. Christopher was right; the bird didn't look well. He appeared listless, hanging his head as if he couldn't hold it upright. "Do you suppose he ate some bad seeds or something?"

"Smells like he got drunk," Christopher joked. "I could have sworn I smelled wine when I pulled back the covering."

"Very funny." Justine suddenly remembered the violent incident yesterday between the two birds. She pinned her suspicious gaze on Mini, who was regarding her with an intensity that made the hair on the back of her neck prickle. "Did you do something to him, Mini?"

Mini gave an almost imperceptible shake of her head.

Justine gasped. "Did you see that, Christopher? Did you see her shake her head?"

"Yeah, right. And pigs fly."

"No, she did! I saw her . . ." Justine bit her lip, suddenly realizing how crazy she sounded. It had to have been a coincidence. Yes, a coincidence, or a trick of the light. Some birds were smarter than others, but no matter how smart they were, she knew they couldn't understand her.

"Well, we'll keep an eye on him today. If he gets worse, I'll call Melissa and see what she thinks." Melissa Copeland was the local vet Justine used when the need arose. Exotic animals and birds weren't exactly her area of expertise, but Justine respected her opinion.

The box of candy arrived at noon. Justine accepted the ribbon-wrapped box from the florist with a frozen smile and a feeling of dread. She was beginning to think she'd made a serious mistake in encouraging Barry. If he called her once a week when she said no, sent her roses and flowers when she said yes, what would he do when she actually went out with him again?

She read the card without much interest. *"So glad you changed your mind."* He was beginning to sound like a broken record, as well. How would she get through dinner with this man? Had she really once believed herself in love with him?

Her reluctance continued to build throughout the day. The only highlight was the lovebird's apparent recovery, for which Justine was very thankful. Despite their peculiar nature, she'd grown fond of the birds. She would find someone very special for two special birds.

By the time she closed the shop and trudged up the snow-covered stairs to her apartment to get ready for her date with Barry, Justine's feet were dragging.

Zack was running late. He'd called a meeting at the local pizza parlor to go over the team's strategy for the upcoming game Monday night and had lost track of time. Zack grinned as he recalled their enthusiasm. The boys were geared to win—he felt it in his gut.

Humming a jaunty tune beneath his breath, Zack turned the shower on and stripped his clothes off, anticipating a good hot spray to take the chill from his body. At least it wasn't snowing today, he thought, stepping beneath the water.

The water was frigid.

Not lukewarm—hell, he was used to that—but icy cold. *Frigid.* Gritting his teeth, Zack quickly soaped himself from head to toe and rinsed off. He wrenched the faucets so hard they squealed in protest before he stepped out of the shower. Well? What had he expected? He'd declared war when he left the man dripping in the hall like a fool.

Cursing beneath his breath, Zack dried himself and stomped to his bedroom. He was dressed and ready to leave in record time, and a quick glance at his watch told him that he just might make it by eight-thirty.

Despite the late hour, the Rawhide was crowded. Zack wasted precious time finding a suitable parking space, then another five minutes waiting in line before he caught a passing waiter's attention.

"I'm supposed to meet Justine Diamond here," he told the young boy.

The waiter shook his head. "Don't know her, but you're welcome to look around." He hurried away before Zack could ask him where the nonsmoking section was located.

Left on his own, Zack strolled casually into the spacious dining room and looked around. He spotted Justine seated at a table against the south wall. Anticipating her smile, he moved through the tables until he reached her. She hadn't noticed him, intent on the salad before her.

"Fancy meeting you here," he teased.

With a visible start, she glanced up. "Zack!"

Zack's smile died before it began at her surprised expression. Why would she be surprised to see him? They had a date! Her next words added to his confusion.

"What are *you* doing here?"

"Yeah, what are *you* doing here?" a familiar voice demanded belligerently behind him.

Zack turned to find none other than his neighbor glaring at him. He held a glass platter piled high with salad greens and topped with a rancid-smelling dressing. Zack glared back; he hadn't forgotten the cold shower he'd taken a short while ago. "*I'm* here to do what people normally do in a restaurant—eat dinner."

"You two know each other?" Justine squeaked, throwing her napkin aside and rising.

Zack looked at her in surprise. "Do *you* know *him?*"

"He's . . . he's my date," she informed him. "Zack—this is Barry Fowler. Barry—"

"I know who he is," Barry interrupted. "The question is, how do *you* know him?"

Zack wasn't listening. She'd called Barry her date. Worst of all, she didn't sound the least bit remorseful for the cold-blooded stunt she'd pulled. It had all been a setup on her part, he realized, more than a little stunned to discover the woman he loved was capable of such a brutal maneuver. She'd wanted him to see her with Barry, wanted to rub his nose in it.

Wanted to convince him she didn't care? Zack pondered the question as Justine and Barry discussed him as if he wasn't there. Why would she go to such lengths when all she had to do was ignore him? He'd eventually get the point. Unless . . . unless it wasn't just *him* she was trying to convince.

The possibility made Zack more determined than ever to find out why Justine was afraid of him—of their feelings for each other. Why did she fight it? What happened to change her mind?

"Well, that settles it, then," Barry said gloatingly. "The lady told you she already had plans for the evening, and as you can see for yourself . . ."

Zack cleared his mind and focused on the jerk standing before him. So they thought he'd apologize, excuse himself, and just walk away? Over his dead body.

"I'd be more than happy to join you," Zack said, deliberately misconstruing Barry's words. He signaled a passing waitress and pulled out a chair. As he opened the menu the waitress set before him, he glanced at Justine. She looked so horrified, he had no trouble summoning a smile. "Sorry about the mix-up. I guess I didn't get your message when you called to cancel."

"I didn't call to cancel," Justine whispered furiously.

"Ah, but you said you told me you already had plans—"

"I never accepted in the first place!" Her voice rose on the last octave, drawing several interested gazes from tables nearby.

Zack cocked an admiring brow. "I never knew you were such a good liar, Justine." As she sputtered indignantly, he lifted the menu and pretended to study it. He saw nothing but red and was amazed his anger didn't show. "So, what's good? Has anyone ordered yet?"

"This is ridiculous!" Barry announced, an angry red flush creeping up his neck. He threw his napkin aside and came to his feet. "I refuse to eat with this—this—"

"Hot water stealer?" Zack supplied helpfully. "But then, that would be like the pot calling the kettle black, wouldn't it?"

"I've lived in that apartment for five years!"

"Ah, territorial, are we?" Zack clicked his tongue and shook his head. "In the lease I signed, I don't recall reading anything about *you* having first dibs on the hot water."

Justine didn't know which man she wanted to strangle the most. She cleared her throat—loudly. When that didn't get their attention, she banged her spoon against her glass. They already had the attention of at least a dozen or so diners, so what did a few more matter? "Excuse me? Boys? Gentlemen?"

"What about that dirty trick you pulled on me yesterday?" Barry demanded as if he hadn't heard Justine.

"Wasn't any worse than the trick *you've* been pulling on *me* since I moved in. Yesterday was the *first* time I've enjoyed a hot shower, thanks to you."

"Ha!"

"Ha, yourself."

"Wait a minute!" Justine shouted. That got their attention. She lowered her voice to a furious growl. "If you don't quiet down, we're going to get thrown out of here."

A shadow fell across the table before she finished her warning. Zack and Barry fell silent, both scowling as they turned to see who had dared to interrupt them. Justine turned as well, nearly missing the satisfied glint in Zack's eyes.

It was the manager, and he didn't look happy.

Justine groaned, her face heating with embarrassment. Cannon Bay was about to experience its first double homicide, was her dark thought.

Seven

Getting thrown out of a busy restaurant wasn't Justine's most embarrassing moment, but it was close.

She was mad enough to spit ice cubes. It was partly because she felt humiliated, she admitted to herself. Barry and Zack had not been fighting over her, but over hot water. *Hot water!* She stifled a dry, disbelieving laugh. How flattered could a girl be?

"Come on, Justine." Barry grabbed her arm. "We'll just go to another restaurant."

"She's going with me." Zack grabbed her other arm, and to her amazement, they began to tug her back and forth.

Had she really been humiliated a moment ago because they hadn't been fighting over her? What irony. She wrenched both arms free, glaring at Barry, then at Zack. "I'll take a cab, thank you."

"But you came with me!" Barry protested, stamping his feet against the cold.

Zack dared to close his fingers over her arm again. "We've got things to talk about. You're coming with me."

Of all the *nerve*! First he crashed her date, then got them thrown out of the restaurant, and now he was *demanding* she go with him? Justine blew out an angry breath; it frosted in front of her, reminding her that it wouldn't be long before they all froze to death. She knew two men whose deaths she wouldn't mourn!

Jerking her arm loose again, she ignored Zack for the moment. "First of all," she told Barry, her tone as icy as the weather, "I agreed to have dinner with you, and since we can't have dinner, the date is over."

"But—"

Justine held up a detaining hand. "Apparently hot water was more important to you than having dinner with me."

"But, *he* started—"

"I don't care *who* started it," she interrupted furiously. She couldn't believe that she had never noticed Barry's lack of maturity—or Zack's, for that matter. "All I know is that you both embarrassed me in front of a crowd, and some of those people are people I'll have to face next week *as customers*." Now would have been a good time for Barry to apologize.

She should have known he wouldn't.

"Well, then. If that's the way you feel." Barry drew himself up, yanking the collar of his London Fog over his red ears. "Good night, Justine."

Justine watched him stomp through the snow to his sleek new Altima. When he'd gone in a spin of tires, she let out a shaky breath. What a night! One down, one to go.

"You won't get rid of me that easily," Zack said, as if he could read her mind. "We need to talk."

Justine managed to lift a cool brow. "The same kind of *talking* we did last night? I don't think so." She started back inside the restaurant to call a cab. Before she reached the door, she heard his low, angry voice in her ear.

"I think you owe me an apology."

His outrageous comment startled a disbelieving laugh out of Justine. Eyes wide, she swung around to face him. "Are you out of your mind?" He must be, she decided. Completely. "Me apologize to you? *You* crashed my date. *You* also deliberately started a fight with Barry." She knew she had hit a nerve when she saw his jaw tighten. So it was true!

"I didn't crash your date." The look he gave her was unmistakably skeptical. "Don't tell me you don't remember calling me from the store last night and telling me you changed your mind."

Justine gaped at him. "I did *not* call you last night! You called me. Furthermore, I couldn't have called you from the store because I was in my apartment." *Put that in your pipe and smoke it!* Justine silently added. Did he really think she would believe him?

"I have the proof on my Caller ID."

His smug expression sent a chill down Justine's spine. For the first time since the argument started, she realized he was serious. He truly believed she had called him. The thought prompted a puzzling question that had been nagging at her all day, one she had meant to ask Barry. "Zack, there was a rose on my doorstep—"

"So you *did* get it."

"You sent it?"

"Who else would talk about being glad you changed your mind?"

Another chill skirted down her spine, leaving an icy trail behind. She shivered. "I'd like to see for myself, if you don't mind." If the store's number was on his Caller ID, then it meant someone had called him from the store. Which meant . . . someone had to have been *inside* the store last night.

And from what she could gather, that someone had pretended to be her.

Mini snatched the crystal ball from Reuben's hands. "What are they talking about? What's a 'Caller ID'?"

"I'm as lost as you are," Reuben said with a puzzled frown. "But whatever it is, we've got to get rid of it."

"But we *can't*, Reuben," Mini wailed. "I doubt our magic will reach that far, and we can't go flying around in this kind of weather! The Peacemaker warned us that we are far more vulnerable as birds because of our diminished powers."

"We could use a warming spell," he suggested. "I could fly like the—"

"You?" Mini blinked away sappy tears. "You would do this for me?"

"For us," Reuben corrected. "We're in this together, remember?"

Mini was suddenly gripped with a terrible fear. "No, it's too dangerous. I won't let you." She flung herself into his arms and wrapped her wings around him as if to physically hold him in place. "I couldn't stand it if something happened to you!"

"Now, now, dear. Nothing will happen to me. I'll be back before you know it." He gently disengaged her wings and pushed her back. "You do the warming spell. You're much better at that type of thing."

His compliment made Mini blush. She gave a shuddering sigh, realizing that Reuben was determined to go through with it. She knew better than anyone how impossible it was to change a warlock's mind once it was made up. Well, she'd just have to make sure he stayed warm during the trip. Folding her wings across her breasts, she closed her eyes and began to chant. When she was finished, she swept her wing in the direction of the front door. The lock clicked open.

Reuben stroked her cheek. "I'll be back in a flash."

When he'd gone, Mini withdrew her tiny crystal ball and anxiously followed his progress. She knew she wouldn't relax a single feather until her husband was safe and sound again.

Zack unlocked his apartment door and had just stepped inside when he heard the noise. He paused. Justine bumped into him, her soft gasp cut short as he put a finger to her lips. "Stay here," he whispered. "I heard something."

"What is it?"

"Just stay here," he commanded again. Before he'd taken his first step, she thrust a small cylinder-shaped object into his hand. It was ice cold.

"Pepper spray."

"Thanks."

"You're welcome," she whispered back.

He crept down the dark hall to the living room, wishing he had something more substantial than a can of pepper spray and his car keys to use as a weapon.

The light switch lay to his left. Stretching his hand along the wall, he felt around until he found it. He flipped it on. Harsh light illuminated the empty room. Next, Zack searched the kitchen, and then the bedroom before he was satisfied they were alone.

"You can come on in now," he told Justine. When she came into sight, he pointed to the floor. "They're gone, but someone was in here. They knocked the Caller ID from the table and left the window open." He retrieved the Caller ID, cursing when he saw that it was dead—and his proof with it. Imagine that.

"You're on the second floor. How could someone have gotten in?" She shivered as a draft of cold air blew across the room, but he noticed that she didn't look frightened.

Zack strode to the window and slammed it shut. "Fire escape right outside," he explained shortly, although he highly doubted anyone could have navigated the slick, icy surface coating the frame.

Everything looked damned convenient, even to *his* eyes. He could only imagine what Justine was thinking.

"Would you like something to drink?" he asked, bracing himself as he turned. He fully expected an accusation, but instead she nodded, looking every bit as puzzled as he felt.

"Anything warm would be fine. Zack, do you have any idea who it could have been and what they could have wanted? Is anything missing?"

Although Zack was pretty certain nothing *was* missing, he gave the room another glance. "No, nothing that I can see. As for a suspect, I haven't a clue. Motive?" His lips twisted in a derisive smile. "They wrecked the Caller ID, erasing my proof that you called me last night."

"But who—"

"No one knew about it. No one *could* have known about it." He moved to the kitchen, flipping the light on as he put water on to boil for hot chocolate. "Probably a kid snooping around. Got scared when he heard us come in and knocked the ID over on his way to the window."

Zack didn't believe it for a moment, but then nothing else sounded rational, either. He opened a cabinet door and took out two mugs, slamming them onto the counter before reaching for the box of instant cocoa. From the corner of his eye he saw Justine approach. She'd taken off her coat, and not for the first time that night Zack noticed how the dark blue velvet dress hugged her waist and hips.

"I know why you're so angry," she said. She took the packets from his unresisting hands and tore them open, dumping the contents into the mugs. "You're angry not only because someone was in your home, but also because you don't think I believe you now."

His laugh was abrupt and without humor. "Why should you? If I were you, I probably wouldn't believe me, either."

Justine cocked her head, considering his words. Either he was very good and she was a damned fool, or something very strange was going on. Strange . . . like the muzzle on the parrot and the sprinkler system coming on without rhyme or reason. And she hadn't forgotten how the covering on the birdcage had mysteriously changed textures *twice*.

A string of odd coincidences, or was someone pulling a few rather clever tricks? Finally, she sighed. "I expected you to believe *me*, didn't I?"

Zack laughed again, but this time he seemed genuinely amused as he pointed out, "We can't agree to believe each other, because one of us has to be wrong." He poured hot water into the mugs and carried them to a small dinette table, pulling out a chair for her before seating himself. "Either I'm lying about you calling, or *you're* lying about not calling."

She followed and took a seat across from him, determined to keep her temper in check until they figured this thing out.

Maybe she was a fool to believe him, but every instinct told her he was telling the truth.

But . . . so was she.

"Zack, are you *certain* it was my voice you heard?" When he looked up at her, her breath caught in her throat at the raw emotion in his eyes. He effectively masked it, leaving her to wonder if she had imagined it. She decided after a brief moment that she must have, because if he cared, why would he have walked out on her without a word? *Stop it! You know how dangerous it is to think about then, especially with him sitting across from you!*

He lowered his gaze, absently stirring the dark liquid. "I know your voice like I know my own," he said softly. "Or at least I *thought* I did."

Justine leaned forward. "What do you mean?"

"Well . . ." Zack rubbed his jaw, then sighed. "You did sound a little strange." His gaze met hers. "And you hung up without saying good-bye."

"Zack, I didn't call you back." She felt an urgency to convince him, because in convincing *him*, she hoped to restore her own slipping sanity. "I swear."

"I believe you," he said slowly. "But if *you* didn't call me, then who was it? Does anyone else have a key to the store?"

Christopher. Christopher had a key, and so did Clay in case something happened to her and he needed to get inside to see to the animals. "Yes, but I trust them totally."

She did. To consider for one moment that Clay would pull an immature stunt like that was ludicrous. Christopher wouldn't either, she was sure of it. He was young, but she'd known him since he was a small boy, and he'd never been the trickster type.

"What about your nephews?" Zack asked abruptly.

Justine bit her lip. She hated to consider it, but she supposed it was possible they could get Clay's key. "Drew would think such a stunt immature. Colby might, but I happen to know he was at basketball practice around the time you think I called." She hesitated. That left . . .

"And Jordan?"

"If any of my nephews were responsible, there was no malicious intent," Justine said defensively. She took a sip of her cocoa, hoping he'd let it drop. The last thing she wanted to do was tell Zack that Jordan had been the only nephew unaccounted for Friday night.

"Is Jordan angry with me, Justine?"

Damn his soft voice. It was incredibly hard to be mad at someone who could turn her knees to jelly with a few soft-spoken words! She licked the chocolate from her lips, sensing his gaze following the movement. Heat flared in her belly. She quickly stanched it. "Of course he's mad at you, but he didn't even *know* about us, so he couldn't have made the call." To her relief, he nodded and gave her a boyish, lopsided smile.

"Back to square one."

Justine mentally hardened her heart against his charm. If she wasn't careful, she'd find herself forgiving him. She shuddered just thinking about falling in love with Zack all over again. In her opinion, heart pain was the worst kind of pain, and in this instance, avoidable.

"Justine, I want to say—"

"Don't." Justine forced a bright smile. She didn't want to hear an apology or an explanation or both; too much time had passed for it to matter. "Let's not drag up the past. We can start over . . . as friends."

"Friends?" Zack echoed.

Justine stiffened as he rose and came around the table to stand behind her. When his hands descended onto her shoulders, it was all she could do not to clear the chair and run for her life. Somehow she managed to remain seated and to keep her trembling to a minimum.

Or so she thought.

"I feel you trembling, Justine," he whispered as his magical fingers kneaded her tense muscles. "Are you afraid?"

She shook her head. "Afraid of what?" *Of you? Of the way you make me feel? Of the power you wield over my heart? Yes!* But she wasn't about to admit it. As long as she didn't admit it out loud, she could fight it.

His fingers continued to work their magic, sliding onto her collarbone and tracing delicate patterns on her skin. "Then what is it? Why won't you talk about what we—"

Justine stood abruptly, dislodging his hands. Her breath came out in a rush. She could feel him staring at the back of her neck—undoubtedly disappointed to find she was much stronger this time around. "Take me home," she said, facing him.

"Justine . . ."

Something in her expression must have convinced him that she meant business, for he clamped his lips firmly shut. Justine took the opportunity to retrieve her coat from the living room sofa and make for the door.

Outside, the night was still, the air cold enough to sear the lungs. A thin layer of ice covered the hard-packed snow, causing their shoes to crunch loudly as they walked to his Explorer. The streetlights made the ice-covered snow glisten like a winter wonderland.

When they reached her street, Zack insisted on walking her to the door of her apartment. Justine shrugged with admirable indifference and left him to follow her up the slick stairs. At her door, she turned and summoned a polite smile. "Thanks for seeing me home."

Zack braced an arm against the door and leaned close, capturing her gaze in the dim light of the streetlamp at the corner of the building. Justine tensed, wishing he wouldn't stand so near.

"You're welcome." His lips curved in a slight smile. "I guess this is a mystery we failed to solve."

Justine managed to keep her voice steady. "I guess it is. Good night, Zack."

He brought his head closer, his warm breath fanning her cold cheeks as he placed a brief kiss on her lips. When he lifted his head, she could see a warm flame burning in his eyes. She suspected her own weren't as cool as she'd like them to be.

"Good night, Justine."

Justine let herself into the apartment and leaned her back against the door. She let out a shuddering breath. Her legs shook, and her lips tingled as if from an electric shock—although his mouth had barely touched hers.

Nobody but Zack could make her feel this way. Nobody ever had, and she sadly suspected nobody ever would again.

In the dark store below, Mini silently stared at the crystal ball and contemplated the scene she had just witnessed. She wasn't sure *what* to think. Maybe when she replayed the scene to Reuben, he'd have the answers.

Turning the round globe to the opposite side to check on Reuben's progress, she uttered a dismayed shriek when the image of the flying lovebird came into view. She could clearly see the icicles forming on his wings and beak! Apparently her warming spell hadn't lasted, and now Reuben was in danger of freezing in mid-flight!

"Come on, Reuben, my darling hero," Mini urged softly. "You can make it. Just a little longer . . ."

By her calculations, he was only minutes away. To prepare for his arrival she waved her wing and unlocked the pet store door, swinging it wide. The temperature in the shop immediately began to drop, but Mini paid no attention. She closed her eyes and began to chant the words for the warming spell. The moment Reuben drew close enough, she knew the spell would once again take effect.

A rustling noise at the door caused Mini to pause in her chanting. "Reuben! Oh, darling, you made it. I was so—"

"Who's there?" a deep, unfamiliar voice demanded from the doorway.

Mini's eyes flew open.

"All right, come out with your hands up! Nice and easy."

She uttered a shriek and threw up her wings. It wasn't Reuben. It wasn't even a bird.

It was a mortal!

Eight

"Are you certain you heard voices, Mac?" Justine wandered around the store as she spoke, making sure nothing had been taken. When the officer knocked on her apartment door a few moments ago, she'd been stunned when he told her he found the door of the store standing wide open.

She was positive she had locked it.

Mac nodded vigorously. "Sounded like a woman's voice. She must have gone out the back way."

"Did you check the back door?"

His dismayed expression told its own story. Quickly he started in that direction, his hand on the butt of his gun, his nightstick banging clumsily against his leg. "You stay here, ma'am."

"Okay, Mac." Despite the somber circumstances, Justine couldn't help but smile at his serious tone. She'd gone to school with Mac and had known him most of her life. It was hard to take him seriously, even in a smart suit and a shiny badge.

He returned, his boyish face creased in puzzled lines. "The back door's locked solid. In fact, the front door didn't look tampered with, either. Doesn't make sense!"

Justine chose her words carefully, mindful of Mac's feelings. "Mac, did you close the front door before you took a look around?"

The color drained from his face, then turned a fiery red. "I thought it would be best to leave it open, in case there was more than one perpetrator." He thrust his shoulders out and added defensively, "Procedure, ma'am."

"Can't you just call me Justine?" she asked with mild exasperation. Being called 'ma'am' made her feel old, and she and Mac were the same age. "Do you think they could have slipped out when your back was turned?"

"I guess maybe they could have," Mac admitted, shamefaced.

Justine gave her head a mental shake. It still didn't make sense . . . any more than the break-in at Zack's apartment made sense. Nothing was taken, and nothing looked out of place. Her gaze wandered to the cage housing the lovebirds. It was the only thing she hadn't checked, but why would anyone steal a pair of birds? Not that they weren't valuable . . .

Walking to the cage, Justine peeped between the part in the cover, her gaze seeking the two lovebirds on the perch. Reuben was shivering uncontrollably—probably because of the open door, she mused. The female lovebird, Mini, looked as if she were attempting to warm him with her wings. Sometimes their actions were so humanlike it was uncanny.

Justine studied them a moment longer before letting the cover drop into place, a *satin* cover, she noted with a great deal of relief. Maybe she wasn't losing her mind after all. Frowning, she dabbed at the small puddles of water, leaving a trail along the counter to the cage door.

She shook her puzzled head and turned back to Mac. "Well, there's nothing missing that I can tell, and nothing's been vandalized." *Just like Zack's apartment,* she thought, with the exception of the Caller ID, which could have been an accident.

Still, the two incidents were related in some way; of that

she was certain. She just didn't know how or why. The urge to call Zack and tell him what happened was strong, but in the end her pride won. The last thing she wanted was for Zack to think she needed him or depended on him.

"If you'll lock up nice and tight, I'll escort you back to your apartment," Mac offered.

"Thanks, Mac. And thanks for keeping an eye on the store." She flashed him a grateful smile. "If you hadn't noticed the door open, I probably would have had a shop full of frozen critters by morning."

Mac blushed and ducked his head. "It's my job, ma— Justine. I just hope whoever it was doesn't decide to come back." He looked at her, frowning so sternly Justine had to bite her lip to keep from smiling. "I'd get those locks changed tomorrow if I were you."

Tomorrow was Sunday. Justine didn't think she'd get a locksmith until Monday, but she didn't share her thoughts with Mac. He was a dedicated policeman and probably wouldn't sleep a wink if he knew.

She wasn't entirely certain *she* would.

The moment Justine and the uniformed man she had called Mac left the store, Mini quickly chanted a warming spell for her frozen husband. Mac's startling appearance had frightened her into silence, and while Mac took a look around, Reuben had flown in through the open door, icicles melting from his wings as he stumbled along the counter to the cage. But prudence had kept Mini silent until the mortals had gone, despite her wifely concerns.

Within seconds after she finished chanting the warming spell, Reuben was enveloped in a cocoon of warmth. He let out a thankful sigh and fluffed his damp feathers. "That feels wonderful! Thank you, my dear." He shot her a questioning glance. "What happened? Who was that mortal waving a gun around?"

"Justine called him Mac. I think he's a policeman."

"What was he doing here? Did he threaten you? If he did, I'll—"

"No, no. He didn't hurt me." Mini produced a towel and began to dry her husband's feathers. "When I saw you in distress, I opened the shop door to let you in. In your frozen state I was afraid you wouldn't have the strength . . ." She winced inwardly, realizing her blunder too late. It wasn't wise to question a warlock's strength.

Reuben's eyes narrowed to slits. Mini mentally kicked herself.

"I could have opened a measly door!" He sniffed, slapping at the towel until she gave up. "And no matter *what* the danger, I certainly don't need a witch to do it for me. Nor do I need to be towel-dried like a babe just getting out from his bath!" he added irritability.

Holding onto her temper by a slim margin, Mini threw the towel aside; it vanished into thin air. "I'm your wife, Reuben. You said we were in this together."

An edgy silence fell between them. She waited, her heart sinking with each moment that passed. Had her hopeful imagination conjured the feeling that things had improved between them?

"You're right, I did say that," Reuben finally conceded, sounding slightly ashamed.

Mini slumped in relief.

Sunday was the one and only day Clay didn't go into the office, and refused to answer the phone. Bea always cooked a huge midday meal, and Justine had a standing invitation. Since he joined the law firm and she opened the pet store, she rarely saw Clay anymore, so she made it a point to eat dinner with the family each Sunday. Besides, she loved the noise and smells, the laughter and the fighting, and Bea's friendship.

Today it was like a balm to her raw nerves, though she supposed a few people might consider her crazy. Colby and Drew fought as they usually did for Clay's attention, but

Justine noticed Jordan was quieter than normal. His expression—when he decided to look at something other than his plate—was that of a sullen, angry teenager.

Justine glanced from Jordan's drooping chin to Bea's frowning face. Hoping to draw her nephew into the conversation, Justine nudged Jordan's elbow. "Would you please pass the garlic bread?" She was on her third helping of Bea's delicious spaghetti, not realizing until she forked the first bite into her mouth how ravenous she was. Of course, that was because she'd missed dinner last night, thanks to Barry and Zack.

Jordan put his fork aside and grabbed the platter of garlic bread, silently handing it to her. He then resumed playing with his pasta.

"Thanks," Justine said, taking a slice of crusty garlic toast and handing the plate back to him. She hid a smile as he scowled and took the plate. Jordan was about to be reminded that his aunt had inherited the same stubborn genes that his father possessed. "Your mom outdid herself today with the spaghetti, don't you think?"

"Yeah, I guess."

Justine rolled spaghetti noodles around her fork and took an unladylike bite. She chewed and swallowed before tapping her fork against his plate to get his attention. "So, what did you do this weekend? I noticed you didn't come into the store on Saturday." For a long moment, she thought he wouldn't answer. Finally he let out a sigh and set his fork aside again.

"I went out with the guys," he muttered, crumbling a piece of toast over his uneaten spaghetti. He still refused to look at her.

"Oh? Who?" she persisted with cheerful innocence. She was beginning to understand why Bea was so concerned. Jordan usually ate like a horse, talked nonstop, and was rarely ever rude.

This quiet, sulky boy wasn't the nephew she knew.

"Just the guys. You don't know them."

Justine sensed that Bea and Clay were listening intently, although they kept a running conversation going with Drew and Colby. She pasted a determined smile on her face. "Maybe I do know them. This is a small town, and a lot of teenagers come into the store and browse around."

"Whatever."

At his uncharacteristically rude reply, the conversation at the other end of the table ground to a halt, proving that Bea and Clay *had* been listening. Justine glanced at their shocked faces and gave her head a slight shake, hoping they'd take the hint. She breathed again only when their conversation resumed.

"I take it none of these guys are football buddies?" Justine asked bluntly. She forked spaghetti onto her toast, watching Jordan's expression from the corner of her eye. His face was slowly turning a dull, angry red. Good, she thought smugly. Now maybe she'd see some *real* anger. She didn't think it was healthy for him to keep it bottled up inside.

Apparently Jordan had other ideas. He pushed his chair back and came to his feet, looking at his mother. "May I be excused?"

Bea's voice shook with simmering anger. "Not until you apologize to Aunt Justine."

"For what?" Jordan demanded belligerently. His fists were clenched at his sides, and a vein pulsed in his neck.

Justine's heart went out to him. She felt helpless and frustrated. It was obvious to all that something was wrong. Why wouldn't he talk about it? What happened to the old Jordan, the one who wouldn't hesitate to state his opinion or talk about his problems with his family?

Clay answered, anger sparkling in his brown eyes, eyes a few shades darker than Justine's own. "For being rude to Justine. She's a guest in our house—"

"Does that give her the right to stick her nose in my business?"

Bea gasped; Drew and Colby stared in shock. Clay pushed back his chair and threw his napkin on the table, his gaze narrowed dangerously. He reminded Justine of a hard-boiled lawyer drilling a frightened witness.

She felt awful for disrupting dinner and, from the looks of it, getting Jordan into trouble. She opened her mouth, intent on distracting her brother and perhaps easing the way for Jordan, but Clay caught the movement and effectively stilled her words with a single sharp glance.

"Wait for me in the study," Clay instructed Jordan.

"Clay—"

"No, Bea. We've been patient and have tried to give him some breathing space, but I won't stand for this type of behavior. He'll apologize to Justine or he'll suffer the consequences."

Jordan stomped out of the room. Justine started to slump into a miserable ball, but her brother's sharp words jerked her straight again.

"And don't you dare blame yourself, Justine. You were just trying to find out what we've all been dying to know— what's eating Jordan."

"I think that's supposed to be 'what's eating Gilbert Grape,' Dad," Drew corrected, straight-faced.

Colby snickered.

A glance from their father sobered them quickly. "If you boys are finished, I believe the garage needs to be cleaned."

Neither boy protested. They dutifully took their plates to the counter before disappearing through the back door leading into the garage. After Clay had gone, Justine and Bea were left alone at the table. Justine cleared her throat, feeling miserable despite Clay's attempts to alleviate her guilt.

"I didn't mean to get him into trouble," she mumbled, staring morosely at her plate.

"If you ask me, it's about time." Bea rose and began to clear the table, her quick, jerky movements revealing her agitation. When Justine popped out of her chair to help her, Bea waved her back down. "No, don't even think about it. From what I hear, you had the weekend from hell. I've been waiting all morning to hear about it."

Justine stared at her, slowly sinking into her chair again. "How did *you* know?" More to the point, how *much* did she know?

"Carmella was at the Rawhide last night when you got thrown out. She told Sue, and Sue called this morning. She said that Carmella said two men were fighting over you." Bea scraped plates and stacked dishes as she spoke, casting a worried glance now and then at the hallway leading to the study.

"And Carmella didn't recognize the two men?" Justine asked with mild sarcasm. She handed Bea the leftover bowl of spaghetti from the opposite end of the stable. "I'll bet she's pulling her hair out waiting for you to call her back."

Bea laughed, but it wasn't her usual boisterous laugh. "She'll be bald, then. You know how I feel about gossip."

"Unless it's about your sister-in-law."

"Unless it's about my *best friend*," Bea corrected, then added honestly, "and my sister-in-law. Besides, Carmella thought she recognized Barry Fowler, and she described the other guy as tall, dark, and handsome."

"How original," Justine murmured. And how true. She watched as Bea paused in her cleaning to prepare the automatic drip coffeemaker. "So, have you guessed who the other guy is?"

"Been guessing all morning, and I keep coming up with the same answer." Casting a conspiratorial glance in the direction of the hallway, she lowered her voice to a near whisper. "Zachary Wayne."

"Good guess, only he wasn't supposed to be there," Justine whispered back. "I accepted a date with Barry hoping Zack would take the hint."

Bea's brow climbed, emphasizing the tiny lines in her forehead. "And he crashed your date?"

"Not only that, but he insisted that *I* told him to meet me there. By the way, why are we whispering?"

"Because if Jordan finds out you're seeing Coach—"

"I'm *not* seeing Zack," Justine quickly assured her. She

hesitated, then plunged on. "Bea, does Jordan know about . . . the cruise and Zack?"

Bea looked puzzled. "If he does, he didn't hear it from me! Why?"

"Because Zack swears that I called him from the store Friday night and told him that I changed my mind about dinner. I never left my apartment after I got home."

"So? He could have been lying." Bea's gaze suddenly narrowed. "Is he implying that Jordan had something to do with this?"

Justine quickly told her about Zack's uninvited houseguest, the broken Caller ID, and the mysterious break-in at the store. By the time she finished, Bea's defensive expression had crumbled. "No one's accusing Jordan," Justine stressed. "We're just trying to get to the bottom of this. And if by some *slim* chance it turns out Jordan was involved, no harm was done."

Bea was quiet as she filled two cups with coffee and set the cream and sugar on the table. She set a cup in front of Justine, then took a seat, looking dazed and a little frightened. "We're not talking about a prank call here; we're talking about breaking and entering."

"I would never press charges against my own nephew!"

"I'm not talking about you," Bea said. "I'm talking about Coach Wayne."

"He doesn't have any proof of anything."

"But he suspects him, doesn't he?" Bea guessed shrewdly. "He's thinking Jordan might be after a little revenge for kicking him off the team. What about fingerprints? If Coach Wayne tells the police about his suspicions, they could take Jordan in for questioning. If they find fingerprints on the Caller ID—"

"Whoa!" Alarmed at her words, Justine held up her hand. "You don't really think Jordan was behind this, do you?" She hadn't believed it either, but the fact that Bea was considering it frightened her.

Bea sighed and shook her head. Her eyes were suspiciously bright. "I don't know. Before tonight's display, I would have snapped your head off for even *hinting* at it. Now I just don't know. I've never seen him this angry, and if he *does* know that you're involved—*were* involved—with Coach Wayne, he might be mad at you, too." Absently she dumped three spoonfuls of sugar in her coffee and took a drink without stirring it. "Did you get a chance to talk to Coach Wayne about Jordan?"

Justine groaned inwardly. She had hoped Bea had forgotten about it. "I mentioned it," she admitted reluctantly.

"And?"

"And he refused to discuss it."

Bea's spoon clattered to the table. "He didn't even give you a reason for not talking about it?"

Shaking her head, Justine recalled his expression at the time. He'd looked as if . . . he knew something that she didn't. But it was just a suspicion, not something she felt comfortable sharing with Bea. "No. He just clammed up and wouldn't talk about it."

"So where do we go from here?"

Justine wished there was something she could say to erase Bea's miserable expression.

Unfortunately nothing came to mind.

"Poor kid," Mini whispered as she gazed into the crystal ball at Justine and Bea. She glanced sideways at her husband and saw from his expression that he shared her sympathy for the young mortal, Jordan. "And I thought by creating a mystery we'd found a way to bring Zack and Justine together, at least for a short while. Now they're blaming Jordan for what *we* did. We can't allow this to continue, Reuben. The poor mortal child has enough on his mind."

Reuben stomped his foot on the perch and muttered, "Wretched mortals! Why do they have to *think* so much?"

"Because they're mortals, darling," Mini explained patiently. "They don't use magic, so they have difficulty believing it exists. Therefore, in their minds everything that happens must have a logical explanation."

"Are you saying they have no imagination?"

"No, I'm not saying that at all. If they actually *saw* magic, then they might believe in it."

"*Might* believe in it?" Reuben repeated incredulously.

Mini nodded. "It's true. Some mortals refuse to believe in magic even when they *do* see it for themselves."

"What about Justine and Zack?"

She tipped her head, staring at Reuben suspiciously. "If you're thinking what I *think* you're thinking, you can forget it. We can't have mortals knowing about us, darling."

"Why not? Why not just tell them exactly what happened aboard the cruise ship—show them on the crystal ball." Reuben tried to snap his fingers, growling an oath when he only succeeded in loosening a feather. "Our mission would be over, our sentence reduced. We could go home."

"Reuben—"

"I don't like it here, Mini." Reuben's voice took on a familiar grumble she'd hoped never to hear again. "I hear things at night, slithering, hissing sounds. I think—I think she might have *rats.*" He shuddered. "I haven't slept a wink since we got here."

Mini laughed outright, unwilling to confess the true nature of the slithering and hissing. Her husband had yet to find out about the reptile room. "*I'm* the one who doesn't sleep at night. You snore loud enough to wake the dead."

Reuben looked intrigued. "You think so? I tried raising the dead once, but the spell mentioned nothing about snoring." He pressed his wing tip to his chin in thought. "Perhaps *that's* why the spell didn't work."

He was serious! With a gasp, Mini said, "Reuben, do you know the penalty for raising the dead?"

"I wasn't aware there *was* a penalty."

"There is." Mini paused a beat, then added fearfully, "They take away your powers."

"No!"

"Yes."

"No! For how long?"

"Forever."

Reuben thrust his chest out in an act of bravado, but Mini noticed his eyes had widened in shock. "Well, I was a nasty warlock at the time. They can't hold my past transgressions against me . . . can they?"

"They could, but they don't. They can, however, watch you very closely because of your past . . . transgressions. Now, back to why we can't clue Justine and Zack in on the fact that we're witches—"

"Ahem."

"A witch and a *warlock,* although I can't imagine why you still insist on being called a warlock." Mini sniffed to show her disapproval. "As I was saying, showing ourselves to Justine and Zack and telling them the truth would be too easy."

"What's wrong with easy?" Reuben demanded.

"We're being punished, darling. I don't think the witch's council will reduce our sentence just for delivering a message *any* witch could have delivered. Justine and Zack must resolve this issue themselves."

"Then why are *we* here?"

Mini frowned at his sarcastic tone. "We're here to make sure they have an *opportunity* to resolve their differences."

She wasn't about to explain to her husband that she had taken the assignment for other, more personal reasons, such as finding out why Reuben had changed over the past hundred years or so from a happy, loving husband to a restless, grumpy warlock. Or that she hoped the courtship between Justine and Zachary would remind Reuben of what *they* once had.

"Well," Reuben sneered, back to his old nasty self. "So far all we've managed to do is create more *problems.*"

Unfortunately, Mini thought gloomily, thinking of Jordan, he was right.

Nine

When Justine came into the shop Monday afternoon after a quick visit to the bank to make a deposit, she walked into a scene that made her question why she had chosen *this* particular line of business over something staid and normal . . . like a flower shop or a clothing store.

Christopher, whom Justine had always admired for his cool, unflappable reaction in the face of disaster, was hysterical to the point of wringing his hands. And who wouldn't be? Justine reasoned, staring openmouthed at the enraged monkey hanging from the overhead light fixture.

The little monkey glared at them, pointing and chattering and occasionally baring his teeth in what might have been a smile, but which to Justine looked more like a grimace. Black with the exception of his face and throat, he had anchored himself to the fixture by curling his long tail around the protruding base.

He didn't look as if he planned to come down anytime soon.

Justine closed her eyes and slowly counted to ten. If she believed in witches and curses, she would have considered the possibility that she had offended someone with the power

to make her life miserable. The sprinklers, the break-in . . .
now *this?*

She opened her eyes to find the monkey staring at her with
bright hostility. "Christopher, call Melissa and ask her to
come down here. Tell her it's an emergency."

"Okay, but I swear I didn't realize there was a monkey in
that crate," Christopher began to babble. "I thought it was
the shipment of ferrets you ordered. When I opened the crate,
he jumped out and scared the daylights out of me. Before I
could grab him, he—"

"I'm not blaming you," Justine interrupted. But the deliveryman would certainly get an earful when he returned,
which wouldn't be for . . . two weeks? She gritted her teeth
in frustration. What in the world would she do with a monkey until then? She knew little about monkeys, wasn't sure
she was licensed to handle them! Perhaps whoever had been
expecting him would trace the delivery back to her store.

As Christopher went to call Melissa, the door opened and
Bea and Jordan came rushing in, bundled against the cold in
heavy coats and toboggans. Hiding her surprise at their unexpected visit, Justine quickly pointed to the monkey and
warned them to stay by the door. "I don't know if he's dangerous, but I don't want to take any chances."

She noticed Jordan's interest had sharpened at the sight of
the monkey. All three of her nephews loved animals, but
Jordan had a special way with them that always made Justine's chest swell with pride. Maybe he could help her with
the monkey, she thought hopefully.

"So, what's up?" she asked, keeping a cautious eye on the
primate. He'd grown quiet, regarding Jordan with equal curiosity.

Bea pulled her amazed gaze from the sight of the monkey
and gave her head a disbelieving shake as she looked at
Justine. Her lips curved upward, but Justine noticed it wasn't
Bea's usual full-fledged smile.

"Jordan would like to help you in the store after school
this week," Bea announced.

Justine quickly translated, and her heart sank. Clay was forcing Jordan to help her as punishment for his rudeness yesterday at dinner. Didn't her brother realize he was only making things worse?

She summoned a warm smile for her nephew, but Jordan's fascinated gaze remained glued to the monkey. Justine pretended not to notice that he was ignoring her. "Wonderful! I could use an extra hand this week. Christopher won't be here on Wednesday or Friday because his parents are going on vacation and he's house-sitting." She turned to Christopher as he joined them. "Isn't that right, Christopher?"

"Yeah, that's right."

"Then he won't be in the way?" Bea asked anxiously.

"Not at all." Justine felt a draft of cold air and looked around to see that the local vet had arrived. From the looks of her reddened cheeks, she'd run the block and a half from her office to the pet store.

Melissa was a pretty woman in her early forties, with curly black hair that seemed to have an energy all its own. She shrugged out of her heavy coat and laid it on the counter next to the covered cage housing the lovebirds, making herself at home.

"It's like a sauna in here, but it feels good after being outside." Melissa rubbed her cold hands briskly together. "Now, what's the emergency?"

Justine didn't have to explain. The monkey, agitated over the newcomer's arrival, began to screech and chatter. The light fixture swayed dangerously as he crawled from one side to the other, then back again. He glared down at the group, pointing his long finger as if accusing them.

Melissa's mouth opened in surprise. "Where did you get a capuchin?"

"A what?" Justine asked, frowning.

"A capuchin, native to Central America." Melissa pointed to the black fur covering its body, then to his snowy white face and throat. "They're named after a Capuchin monk because of their black cape of fur that resembles the cowl the

Capuchin monks wore. Some experts say they're considered the most intelligent monkeys in their species."

"The deliveryman left him by mistake," Christopher informed her, flushing a guilty red. "He was in a hurry, so I let him leave before I finished checking the inventory."

"Stop blaming yourself," Justine ordered. "I've done the same a dozen times." To Melissa, she said, "Well, what do you think? Is it dangerous? Rabid? Or just plain ole frightened?" Justine was experienced enough to keep her voice low and even to keep from startling the monkey. He'd fallen blessedly silent again, watching them intently. If they didn't get him down soon, she thought with growing concern, he might work the wires loose from the ceiling and electrocute himself.

Melissa walked around the monkey, studying him from every angle. Finally she sighed and shook her curly head. "He looks healthy enough, from what I can tell. A young monkey, too. I'm not an expert on monkeys, though. You might consider calling the Animal Control Center—"

"No!" Jordan burst out, speaking for the first time. "Please don't do that, Aunt Justine."

Justine gave him a reassuring smile. "I won't unless I absolutely have no choice." Her smile faded. "But if he turns out to be vicious, I'll have to call them. I can't afford a lawsuit."

"Well," Bea said, darting a worried glance from Justine to Jordan, then back again. "I hate to leave all of this excitement, but I've got a million errands to run today. I'll pick Jordan up at closing."

When Bea had gone, Justine tilted her head to study the monkey, conscious of Jordan standing beside her. Obviously the monkey couldn't remain attached to the light fixture, as secure as he seemed to feel. She glanced at Christopher, then Jordan, and finally Melissa. "Anyone have any ideas about how to get him down?" she asked hopefully.

Before anyone could answer, the door opened again, sweeping the room with a chilling blast of cold air. Four pairs of eyes swerved to look at the newcomer.

Justine sucked in a sharp breath as Zack's broadshoul-dered, handsome form filled the doorway. Her heart began to trip-hammer against her chest. Her forbidden delight at seeing Zack quickly turned to dismay as she remembered Jordan standing beside her. As Zack's gaze met Jordan's, she could literally feel the tension leap and sizzle between the two.

The capuchin monkey was momentarily forgotten as the drama unfolded before her. She braced herself, more than ready to defend her nephew against a man who had ruthlessly trampled her heart—and seemed determined to do it again.

Zack allowed himself to pause no more than a heartbeat when he realized the identity of the tall, lanky teenager stand-ing beside Justine. His jaw hardened, his resolve to stand firm miraculously overriding his unruly libido. "Justine, Jor-dan." Briefly his glance fell on the dark-haired woman, then the young man standing behind Justine.

The young man stepped forward, his boyish face crinkling in a hesitant smile. "You're Zachary Wayne! I recognized you from your pictures."

Zack automatically took the hand extended.

"Christopher Marshall, Justine's assistant." He jabbed a finger at the dark-haired woman Zack hadn't recognized. "That's Melissa, the vet here in town. I guess you know Jordan and Justine."

Melissa gave his hand a brief shake, regarding him curi-ously. Christopher shook his head, grinning. "Man, I can't believe I'm meeting you in person! You were a great . . . quarterback." His grin faltered, his face turning crimson. "I heard about your injury. Tough luck, huh?"

"Yeah, tough luck." For once, Zack didn't feel the twist of the knife similar comments usually produced. Maybe he *was* accepting his fate.

"Heard you were coaching Cannon Bay's team," Christopher continued, obviously unaware of the heightened tension—and Jordan's expulsion from the team.

When Christopher poked Jordan with his elbow, Zack winced. He looked at Justine and saw that she, too, had blanched at the painful reminder. But she recovered quickly, her chin lifting, her gaze faintly accusing as she stared at him. Great. She was mad, and he'd only just arrived.

"Say, Jordan. How does it feel having a pro coaching your team? Must be something, huh? Coach Abernathy's good, but he doesn't have Mr. Wayne's expertise. I mean, you've got a real *pro* teaching you the ropes!"

It wasn't going to get better, Zack realized, as long as the assistant kept talking. Jordan looked as if he would blow any second.

Zack opened his mouth to interrupt him, but instead of words, a screeching sound emerged. Only it wasn't him, he realized, tilting his face to the ceiling where the sound had originated. His gaze widened at the sight of a monkey hanging from the overhead light fixture.

Of all of the things he expected to see, a monkey wasn't one of them. But why should it surprise him? he asked himself. He'd been stalked by an overgrown iguana, attacked by an overweight cat, and taunted by a slithering snake.

A monkey shouldn't shock him in the least.

"Well," Zack drawled with a casualness he didn't exactly feel, "I don't think *he's* a happy camper."

"No, he's not," Justine said, taking his arm and moving him closer to the door. "I have no idea what he's going to do next, so if you'd just stand by the door while we figure out—"

Zack had been watching the motion of her cherry-red lips, but when her words stopped abruptly, he followed her gaze to the monkey just as it uncurled its tail and leaped in his direction.

He didn't have much time to think; he just reacted, catching the flying monkey as it landed in his arms. Yes, he had to admit—at least to himself—that his heart literally stopped beating for a moment or two, but when the monkey did nothing more than wind his long, hairy arms around his neck and press tightly against him, Zack relaxed.

"Don't move," Justine ordered softly, her voice edged with anxiety. "I'll call the Animal Control Center. It shouldn't take them long to—"

"Aunt Justine, no!"

Zack held himself very still, watching over the monkey's shoulder as Jordan grabbed the sleeve of Justine's sweater, the boy's expression a mixture of anxiety and anger. He could feel the monkey trembling, long fingers gripping his neck in a desperate hold that made Zack experience a surge of protectiveness that was totally foreign to him.

And very probably misplaced.

"He's not hurting Coach Wayne, can't you see?" Jordan pleaded. "He's just scared."

Justine brushed his hand aside, her face set in stern lines Zack had never seen before. Another facet of her personality. He suspected there were many and, God willing, he would discover each and every one of them. That is, if he didn't die of strangulation first.

"Jordan, I sympathize with your concern, but he might—"

"Don't," Zack heard himself say in a low, croaking voice that made the monkey stir restlessly against him. To his continued amazement, the monkey pressed a wet nose against his neck as if seeking comfort. Zack swallowed hard, hoping he was doing the right thing. Sometimes instincts were wrong, and if this was one of those times, the results could be ugly. "He's not hurting me."

Justine looked uncertain, stretching her hand out as if to touch the monkey's back. Another odd instinct kicked in, and Zack quickly shook his head in warning.

She pulled her hand back. He sighed his relief, catching and holding her confused gaze. "Do you have a cage I can put him in?" he asked softly, unconsciously rocking the monkey. When she nodded and turned, he followed her, carrying the monkey. Not that he had a choice, he mused wryly. The monkey was plastered to him like a coat of paint.

When she opened the door of an empty cage, Zack gingerly grabbed the monkey around the waist and pulled. The poor little critter was frightened, but Zack was ready to unburden himself; he'd come for a turtle, or perhaps a kitten, not a monkey!

It was like trying to remove bubble gum from the bottom of a rubber shoe. The more he pulled, the harder the monkey gripped him. In danger of choking from the tight squeeze of the long arms circling his neck, Zack finally relented. The moment he did, the monkey relaxed against him.

"I guess maybe we should give him a few moments," he suggested, dropping his arms to his sides. The monkey, wrapped around him as he was, didn't need assistance in staying put. Zack hated to admit he was at a loss, especially when he'd come here with the express purpose of showing her that he didn't dislike—or fear—animals.

"Maybe I could try to take him?" Justine offered.

Melissa came into sight, followed by the mouthy assistant. "You want me to tranquilize him?"

The monkey, apparently feeling crowded, tightened his hold.

"No, no. I'm fine," Zack assured them hastily. "If you could just . . . back away a little." When they did as he asked, the monkey once again relaxed its hold so that Zack could breathe. He could feel the mad beating of its little heart against his chest. The poor thing was scared to death.

Justine stood back and folded her arms, her slim face creased in a perplexed frown. No doubt trying to figure out what the monkey saw in him, Zack thought, wondering what in the hell he was going to do now. Obviously he couldn't hold the monkey indefinitely.

"Jordan, why don't you go to the library and see what you can find on monkey behavior?" Justine suggested. "Maybe we can get some idea of what to do next."

"I still think we should tranquilize him," Melissa repeated, looking concerned. "I've heard monkey bites can be—" Her words ended on an *oof* as Justine poked her in the ribs.

Zack silently thanked Justine. His gaze landed briefly on Jordan's sullen, slump-shouldered figure as he left the store. Obviously the boy hadn't taken his advice yet, Zack thought with an inward sigh. Only time would tell . . . Meanwhile, Justine still blamed him for Jordan's unhappy state.

"If you don't need me, Justine, I'll be getting back to the clinic, I've got a Saint Bernard just out of surgery that should be coming around, and he's going to be a handful."

"Thanks for coming," Justine said, throwing her a grateful smile.

"That's my job. If you need me, you know where to reach me." She gave Zack and the monkey one last, worried glance before shrugging into her coat.

When the door shut behind her, leaving Christopher, Justine, Zack, and the monkey, Justine found Zack a chair and urged him to sit. Zack didn't argue. The monkey probably didn't weigh more than seven or eight pounds, but the entire incident had left his legs shaky.

"Do you want a cup of coffee or something?" Justine asked.

Zack carefully shook his head. Was he imagining the sparkle of admiration in her eyes when she looked at him? And did her voice actually sound warmer, or was that also wishful thinking?

All because he wasn't freaking out that a monkey had jumped from a light fixture into his arms? Actually, it had scared the hell out of him, but she didn't *have* to know that, right? He decided to test his theory, keeping his voice soft as he managed a rueful grin. "When I came in to buy a pet, this wasn't exactly what I had in mind."

"You came in to buy a pet?" She pulled up a chair and sat across from him, folding her hands over her knees. Christopher went to help a customer, leaving them alone in a room full of puppies and kittens.

Definitely warmer. Zack decided to see how warm she

could get. He nodded. "I was thinking maybe a turtle or a kitten. Something that wouldn't need around-the-clock attention." Unlike an insecure monkey.

She propped her elbow on her knee and her chin in her hand. Her gaze lingered for a moment on his mouth, then jerked upward to his eyes as if she realized she'd been staring. "What made you decide to get a pet?"

A tricky question, and one he couldn't answer truthfully, not unless he wanted the temperature to drop to sub-zero. And he liked it the way it was just fine. Now, if only motor mouth would stay away, maybe he'd recover some lost ground.

The lie came easier than he expected. "I had a dog when I was a kid." Okay, so it had belonged to his brother, but he'd played with it once in a while and he'd lived in the same house. "I figured I could use some company, now that I'm home more." When she smiled, the temperature of his blood moved up several degrees. Fast. As Thomas would say, he had it bad. Of course, he'd known that the moment he decided to take up stalking as his new hobby.

"And you think a turtle would keep you company?" she asked in a soft, teasing voice that had Zack slumping in his chair.

The monkey whimpered a protest. Zack straightened, absently patting the monkey on the back. He'd begun to sweat in his heavy coat with the monkey lying against him, but he wasn't complaining. He and Justine were having a nice, normal, noncombative conversation for a change, and that was worth any discomfort.

"Maybe a kitten would be better." Anything but a monkey. Or a toe-eating iguana. As a matter of fact, Squeeze wasn't his type, either. A cat like Rogue he might learn to tolerate— minus the claws. "What do you suggest?"

"I suggest," Justine said slowly, "that you start carrying a change of clothing around with you."

Her gaze dropped to stare pointedly at his crotch area, but

Zack realized right away that there wasn't anything sexual in her look. He groaned as the warmth and the wetness finally seeped through his jeans.

His newest fan apparently was not potty trained.

Ten

"Reuben, you're a genius!" Mini pulled him close and clicked her beak against his. Oh, for a set of real lips so that she could give him a proper kiss!

Her instincts had been right; this assignment was the best decision she'd made in a long time. Not only was Reuben participating, he was beginning to enjoy it!

Reuben preened like a peacock at her praise, swaggering back and forth on the narrow perch. "Just a little love spell, dear. Nothing death-defying."

She heard the tiny note of disappointment in his voice, but chose to ignore it. "But to think to cast the spell on the *monkey*! It was brilliant, just brilliant. What do you think will happen next? Will Zack take the monkey home?"

With a wicked chuckle, Reuben said, "I don't think he'll have a choice. The monkey is totally enamored of Zack, and he won't let anyone else come near him."

"What if Melissa returns with a tranquilizer?"

"If she does, we'll take care of it."

Mini felt like dancing a jig. Because of Reuben and his spell casting, Justine might now question her harsh judgment of Zack. Mini knew Justine's heart had already softened just watching Zack and the monkey together—she didn't need magic or her crystal ball to decipher the expression on Justine's face; the mortal woman had been thinking of mortal babies—hers and Zack's.

If Zack actually took the monkey *home*—Mini snapped her beak closed on an excited squeal, mindful of the mortals close by—Justine would further be reminded of the strong, tender man she fell in love with on the cruise ship!

"Maybe now these two hardheaded mortals will talk about that blasted cruise," Reuben muttered as if to himself, striding arrogantly along the perch.

But Mini wasn't listening; she was staring at the eye peeping between the cage covering. A *mortal* eye. Large and brown—Jordan's, to be exact. He'd returned without them being aware of it.

"Reuben," she whispered urgently, not daring to take her gaze from the eye. After her frightening experience with the policeman last night, she should have been more careful!

". . . and work things out. I'm ready to leave this smelly place, get out of this cage, shed these feathers, and get back to some *real* action." Reuben, oblivious to his wife's frozen state, pivoted on the perch and marched back to her. "What do you think, darling? How does exploring the pyramids sound to you? It's been years.... "

Mini's heart sank at his words, but right now she had bigger problems. Very big, with a black pupil dilated with shock. "Reuben, please shut up," she ordered, trying to speak without moving her beak. "We have company."

"Company?" Surprised, Reuben finally stopped pacing. "You say we have company? Who is it? Someone from the witch's council, here to check on us?"

He craned his head around the cage, his gaze passing over the eye peeking through the covering. His head jerked back to the eye. His beak fell open, then slammed shut. Gathering himself, he began to whistle and fluff his feathers.

Mini might have laughed at his sudden transformation from cocky warlock to happy lovebird if the circumstances hadn't been so dire—and he hadn't been whistling "Dixie!"

She remained frozen, undecided. How much had Jordan heard of their conversation? Did he know about the love spell Reuben had cast on the monkey? Did he actually believe, as only a few mortals would, that they really had been talking?

The eye blinked, then disappeared. Mini let out a long, shaky sigh. Oh, dear. What would they do? Was her magic powerful enough to make Jordan forget the last few minutes? Before she could recall the spell of forgetfulness, one side of the cage covering lifted, revealing Jordan's stunned face.

Beyond the amazement, beyond the fear, Mini found what she was looking for—doubt.

Jordan didn't believe . . . at least not fully.

She stifled a pang of disappointment, knowing it was for the best. Moving closer to Reuben, she rubbed her breast against his, ignoring the young mortal as she joined her husband in reversing the damage their carelessness had wrought.

In the blink of an eye, they were once again just two ordinary—well, maybe peculiar—lovebirds.

After a few tension-fraught moments, Jordan let the cover drop. Mini's skinny legs nearly buckled with relief. She swiped a trembling wing over her brow and let out a low whistle. What a close call!

"I think he's asleep," Justine whispered, swallowing a silly lump in her throat as she watched Zack rock the monkey gently back and forth. He was a natural, she thought. If things had gone differently . . . *No, don't think like that!* Justine put a brake on her dangerous thoughts, surging to her feet. She opened the door to the cage she had shown him earlier. "Do you want to try to put him in here?"

Zack hesitated, then nodded, easing slowly to his feet. She watched him as he pulled the monkey's arms from around his neck and cradled him like a baby. Gently he laid the sleeping monkey in the cage. As she closed the door and turned the latch, she noticed that his eyes lingered on the monkey.

That curious lump returned to her throat. To distract herself, she dropped her gaze to the wet patch on his jeans and she had to bite her lip to keep from smiling. "Um, we'd better get a hair dryer on that before you leave, or you'll freeze your . . . butt off."

He arched a dark brow. "Very funny."

Justine laughed and led the way through the door leading into the main store. Christopher was nowhere to be seen. Probably checking inventory, she mused. Jordan, however, was standing near the birdcage on the counter. When he saw them he gave a guilty start and moved away.

Her steps faltered. "Jordan? Are you all right?" His brown eyes, so like his father's, looked huge against his pale face, as if something or someone had given him a nasty fright.

Justine gave herself a mental shake. The Jordan she knew feared nothing. She was just being overly protective.

"Of course I'm all right," Jordan scoffed, but his Adam's apple bobbed up and down, and his voice came out squeaky and high. The glance he threw Zack's way was full of resentment and something else she couldn't define.

What had she expected? By kicking Jordan off the team, Zack had taken away his greatest joy and, if she wasn't mistaken, had put a considerable dent in Jordan's pride as well. She could hardly blame him for being upset, could she? Her nephew believed he'd been treated unfairly, and until she had proof otherwise, she would continue to believe the same.

Until she had proof? Justine frowned. Was she, then, considering Zack had *cause* to kick Jordan from the team? Just the thought made her feel disloyal. Yet she couldn't forget the look on his face when she asked him about it, a look that had said, *"You don't know the whole story."* Jordan interrupted her disturbing thoughts, the taunt in his voice unmistakable. She half expected his lip to curl in a sneer.

"Hey, Coach Wayne, did the monkey scare you *that* bad?"

His scornful laugh made Justine want to pinch him. She didn't have to follow the line of his gaze to know that he had noticed the stain on Zack's jeans and had drawn his own gleeful conclusions.

Apparently she'd misread his expression when she first saw him: Jordan wasn't frightened; he was angry. Angry enough to insult his football coach, and possibly destroy his chances of getting back on the team. Not only did she feel dismay at the possibility, she felt a surge of irritation on Zack's behalf. Her reprimand came out sharper than she intended. "Jordan!"

"It's okay." Zack curled his fingers around her arm and gave it a warning squeeze. He held Jordan's defensive gaze as he explained, "The monkey had an accident while I was holding him, but I have to admit he did scare the hell out of me."

Although Justine didn't understand why Zack was bothering to explain, she was grateful for his patience. Before anything further could be said, she jumped into the breech. "Jordan, would you mind watching the store for a few moments? I think Christopher is checking our supplies in the storeroom."

He shrugged his wide, boyish shoulders. "Guess I can. Are you going with *him?*"

He knows, Justine realized suddenly. *He knows about Zack and me and he's furious.* It explained *why* he was behaving badly, but she couldn't excuse his surly attitude. Zack had entered the store as a customer; he deserved a little respect.

Coolly she said, "As a matter of fact, I am. He needs to get dry or he'll catch pneumonia."

She chose to ignore his snort, grabbing Zack's arm and hustling him from the store. However much she loved her nephew, she wasn't about to let him run her life or make her feel guilty for a simple act of kindness. Besides, if Zack hadn't come into the store, they might all still be standing around wondering how they were going to get the monkey down from the light fixture.

For some reason, the monkey had taken to Zack.

Still puzzling over this amazing fact, Justine unlocked her

door and entered her apartment. Zack followed. From the corner of her eye she saw him cast a wary glance around the empty living room. She couldn't resist a chuckle. "They're as frightened of you as you are of them."

"That's because I have my shoes on," he muttered.

When he removed his coat, Justine did the same, hanging them on a shaky wooden coatrack behind the door.

"I'll get the hair dryer. I think there's an outlet by the couch, if you want to have a seat."

Zack stayed by the door for a moment, taking a good look at the worn, comfortable sofa. Next, he craned his neck and glanced in the kitchen. No sign of a lizard, a cat, or a calico snake. Or was it a rainbow boa? He couldn't remember. Bracing himself, he eased cautiously onto the sofa.

He hadn't been still more than a few seconds when his eye caught a movement under the chair—the one place he hadn't looked. He cursed silently as the brilliantly colored snake uncoiled from its hiding place beneath the chair and began to slither across the floor in his direction. A slim pink tongue flickered in and out, almost hypnotizing in its rhythm.

The boa had nearly reached his legs when Zack felt sharp claws dig into his shoulders. Rogue the cat, he presumed, bracing himself for the pain.

But the cat didn't stay on his shoulder long. With an arching, graceful leap Zack couldn't help but admire, the cat landed on floor in front of the snake, effectively blocking its path. Squeeze didn't look too happy about the interruption. The snake recoiled with an angry hiss, it's triangle-shaped head swaying back and forth.

Rogue held his ground, batting at the snake until it apparently decided the bounty wasn't worth the battle. With a smooth motion, it turned and slithered in the direction of the kitchen. Zack didn't realize he'd been holding his breath until the snake was a safe distance away. With a soft explosion, he let it out, only to suck it back in again as Thor came waddling around the corner of the sofa. His dorsal crest of soft spines added to his fierce appearance.

The iguana dug his evil-looking claws into the cushions and climbed onto the couch with slow, cumbersome movements, pausing once to give Zack an unblinking stare that set Zack's teeth on edge. Where in the hell was Justine? he wondered, glancing hopefully at the cat.

Rogue seemed unconcerned about this new threat. He calmly licked his paws, then swiped them over his face, repeating the motion again and again.

Meanwhile, Thor advanced toward him one claw at a time, as if each limb had been dipped in cement. Zack pressed himself against the sofa, refusing to give in to the cowardly urge to get up and move. If the woman he loved could *live* with this . . . overgrown lizard, then he could learn to tolerate it.

Maybe.

Thor reached him but didn't stop. He climbed onto Zack's lap and then onto his chest, planting his weighty claws directly over his heart. Then he froze as if someone had flipped a switch.

Unfortunately Zack knew Thor was not an animated toy.

Zack dared to move his eyes, glancing at the closed bathroom door. *Where in the hell was Justine?* In the bathroom peering through a crack in the door and laughing, no doubt. The thought gave him courage. If she *was* observing him with her odd assortment of critters, then she would discover he was tougher than she thought.

He'd calmed a wild monkey, hadn't he?

Offering a quick prayer for his survival, Zack lifted his hand and stroked his fingers along the iguana's side. The skin was rough and cool, but not unpleasant.

Marvel of marvels, Thor's eyes slowly closed, as if in ecstasy.

Zack felt a grin stretch his lips. He grew bolder, raising his hand to scratch the iguana's head. Rogue jumped onto his shoulder, but instead of digging his claws into Zack's skin, he settled down and began to purr as if he approved of what Zack was doing. The rumbling vibration and Rogue's soft fur relaxed him further.

Two down, one to go, Zack thought, wondering if he'd gone totally crazy. He had a feeling ole Squeeze wouldn't be an easy victory.

"Well, well, well. Aren't *you* turning into a regular Dr. Doolittle."

Zack jumped at the sound of her soft, drawling voice. Thor's eyes popped open. With a speed that amazed Zack, Thor crawled from his lap and headed in her direction. He didn't blame the iguana; he wanted to do the same. Her jeans fit snugly today, and the cinnamon red sweater she wore clung in all the right places.

She reached down and obligingly scratched Thor's head. "Sorry it took me so long," she said, handing him the compact hair dryer and flashing him a rueful grin that made him want to pull her onto his lap and get busy loving her. "I think Thor's been playing in the toilet again."

He was thankful she moved away after plugging the cord into an outlet; Zack felt silly enough pointing the thing at his crotch without her watching him. However, her watching might generate more heat than he could tolerate.

He flicked the switch on the hair dryer. Rogue shot from his shoulder and galloped to the bedroom; Thor moved faster than Zack thought he could, heading in the same direction, and just around the corner of the island bar, he saw the boa slither behind the curtain hanging in front of the washer and dryer.

When Zack realized they were frightened of the small appliance he held in his hand, he grinned. Maybe he could find one small enough to fit in his back pocket.

After a few moments he shut off the dryer. His jeans were still damp, and they smelled, a musky odor that made Zack think of rotting leaves and ammonia, but he figured he could make it home without becoming an icicle.

"That should do it," he said, unplugging the dryer and placing it on the couch. Justine appeared from the kitchen and leaned against the bar, her gaze lingering for a brief moment on the still-damp circle on his jeans. When she looked at him, her golden eyes were warm with gratitude and . . . the same old wariness.

Not exactly what Zack had in mind. Hot and needful would suit him better. *Much* better.

"Thank you."

"For what?" Zack successfully hid his frustration. How did she just *forget?* he wondered.

She shrugged. "For your patience with the monkey, and with Jordan. He was inexcusably rude."

"Well, I—"

The apartment door burst open. Jordan stood on the threshold. "The monkey's gone crazy again," he announced breathlessly.

By the time they reached the store, the monkey's panic had spread to the other animals; cats meowed, puppies howled, birds screeched and squawked. Above it all, Zack could hear the monkey screaming.

He stopped the moment he saw Zack, pressing his snowy-white face against the bars. With his terror-stricken gaze focused on Zack, he became very still. Zack stood before the cage, amazed and bewildered by the obvious calming effect he had on the monkey. He just didn't get it! And apparently he wasn't alone.

"This is uncanny," Justine whispered, standing behind him, so close he could smell her light perfume.

Jordan and Christopher crowded behind them. "Weird," Jordan said.

Zack shifted back a few steps, parting the crowd. Then he took another step and another. When he reached the doorway to the main store, the monkey began swaying back and forth. A bone-chilling wail emerged from its throat.

Once again, Zack came forward.

The monkey became still and quiet again.

"That settles it," Justine said, shaking her head and looking dazed. "He definitely thinks you're his . . . something."

Christopher clapped him on the shoulder, trying to make a joke of it. "Congratulations, Dad."

Zack didn't see anything remotely funny about the situation. When he realized everyone was staring at him expectantly, he shook his head. "Oh, no. I've got a game to coach tonight."

"You could take him with you. That's a portable cage, isn't it, Aunt Justine? He could be the team's mascot."

As Justine nodded and looked at him hopefully, Zack resisted the urge to reach out and choke Jordan. He'd caught Jordan's subtle challenge even if the others hadn't. To leave the monkey now would be the act of a heartless coward—at least he was certain Justine would think so.

Zack swallowed a curse. "All right. I'll take him with me."

"Here, you'd better take these," Jordan said without a hint of his earlier hostility. In fact, he sounded disgustingly cheerful. "You might need them, since he'll be going home with you."

Automatically Zack took the pile of books and glanced down. The top title was *Old and New World Monkeys*. Reference books, he realized, wishing for the first time that he'd never come to Cannon Bay.

How much simpler it would have been if he had just paid someone to kidnap Justine and bring her to Miami.

Eleven

"You really hate Zack, don't you?" Justine asked softly.

Jordan shrugged but didn't answer. Instead, he turned his face toward the storefront window, the hard, stubborn set of his jaw telling its own story. He reminded her of Clay. Her brother didn't get angry often, but when he did he could dish out the silent treatment for weeks.

She braced her hands on the counter behind her and leaned against it, watching her nephew and hoping she sounded neutral about the entire episode. "You deliberately backed him into a corner with the monkey."

It wasn't a question—Justine was positive this was what Jordan had done. She just didn't understand why Zack had accepted her nephew's unspoken challenge. Children answered dares, not grown men who should know better.

"He would have taken him home if *you* had asked him to anyway," Jordan said with a defensive tilt of his chin. "I saved you from having to ask. This way you don't owe him any favors."

"How do you know he would have?" Justine was genuinely curious.

"Because Coach Wayne's got the hots for you."

Justine's face heated at his blunt assessment. She shouldn't have been surprised; Jordan had never been one to beat around the bush. *Did* Zack have the hots for her? Was sex—and, yes, the sex had been good—his motive for taking the monkey? Was he hoping to soften her, to lure her into his bed?

She had to admit, albeit painfully, that it wouldn't take much softening. She wasn't, however, so vain as to think Zack had come to Cannon Bay just to get her in the sack. There were plenty of willing women in Florida, and Zack was a sexy, gorgeous man. He could have his pick. Probably had.

The thought was *not* a pleasant one, she discovered.

Uncomfortable with the current subject, Justine changed it. "How did you find out about me and Zack, anyway?"

"Colby heard you and Mom talking. He told me."

"Oh." So Jordan *had* known about them. It didn't mean he was behind the series of not-so-funny pranks, though, Justine reasoned. The fact that he had a grudge against Zachary Wayne wasn't enough proof in her book. She didn't know what the lawyer in Clay would think, and wasn't anxious to find out.

She shifted around to face the birdcage and absently pulled the satin covering aside, tying it with the tassels. There hadn't been much traffic in the way of customers today, so she thought it would be safe to let them enjoy the evening light before it faded. Tomorrow she would move them back into the bird room where they would be free of drafts.

The colorful lovebirds stood very still on the perch, heads cocked as if they were listening to the conversation. Justine started to smile at her ridiculous thoughts, but Jordan's outrageous comment froze the smile on her face.

"They talk, you know."

Slowly Justine turned, dumbfounded by his words. He was jesting, of course. "Who?"

Jordan pointed to the lovebirds, his voice filled with an eery conviction that made Justine's blood run cold.

"*They* do. I heard them talking earlier."

Justine swallowed hard. "What . . . what did they say?" *Oh, Lord,* she thought, her heart hammering with fear. *Drugs. It had to be drugs making him hear voices in his head.* It would explain his abrupt personality change, the mood swings, and the outbursts. Maybe it was the reason Zack had kicked him from the team!

Her knees nearly buckled as the possibility slammed into her. No, not her Jordan. It couldn't be true! Oh, she wasn't completely naive—she knew drugs were the going thing these days with so many teens, but Jordan had always been anti-drugs. He wore T-shirts that read Just Say No. At a youth rally once he had made a speech encouraging other teens to avoid drugs.

Unaware of his aunt's near-hysteria, Jordan said, "They were talking about you and Coach Wayne, and about the cruise. They also said something—at least, *he* did—about getting out of the cage and shedding some feathers, seeing some *real* action. The female bird tried to warn him I was watching. He said something about the witch's counsel—"

There was a soft gasp behind her. Wide-eyed, Justine whirled around to stare at the lovebirds. No, she had imagined it. Power of suggestion. Group hypnosis. She'd heard about it, and now she believed it because it had certainly *sounded* like a human gasp.

When she faced Jordan again, he wore a smug, I-told-you-so expression that sent chills streaking down her spine. And he wasn't finished, it seemed.

"I think they're witches or something."

Justine gripped the counter to keep from falling. She licked her dry lips. "What . . . what makes you think that?"

Jordan smiled, and, strangely enough, it wasn't the insane grimace she expected. "They put a love spell on the monkey so that it would like Zack."

"Why would they do that?" Justine asked faintly. *Keep him talking. Maybe he'll eventually hear his own voice and realize how crazy he sounds.*

"So you'd be impressed, I guess." Jordan shrugged. "What happened between you two, anyway? On the cruise, I mean."

"That's none of your business." How did she manage to sound so calm when she was falling apart? Not Jordan. *Please God, not Jordan.*

"Well, it may not be *my* business," Jordan said, pointing a finger at the lovebirds, "but I think they've made it theirs."

"I don't understand." Anything. None of it. Most of all why her nephew, Mr. Anti-drugs, had changed his mind. What was it? she wondered frantically. Crack? Pot? Pills? Alcohol?

Jordan approached the cage, his wary gaze trained on the birds. There was a lurking fear in his eyes as well, Justine saw. Paranoia, another symptom of drug use. She clenched her teeth against a cry of outrage. *Not her Jordan!*

"I think they're here to make sure you guys get back together," Jordan continued calmly, looking from one bird to the other. "Aren't you, guys? Is that why you're here?"

Her heart breaking, Justine followed his gaze. The birds were watching Jordan, blinking and cocking their heads like a puppy might do when a human spoke to them, as if they were truly trying to figure out what he was saying. Just two ordinary lovebirds.

She leaned closer as Reuben opened his beak. Now he would whistle or chirp, make ordinary bird sounds that might jar Jordan back to reality. As Justine silently urged him on, Mini slapped her wing across Reuben's face and knocked him from the perch.

The colorful bird landed on the bottom of the cage with an outraged squawk. He scrambled to his feet and fluffed his feathers, hopping nimbly back onto the perch. But Justine noticed that he kept a safe distance between himself and his mate.

"Did you see that?" Jordan asked in an awed voice that made Justine's heart drop to her toes. "She hit him on purpose!"

"It was an accident," Justine said firmly. Telling him about the violent incident on Friday would only fuel his fantasy.

Jordan continued to argue, growing excited. "No, she hit him because he was about to say something. Didn't you see him open his mouth?"

"They *are* capable of mimicking humans, Jordan, and her hitting him was just an accident."

"What was an accident?"

White-faced, Justine turned to look at Bea. She could hear Jordan's agitated breathing beside her and wondered if he would share what he heard with his mother. She wasn't sure *she* could, not right now. Not before she had time to think about it.

"Hi, Mom! I was just telling Aunt Justine that it looked like Mini hit Reuben on purpose."

When he stopped there, Justine let out a slow, shaky breath. Safe for now.

Bea looked bewildered. "Who's Mini and Reuben?"

"The . . . lovebirds," Justine croaked out. She cleared her throat and forced a shaky laugh. "They fight like an old married couple."

"Yeah, and argue like one, too." He grunted as Justine gave him a solid poke in the ribs. "Or they probably would if they could talk," he added hastily. "But of course they can't."

Justine interrupted his dangerous babbling. Bea and Clay would have to be told about Jordan sooner or later, but she preferred it to be later.

She'd much rather jump off a bridge into shark-infested waters.

"It says here that you eat fruit, leaves, insects, birds, and eggs." Zack glanced up at the monkey perched on the ceiling-fan blade. "Sorry, I'm all out of birds and insects, and eggs sound a little too messy. You'll have to settle for an apple."

The monkey glared at him and chattered something in a language only he could understand.

With a shrug, Zack stood and offered him the apple. After a slight hesitation, the monkey took it.

Zack started to resume his seat on the couch when the apple bounced off his head. He saw stars. "What the hell did you do that for?" Zack demanded, gingerly feeling for a lump on his head. Good thing he *hadn't* given him an egg.

He should never have let the monkey out of the cage; he realized it the moment he opened the door and the monkey knocked him flat as he got out. From his dazed position on the floor, he had watched the monkey leap onto the ceiling fan.

If he didn't know better, he would believe the damned thing had laughed at him, like Cheetah in the old Tarzan movies.

"Look," Zack said, feeling more than a little foolish to find himself talking to a monkey. "We've got a game to go to tonight, and you're supposed to come with me."

For an answer, the monkey screamed as he leaped from blade to blade. Zack had to cover his ears, expecting his landlord to beat on the door any moment now. Thank God the walls were thick and well-insulated!

Finally the monkey stopped as abruptly as he had begun. It was a pattern, Zack thought, and it probably meant something, but he doubted he'd ever find out what.

"If you keep that up," Zack warned softly, and very sincerely, "I'll have to take you back to the pet shop." He must have been nuts to take him home in the first place. Either nuts, or crazy in love with Justine.

The monkey was quiet, watching him intently. Zack walked to the fruit bowl and picked up a banana. He peeled it, pretended to take a bite, and made delicious smacking noises he figured even a monkey might understand. Finally he held it up for the monkey to take. If the monkey decided to throw it back at him, at least it wouldn't hurt.

But it made an awful mess, he discovered when the monkey spit the chewed banana onto the hardwood floor.

"Okay. You want to play hardball? We'll play hardball. If

you want anything else to eat, you'll have to come down and get it yourself." And the moment he did, Zack intended to grab him and stick him back in the cage.

What happened to the cuddly, frightened monkey he'd comforted in the pet store? Zack gave his head a bewildered scratch, wincing when he encountered the tender lump. The moment they drove away from the shop, the docile monkey had begun to rattle the cage door and scream loud enough to split his eardrums. Driving hadn't been easy, and he'd thought once they reached the apartment the monkey would calm down.

His first mistake.

His second mistake was in thinking the monkey would calm down once he was out of the cage.

Giving the monkey the apple might have been his third mistake, but by this time Zack had decided to stop counting. He feared there would be many, many more mistakes concerning the monkey. He hoped none of them would require a trip to the emergency room—for him *or* the monkey. He wouldn't relish explaining *that* to Justine.

How had he gotten into this mess? Zack scowled as he remembered *who* instead of how—Jordan Diamond, star quarterback for the Cannon Bay Indians, the most popular boy in school—according to his teammates. Zack had heard rumors that there would be a boycott of the game tonight, a noticeable drop in attendance, and a definite chill in the air created by the faculty.

Let them do what they may, Zack thought. They'd find that Zachary Wayne was made of pretty stern stuff. If hiring him to coach meant sacrificing his values, then he was in the wrong place.

The monkey chattered something at him, gaining his attention. Zack craned his neck and gave him a quizzical look. "Sorry, bud, I don't know what you're saying. Wished I—"

Mistake number whatever; never stand beneath a monkey who can't control his bladder.

Zack cursed and grabbed a roll of paper towels from the

kitchen. He had a bone-deep feeling it was going to be a very long night.

Justine sat in her darkened apartment with the boa curled at her feet, Rogue purring on her shoulder, and Thor in her lap—or half of him, anyway. His tail took up a good portion of the couch beside her.

She'd tried to exhaust herself after closing the shop at five, cleaning cages, scrubbing floors, grooming the kittens and the puppies, and spending an hour just playing with them. She had even finished her inventory.

Yet her nerves still hummed, and her thoughts still tumbled over one another with dizzying speed. Her mind kept zooming in on two things. Jordan was on drugs, and Zack must know. It explained why he didn't want to talk about it, but it didn't *excuse* him for not telling her. She was Jordan's *aunt,* a very loving, concerned aunt. This was not something Zack should have kept from her.

Justine glanced at her watch, realizing for the first time that it was dark. She flicked on the lamp and looked again. Ten o'clock. The game should be over, and Zack should be home. Should she call him or just show up on his doorstep? What if she ran into Barry?

What if she did? Justine was angry for asking herself the question. Barry was old news, and she owed him nothing. *He* had dumped *her.*

Just as Zack had.

With an impatient growl, Justine moved Thor from her lap and slowly rose from the sofa, giving Rogue and Squeeze adequate time to move. She knew she would not sleep a wink until she'd talked to Zack. Maybe she was wrong. Maybe Zack *didn't* know but already suspected. Maybe kicking Jordan from the team had nothing to do with drugs.

One thing was for certain; she wouldn't find out if she didn't ask. Feeling old and tired, yet oddly strung out, Justine put her coat on and left the apartment.

She wasn't going to Zack for comfort, but for information,

she reminded herself sternly on the drive over to his apartment. Besides, if she *did* discover Zack had been keeping something so important from her, she would be furious with him for a very long time.

To her relief, Barry's car wasn't in its appointed slot in the garage beside the two-story house. But Zack's Ford Explorer was. Sitting in her van behind his vehicle, she stubbornly drummed her fingers on the steering wheel until her heartbeat returned to normal. Ridiculous for her body to go haywire at just the thought of seeing Zack! Why, it hadn't been but a few hours since she'd *last* seen him.

Justine caught her breath as his silhouette appeared in the window of his apartment, then let it out in an irritated rush. So what if his shoulders were so broad she might never lay her head in the same spot? She drummed her fingers harder on the steering wheel. And so what if he could work magic with his lips? Not to mention his hands—*Stop it. Just stop it.*

Zachary Wayne would like nothing better if she fell at his feet so he could start shredding her heart all over again. Oh, he would love that.

She would not let it happen. She was steel. She was strong. He would *not* get to her again. Justine Diamond would never be stupid enough to fall in love with the same man twice. *You've never stopped loving him and you know it.*

Justine shook her head at the snide voice, muttering out loud, "No, you're wrong. I loved him once, but I'm over him now. I'm attracted to him—who wouldn't be? And I . . . I can't help but like him. Love?" She gave a scornful laugh for good measure as she got out of the van and locked the door. "Not a chance."

When Zack opened the door to her soft knock a moment later, the last words she expected out of his mouth were, "Did you come to gloat?"

She stared at him. "I beg your pardon?" He was frowning, and a thought flashed through her mind like quicksilver; she couldn't remember him ever frowning at her. In fact, he looked tired and angry and defensive. Apparently she'd caught him at a bad time. She straightened her shoulders and lifted her chin. Well, that was just too bad.

"Didn't you go to the game tonight?" he demanded.

"No, I didn't." In fact, she'd completely forgotten about it. She didn't go to every game, but she tried to go to the majority of them. Bea usually insisted.

"Neither did a lot of other people."

"I'm not following you." Justine looked over her shoulder at Barry's closed apartment door. "Do you mind if I come in?"

He stepped aside without answering, waving his arm in a dramatic flourish that hinted at sarcasm. Justine frowned. "I'm listening if you care to explain." She had questions, but it was obvious he had something on his mind as well. Since it was his apartment and *she* had bothered *him*, the polite thing to do would be to let him go first.

She shrugged out of her coat and watched him as he ran his fingers through his hair.

"You want a cup of coffee?"

"That would be fine. Where's the monkey?"

He paused and glanced back at her. "You came over to see about the monkey?"

Her brow lifted at his irritable tone. She shook her head. "No, I didn't. Just making conversation." Now she *was* curious about the monkey. Slowly she turned a full circle, her gaze traveling over the area. No monkey, and no sound of it, either.

From the kitchen, Zack said, "*Dennis* is asleep. I think he's exhausted from all that screaming he did at the game."

"Dennis?"

"As in Dennis the Menace," he explained grimly, appearing around the corner with two mugs in his hands. He handed one to her, then tilted his head to gaze at a spot above her head.

Justine followed his gaze. The monkey was lying across the blades of the ceiling fan, its tail curled securely around the base. Zack had covered the monkey with a thick towel.

"I take it Dennis doesn't like football?" Her attempt to joke failed to get the expected result. If anything, his mouth looked grimmer.

"At least he had the decency to show."

"Meaning?"

"Meaning there were a lot of people *not* there tonight. Well, they were there, just not sitting in the bleachers. They were walking outside the gates carrying signs and shouting 'We want the Diamond back!' "

Finally Justine understood his needling comments, but wasn't certain she believed him. "You mean there was a boycott at tonight's game because you kicked Jordan off the team?"

"Suspended," he corrected harshly. "I suspended Jordan, along with a few others. Apparently Jordan's an extremely popular boy."

Justine hadn't known about the others, and right now she didn't care to think about the implications or how they were connected to her nephew. Clasping her trembling hands together, she looked Zack straight in the eye. "When were you going to tell me about the drugs, Zack?"

Twelve

Justine's grave question threw Zack.

He'd had the night from hell—make that a day and night—and now Justine was asking him when he intended to tell her about the *drugs*. Despite a gut full of frustration, he laughed. It wasn't just a chuckle, either, but a full-throated belly laugh. Maybe tinged with a little hysteria, but a laugh all the same.

She didn't laugh with him, just pursed her lips tight and glared at him.

It was the rustling noise above them, indicating he'd disturbed the monkey, that sobered Zack quick. He took her arm and led her to the window. "I'm sorry. It's just that after the day I've had, your question struck me as funny."

"There wasn't anything funny about it," Justine snapped, rubbing her forehead as if her head ached. "*Are* drugs the reason you kicked Jordan from the team?"

Startled, Zack gaped at her. "You were talking about *Jordan?*"

"Don't play the dumb jock with me, Zack. You know I meant Jordan. When were you going to tell me? *Were* you going to tell me at all?"

Zack could see there wasn't any sense in arguing with her. For the first time, he began to realize she was serious. Dead serious. He led her to the sofa. She sank onto the middle cushion and he sat next to her. "What makes you think Jordan's involved with drugs?"

"Because the signs are all there," she whispered, her great golden eyes filling with tears.

Resisting the very strong urge to pull her into his arms, he prompted gently, "Go on."

"Well, he used to be so cheerful and *nice,* for starters. You got a taste of the new Jordan today."

"He's sixteen. At that age, their hormones are raging—"

Justine shook her head violently. "No, this was like an overnight thing with Jordan. And then . . . then today he seemed convinced he'd heard the lovebirds talking to one another. He said they put a spell on the monkey, and that they were here to get us back . . . together."

She bit her lip until it turned white. Zack reached out and rescued it with his thumb.

"Personality changes, mood swings, hallucinations."

The tears spilled over and ran down her cheeks. Something twisted sharply, painfully, inside Zack at the sight of her angst. "Justine, are you sure? Jordan doesn't strike me as the type to experiment with drugs. From the few weeks that I worked with him, I got the impression he was a health nut. Health nuts have this thing about not polluting their bodies."

She rested her head against the back of the couch, and the tears kept falling. Zack wished she'd look at him—lean on him. The old Justine would not have hesitated to bury her face against his shoulder and let it rip. Not that she'd done much crying. No, they'd been too deliriously happy for that.

This Justine was determined to keep him at a distance. He wanted the old Justine back with a fierceness that hurt.

She finally looked at him, hopefully, swiping at her wet face with the back of her hand as if the tears irritated her. "So Jordan's suspension from the team had nothing to do with drugs?"

"No. I can tell you that much." It took a lot of willpower to add, "But don't ask me to tell you more."

"Do you swear?"

Zack allowed a faint smile to curve his mouth as he planted his hand over his heart. "I swear that Jordan's suspension had nothing to do with drugs. I further swear that I don't believe Jordan is *involved* with drugs."

"But you said he wasn't the only one—"

"And by that you gathered I'd caught them smoking pot in the locker room or something?" He quirked a chiding eyebrow. "I didn't know you had such a wild imagination, Justine."

"There are a lot of things you don't know about me," she retorted, her gaze narrowing. "And maybe my imagination wouldn't run wild if you didn't keep secrets from me about *my* nephew."

Zack slid his arm along the couch inches from her head, relieved to see that she was bouncing back. "Classified information, ma'am."

"Bullshit."

He clicked his tongue. "If you were my student, I'd—"

"I'm *not* your anything."

Justine knew by the swift darkening of his eyes that she had gone too far. Why did she keep pushing him? Was she subconsciously hoping she'd make him snap? If he kissed her in anger, and she responded in anger, did she really believe it would absolve her of any stupidity on her part?

"You *were* my something once," he said, slowly closing in. He effectively trapped her against the sofa with his arms, his gaze locking on hers. "What happened, Justine? When are *you* going to give up *your* secrets?"

His voice lowered to a seductive whisper. Justine closed her eyes, hoping to break the spell.

It didn't work.

There was still his fingers, which had begun to stroke her neck, and his voice, which flowed over and around her to form a sensuous web she didn't have the strength to destroy.

His scent, so purely male, so wholly Zack, invaded her lungs and made them labor for more.

"When are you going to stop fighting me and admit that you still love me?"

Justine's eyes snapped open. She couldn't let him get away with that remark. "Don't confuse love with lust, Zack."

His brow arched playfully, but his hazel eyes remained dark with blatant desire. "The girl I knew called it love."

"That girl wizened up." She licked her lips, then wished she hadn't when his lids lowered to watch the movement. Why didn't she just push him away? Good question, and one she wasn't ready to answer.

Closer he came, until his mouth hovered a breath away.

"So," she whispered not only breathlessly, but desperately. "You really think I'm wrong about Jordan?"

His sexy smile mocked her attempt to distract him. He trailed his finger along the gentle slope of her breast, creating shivers in its wake. "I really think you're wrong about Jordan."

That wicked, wandering finger paused on the telltale outline of her nipple. His smile widened when she caught her breath.

She wasn't ready to give up. Well, she was more than *ready,* but her mind wasn't. Her mind was the smart one. She licked her lips again—she couldn't help it, he was making them dry with every breath that came sighing softly from his lips. "Then—then how do you explain what he heard from the lovebirds?"

"Maybe it wasn't his imagination," he murmured. "Maybe they really *can* talk."

"That . . . that would be impossible. I mean, they can mimick humans, but they can't carry on conversations!"

"Maybe it's magic."

"You believe in magic?" Despite her helplessly husky tone, she managed to sound incredulous. Zachary Wayne, a believer of magic? No way. He was as solid and as down-to-earth as any man she'd ever met. Gee, was he solid.

He caught her gaze and held it, all hint of humor gone. "I *didn't* believe in magic before I met you."

It was a trap. Justine knew it, but she had to ask. "But now you do?" *Gullible fool.* No, she wasn't gullible. She was just playing along. He could talk nonsense all night long, and she would pretend to listen.

"Now I do."

She meant to laugh, to let him know how corny his remark sounded, but it was hard to do with his wonderful mouth moving on hers, coaxing her lips apart, and consuming her with little effort. She was lost before their tongues met, and completely in over her head when they found each other and began to duel in earnest.

His hands were cool and exciting as they slipped beneath her sweater and splayed over her back. When the clasp of her bra came free, Justine felt a jolt of hot desire shoot through her belly. He was good. So very damned good. To prove it, he slowly worked his way around until his hand cupped her breast. Her nipple hardened, jutting shamelessly toward his palm. She moaned as he gently pressed his thumb and forefinger around it and squeezed, just the way she liked it.

He hadn't forgotten.

The kiss deepened; they both panted like honeymooners after a long abstinence. She reached for the button of his jeans just as he reached for hers. Arms tangled together, but somehow they managed.

She slipped her hand inside his briefs and cupped him, tracing paths she'd traced before, but now seemed new to her all over again, reacquainting herself with his feel, his length. He pulsed beneath her, hot, hard, and ready.

He inched his fingers beneath her panties and made her sob with the first tentative touch. Zack could do that. How could she have forgotten? She hadn't, though. She'd merely put it from her mind so that she wouldn't go insane with missing him.

Now here she was, falling right back into a hole she might

not be able to crawl out of. Zack's arms were that hole. A
wondrous hole, no doubt, but at what price? Another heartache that never died? A long string of painful months waking
in the night and hugging her pillow, crying buckets of useless
tears for a man who got his kicks loving and leaving?

Justine's thoughts made her hesitate, but Zack quickly distracted her by whispering huskily in her ear, "God, I missed
you."

She could hardly doubt his sincerity, as heartfelt as he
sounded, and she wasn't lying when she whispered back, "I
missed this, too." She missed a whole lot more, but she knew
better than to think about it, and her choice of words wasn't
an accident.

"I want to get rid of these clothes so that I can feel your
satin skin against me. Feel *you*, all of you."

Justine's body melted at his talented pillow talk, but her
mind remained clear, her outlook both cynical and cautious.
Before she could think of just *one* reason she shouldn't indulge her starved body while keeping her heart safe, he had
thrust her beneath him on the sofa and had began to tug her
jeans down.

Once she decided to stop fighting him—at least the sexual
attraction part—Justine jumped in with both hands. He was
naked before he'd finished undressing *her*, and she helped
him with the rest. Her urgency spurred his passion. They met
skin to skin, hip to hip, and mouth to mouth.

She quickly showed him the way and clasped him to her.
He sank so deeply and completely into her that a shudder
threatened to rip her apart. Her body wept joyfully at the
union, but her mind ruthlessly recalled the price for such
weak emotions.

Buried deep inside her, he hovered for a moment, still and
trembling. She knew by the tight look on his face that he
was struggling for control. Zack was an unselfish lover, and
he would hate himself if he left her behind.

Without thinking, without considering the consequences,
Justine gave him a slow, wanton smile, a glimpse of the old

Justine, the one who knew which buttons to push and dared to push them. His reaction was a primitive growl that fanned the flames of her desire to a roaring bonfire.

Three powerful strokes and she was gone, lost in the ecstasy only Zachary Wayne could give. He soon followed, whispering her name over and over again with such poignant desperation that Justine had to shut him out or believe.

And she couldn't believe him, not ever.

"Stars above, are they finished?" Reuben demanded, sounding adorably embarrassed.

Mini withdrew the crystal ball and peeped at it with one eye squinted. Quickly. "Justine's getting dressed."

"What's Zack doing? No, wait! Don't answer . . ."

"He's sleeping," Mini said, watching and trying not to smile as her husband strutted along the perch looking extremely uncomfortable. He stopped often to fluff his feathers, as if he were hot. She knew how he felt and why. They had watched the inflamed couple until they noticed Zack's hand tunneling beneath Justine's sweater.

With a gasp and a giggle, Mini had quickly thrust the ball beneath her wing. But the atmosphere leading to that moment had been taut with unseen sparks, and consciously or not, Reuben had been moved just as she had.

This time Reuben asked, "How do you think it went? Well, obviously it went well in *one* way, although I'm surprised at the speed—" Reuben stopped abruptly and cleared his throat. "What I meant was—"

"I know what you meant, darling." Mini shamelessly stroked his ego, her eyes moving up and down his feathered form in a seductive way that Reuben instantly recognized. "And I'm glad you never get in a hurry."

"You are?" Reuben inquired, seeking reassurance. He edged closer to his sweet-talking wife, envisioning her not as a fat-breasted bird but as the beautiful witch she truly was. In her true form, he knew that her hair was a waterfall of black silk, her face was that of an angel, and her lips ruby red and ripe for kissing. Add a body that would excite a monk, and slanted green eyes that could light his shorts with just a glance, and he had the prettiest witch in the universe.

The fact that she had chosen him—a mean-spirited warlock who wasn't half as good-looking as most of the male witches she knew—when she could have had anyone she wanted, still astounded him.

Unaware of her husband's appreciative thoughts, Mini nodded. "Reuben, I don't mean to change the subject, but do you think Zack meant what he said about believing in magic?"

Reuben shrugged, still thinking about the night to come. He wanted to experience the same passion with Mini that he'd witnessed tonight between the two mortals, a passion that was so thick it seemed almost painful. At least he'd learned something tonight. Mini had been right about Zack and Justine; the two mortals *were* soul mates.

"Reuben? Are you with me?"

"Hmm?" Reuben jerked his attention back to his wife. "I'm sorry, what were you saying?"

"I said, do you think we should talk to Zack? Let him know that we're here to help?"

"Why him and not the young mortal?" he asked, recalling how she'd stopped him earlier. She had apologized a hundred times, but he could still feel the sting of her wing against his face.

Mini frowned and shook her head. "I'm afraid it would be too much for Jordan, and too big a secret to keep to himself. You saw how quickly he told Justine."

"No harm. She didn't begin to believe him." Reuben followed his observation with a snort of derision. Justine's total disbelief still irked him.

"I know. Instead, she thought he was under the influence of drugs." Mini looked worried. "I hope she's got that idea out of her head."

"I think maybe Zack distracted her," Reuben said dryly.

"Humph! I think maybe *she* distracted him even more."

Reuben waved his wing and produced a plate of steaming clams. When he intercepted his wife's threatening glare, he waved a resigned wing across the plate and turned it into a disgusting pile of sunflower seeds. Maybe she wouldn't notice the salt.

"Remove the salt, please. It's bad for us."

Maybe she would. With a grunt, Reuben did as she asked. "What I want to know," he said between bites, "is what we're going to do about the monkey." The seeds weren't as bad as he expected. They were quite good, in fact, even without the seasoning.

"I don't know what we *can* do. Just like the warming spell, the love spell wore off when Zack took the monkey out of range."

Reuben couldn't resist an evil chuckle as he recalled the monkey's excellent aim with the apple. The little devil had spirit, and Reuben always admired spirit. If he could get over his . . . *revulsion* of animals—he refused to admit that it was fear—then he wouldn't mind having the little fellow himself.

"Well, I don't think it's fair not to do *something*. You saw for yourself that Zack has a lot on his mind. He shouldn't have to fear for his life as well."

"Maybe he'll just return the monkey," Reuben suggested, quickly conjuring a goblet of clear wine to wash down the seeds. He stole a glance at Mini, relieved to see that she had decided to take a bath and wasn't paying attention.

"He won't, at least not for a while." She sighed. "Something tells me tonight was just the beginning of the battle. Justine will be running scared now that she's allowed herself to indulge in a bout of steamy hot sex with Zack."

Reuben choked at her words. He quickly gulped his wine.

"And don't think I don't know what you're drinking, husband dear," Mini said tartly.

In the blink of an eye, the wine became water. "Sly witch," he muttered beneath his breath.

"I heard that and I'll take it as a compliment."

He looked up just as Mini spread her wings wide, revealing a patch of tender, soft white feathers beneath. His mouth watered. He couldn't believe he was getting turned on by a patch of feathers, but damned if he wasn't!

Sadly unaware of her husband's lustful gaze, Mini dipped forward, using her wings to splash water onto her breast. The move sent her tail high in the air, giving Reuben a tantalizing glimpse of more white feathers covering her perky behind.

Reuben muttered a chant beneath his breath, and the feast of seeds disappeared. He rose and tiptoed across the cage to join his wife in her bath. Tonight was going to be a night Mini would never forget, he vowed.

Thirteen

Tuesday afternoon, while the team warmed up for practice, Zack slipped into the principal's office and called the florist.

He ordered a dozen red roses and a card that read, "Do you believe in magic?" When he thought the florist had enough time to deliver the flowers and the message, he slipped back into the office and called the pet store.

Jordan answered the phone, and after a few moments of shuffling sounds and indistinguishable whispers, Jordan returned to the line and cheerfully informed him that Justine was too busy to talk.

Mildly disappointed, Zack ended practice at four and headed home. They had a game scheduled on Friday, and by then Zack hoped the boys accepted the fact that Jordan Diamond would not be playing, and that they *could* win without him.

Once home he intended to take a quick—and probably lukewarm—shower and take Justine out to dinner. After last night, he figured things would begin to move more quickly. She could hardly deny now that there was something special between them.

Special and timeless.

Smiling at his sappy thoughts, Zack opened the door to the apartment building and stepped into the foyer. He nearly collided with Barry. No matter. Even his wacky neighbor couldn't spoil his mood.

Or so he thought.

"Hello, neighbor."

Barry smirked, ignoring the greeting. "Tell me, Mr. Wayne, does it bother you at all to come in second?"

Zack reminded himself the man wasn't playing with a full deck. He managed to keep his smile as he said, "Is hot water that important to you, Mr. . . . Fowler? Because it isn't to me. In fact, I'm growing used to cold showers, so why don't we just bury the—"

"I wasn't talking about hot water," Barry interrupted, his smirk turning into a full-blown sneer. "I was talking about women. Justine, in particular."

Every muscle tensed at his implication. Zack's smile vanished. Remaining civilized suddenly seemed like a waste of time.

Through his tightly clenched teeth, Zack snarled, "Explain yourself."

"You don't know?" Barry feigned surprise. "I'm surprised she didn't tell you. Justine and I used to be . . . quite close. We were going to be married."

"Is that so?" Zack told himself to calm down, that the man could and was likely lying through his gloating teeth. Maybe he and Justine had dated once or twice, but Zack could not believe Justine would—

"We had a slight . . . misunderstanding, and then she went running off on some cruise instead of letting me explain." Barry's lips tightened. "I don't know what happened on that stupid cruise, but when she came back—"

Zack exploded. He poked a sharp finger into Barry's puny chest, backing him up a few steps with the force. "*I'm* what happened, you wacky mutt! Justine fell in love with *me* on that *stupid* cruise." This time he had surprised Barry, but Barry recovered far too quickly for Zack's satisfaction.

"Ah, but she couldn't have been in love with you, because she was in love with me. *You* were nothing more than a rebound."

Barry's words struck a nerve, arousing a suspicion Zack had so far refused to consider. Justine had told him she was involved with someone. At the time he hadn't really believed her. Now he was forced to admit she might have been telling the truth, but damned if he'd let Barry know. "If she was in love with you, then why was she in *my* apartment last night, instead of yours?"

It was a damned good question, but an immature thing to say. When the man's face turned red, Zack decided it hadn't been a bad idea after all. Could he help it if the man possessed a wild imagination? He hadn't blurted out every sweet, intimate detail—no matter how badly he itched to bury that smirk on Barry's face.

"If you know her at all," Barry's tone implied his doubt, "then you know how fickle she is."

The man simply didn't know when to stop, Zack thought, clenching his fists and wondering if he'd lose his job if he got thrown in jail. It would be almost worth it to feel Barry's bones crunch beneath his knuckles.

Barry continued blithely on. "She falls in and out of love as often as it snows. This week she loves you, next week she'll love me. She gets a kick out of making me jealous."

Zack had reached his limit. He took a menacing step in Barry's direction. Just one little tap on the nose, just hard enough to break his bone and make the blood flow. He couldn't remember the last time he'd felt so bloodthirsty.

He would have hit him, too, if he hadn't noticed the water dripping onto Barry's head in an ever-increasing stream. Barry noticed it, too. He slapped at his head, then with a grimace, looked up. Zack did the same, groaning when he saw the water leaking from the ceiling.

It was coming from his apartment.

•   •   •

"Mrs. Winberry's here for another goldfish."

"So sell her one." Justine kept scrubbing the snake cage, pausing long enough to adjust the young python curled around her neck. Mrs. Winberry was a sweet old lady, but Justine just wasn't up to talking to her.

She wasn't up to talking to *anyone.*

Jordan stroked the python. "She insists on talking to you. She says this time she wants a goldfish that won't die on her."

Justine threw her sponge down, heaving an irritated sigh. The python stirred restlessly. "How many does that make her? Ten, twelve? She's got to be doing something wrong if they keep dying."

"Shall I tell her to stick her money where the sun don't shine?" Jordan inquired serenely.

"No, you may not tell—" She broke off when she saw his smile. It was such a beautiful sight that she couldn't help smiling back. "You rat. Tell her I'll be there in a moment."

Jordan disappeared. Justine rose and washed her hands before making her way to the front of the store. Mrs. Winberry stood by the cash register, her lips pursed in a tight line. Justine groaned inwardly and unwrapped the snake, holding him out for Jordan to take.

"Keep him in the back," she instructed, uncertain how Mrs. Winberry felt about snakes.

As Jordan eagerly took the snake, Justine's eye caught a flurry of movement from the birdcage on the counter. To her shock, Reuben tipped backwards from the perch. He landed on the cage floor, his feet sticking comically in the air. Almost as if . . . as if he'd fainted, Justine thought. Mini flapped her wings and dove to her mate's side, clucking urgently and glaring at Justine as if she were at fault.

"Well, are you going to wait on me, or not?" Mrs. Winberry demanded querulously. "If there was another pet shop in this town, I wouldn't be here." She thumped the counter with a wrinkled fist. "But you guaranteed my goldfish would live thirty days, or I'd get another one."

Worried about the bird, but knowing Mrs. Winberry wouldn't leave until she got her goldfish, Justine hurried to an aquarium and fished out the healthiest-looking goldfish she could find. She darted a glance at the birdcage as she bagged the fish and took it to the counter.

Reuben was back on his feet, but he didn't look well. He leaned drunkenly against the far side of cage while Mini continued to cluck around him like a mother hen protecting her chick.

Mrs. Winberry took the bag from her hand, snagging her attention.

"I hope this one lasts longer," she complained.

"Mrs. Winberry, do you have a cat?" Justine could have kicked herself for not asking before.

"Yes, yes, I do."

"Can he reach the fishbowl?"

"Oh, yes. Frederick enjoys watching the goldfish as much as I do. Why do you ask?" Mrs. Winberry sounded genuinely perplexed by Justine's questions.

"Because . . ." How to put it delicately? Justine cleared her throat, staring into Mrs. Winberry's faded blue eyes. The woman had to be at least ninety. "Well, cats like fish."

Mrs. Winberry didn't take the hint. "Yes, yes, but I *told* you Frederick likes fish."

"No, I mean, cats *really* like fish. To eat." Justine heard a snicker and turned to give Jordan a silent warning.

But Jordan was nowhere in sight.

So where had the snicker come from? Justine frowned, glancing at the lovebirds. Reuben seemed to have made a miraculous recovery, and now they stood together on the perch.

Watching her in that odd, unsettling way they had.

She really needed to move them to the bird room before she started believing Jordan's nonsense about witches and talking birds. Matchmaking lovebirds at that. Ha! Justine laughed to herself and concentrated on Mrs. Winberry.

Mrs. Winberry—who couldn't have been more than five

feet tall—stood on the other side of the counter, glaring at her. She lifted her head, her tone frosty as she said, "Are you implying that my Frederick is a murderer?"

A tiny bray of laughter sounded to her left. It was instantly stifled. Justine didn't even bother to look. She didn't want to know or speculate where it came from. "Mrs. Winberry, would you at least try putting the fishbowl in a place where the cat—"

"Frederick. His name is Frederick. He's orange and white, and I've had him for *ten* years, young lady." Mrs. Winberry sniffed. "If he knew what you were accusing him of, he'd be hurt."

Justine gave up. A goldfish a week wouldn't break her. She wondered how many it would take before Mrs. Winberry realized that beneath Frederick's orange fur there beat the black heart of a goldfish serial killer.

Handing Mrs. Winberry a receipt for the next one, Justine automatically glanced again at the plastic bag holding the fish to make certain she'd left enough air to sustain it. Not that it mattered. The poor thing was cat food the moment Mrs. Winberry turned her head.

Her heart stood still.

She leaned closer, her eyes stretching wide. The goldfish was grinning at her, revealing a mouth filled with evil-looking teeth.

Goldfish *did not* have teeth. Piranhas had teeth, and she did not sell piranhas.

Justine closed her eyes tight, then opened them again. The goldfish had swum to the opposite side of the bag, its fin moving rapidly in the water. She reached out to take the bag from Mrs. Winberry, to get another look to ensure that she had imagined it, but the grumpy woman snatched it out of reach.

"Oh, no you don't. This is my goldfish, and you're not getting it back."

With one last glaring look, Mrs. Winberry pulled her coat together and hurried from the store.

Dazed, Justine felt her forehead. No sign of fever. She rested her elbows on the counter and tried to think rational thoughts.

A snicker, a bray of laughter that couldn't have come from Jordan. A goldfish with tiny teeth and a human smile.

It was stress, she decided frantically. She had thought about last night all day and had mentally flogged herself until she felt physically bruised and sore. Or did she feel bruised and sore because she'd made unbridled, mind-blowing love for the first time in over a year?

With Zack. She couldn't leave him out, no matter how hard she tried, because it wouldn't have been unbridled *or* mind-blowing with anyone but Zack. She was an idiot for thinking she could have simple sex with the man and not involve her emotions . . . her heart. Stupid, stupid, stupid.

What terrified her the most was that she had to tell Zack last night had been a mistake. She had to convince him without giving herself away that there would never be anything between them again. Not even fabulous sex, because with Zack, sex didn't happen without falling in love.

Just seeing him weakened her knees. How could she have been so arrogant to think she could fight it? Him? Her? *Them?*

"Aunt Justine, are you all right?"

Justine rubbed her itchy eyes and tried to smile. It drooped on her mouth like a grimace. "I'm fine. Just tired."

"I finished cleaning the python's cage for you."

"Thanks."

"And I locked the back door. I also fed the python. I know how you hate to do that."

Jordan was right. Feeding live rats to the snakes was the downside of her business. Christopher usually volunteered because he knew how she felt. She flashed her nephew a wan but grateful smile, not so tired that she hadn't noticed the change in him today. He was more like the old Jordan.

"You are an angel." To her surprise, Jordan flushed and

looked away, but not before she saw the stricken look in his eyes.

"No, I'm not an angel. I'm a big dumb chicken, just like Coach—" He clamped his mouth shut and looked at the floor.

Justine felt a surge of anger. Anger was good. Anger would give her the courage she needed when she had to face Zack again.

"Coach Wayne called you that?"

Jordan scuffed his shoe across the floor. "Nah, just the chicken part."

"Want to talk about it?" Justine held her breath. *Please let this be it. Please let him talk to me.*

"Nah. I can't. I just can't," he finished in a miserable whisper.

Gently Justine said, "I know. How about we close this place down and go out for pizza? I could call Bea and tell her I'm bringing you home." When he shot her a wary look, she quickly added, "No questions, I promise."

He looked hopeful for a moment, then his face fell again. "I'm grounded, remember?"

Justine grinned. "I'm your aunt, remember? I can sweet-talk right up there with the best of them when I need to." After all, she'd learned from the best, hadn't she?

The look he gave her was both calculating and mischievous. "You wanna make a bet?"

"You name it."

"If you don't talk them into it, I get to take the python home tomorrow night—just for the night."

"Jordan, you know how Bea feels about snakes."

"Then you don't think you'll win?" he challenged.

Her chin came up. If Zack could revert to his childhood and accept a dare, why couldn't she? Besides, this wasn't exactly a dare. It was a bet, and Jordan was acting like his old self again. She would do just about anything to ensure that he stayed his old self.

"Okay, you've got a deal. But I haven't said what I get if

you lose." When he immediately looked wary again, she shook her head. "No, not questions."

"What, then?" Suddenly his eyes widened in horror. "I'm *not* cleaning the litter boxes!"

Justine laughed at his expression, then took a deep breath. "You have to go to the game with me Friday night and show your support for the team."

Jordan made a face. "Yeah, I heard what happened last night. Pretty dumb, huh? They act as if I'm the only one who can play football, and it takes all of us to win the game." He stared at the floor for a good long while before finally nodding. "Okay, I'll go if you win."

Justine locked the front door and went to call Bea.

Five minutes later she emerged from her office, smiling from ear to ear. Even the thought of confronting Zack later failed to dampen her triumph.

She had won.

The best part was that Jordan didn't look all that disappointed about losing.

When Justine and Jordan had gone, Mini fixed Reuben with a suspicious glare that made him squirm. Good. She wanted him squirming. Maybe she'd get the truth out of him. "Reuben, what did you do?"

"I was clumsy and fell from the perch. I must have knocked myself—"

"I'm not talking about your *fainting* spell over seeing the snake."

"I did not faint," Reuben insisted, raising his voice. "I fell. And just when were you going to tell me about those . . . those creatures? You know that if I had known, I would not—"

"Have slept a wink. Which is why I *didn't* tell you." Mini refused to feel guilty, and she wasn't a fool. "Don't think you can change the subject, dear husband. What did you do to that goldfish? Justine looked as if she'd seen a ghost!"

Reuben made the mistake of grinning. When he met his

wife's icy gaze, he immediately wiped the grin from his beak. He tried to sound righteous. "I gave the poor fellow a chance against that nasty, bully of a cat, that's what I did."

"And just how did you do that?" Mini inquired with deceptive sweetness.

Reluctantly Reuben confessed. "Oh, I gave it a few . . . teeth."

Mini groaned. "That's all?" she persisted, sensing there was more. She hoped she was wrong.

She wasn't.

"And . . . a little intelligence so he'd know what to do with those teeth."

"Reuben, you are the most exasperating, impulsive—" Mini stopped, her anger deflating as she remembered that once the recipients of their spells traveled out of range, the spells lost their power. Almost gleefully she reminded her husband.

"This is true. In this case, however, I don't think that's going to happen."

Mini froze. "What do you mean?"

"I mean that Mrs. Winberry lives in a house directly behind this store, separated by a small alley."

"And just how did you know this?"

Reuben hesitated, then rolled his eyes. "I caught a thought or two from Mrs. Winberry."

"I thought we agreed not to violate mortals' privacy by reading their minds."

"You said we shouldn't invade Justine's and Zachary's thoughts, and I agreed. We have the crystal ball, so there's no need. You mentioned nothing about the other mortals we encounter."

He was like a child, Mini thought, splitting hairs to justify his actions when he knew he was wrong.

Just as Justine had finally given up trying to convince Mrs. Winberry that her cat was responsible for her dying fish,

Mini gave up trying to make her warlock husband admit he was wrong.

She and Justine had a lot in common, she mused, shaking her weary head.

Fourteen

Zack could hear the sound of running water as he fumbled with his key. He cursed under his breath. A broken pipe? It had to be. Why him? Why not Barry? Or the landlord, who lived in the apartment directly below him. At least *he* was on the ground floor.

The ground floor . . . beneath him. Which meant the water was probably seeping into his landlord's apartment!

"Shit." Zack twisted the knob and swung the door open, fully expecting to find a busted pipe gushing water, perhaps in the kitchen beneath the sink or in the bathroom.

There was no busted pipe, but there *was* running water.

In the bathtub.

Both faucets were going full blast with the plug on the drain firmly closed. Zack sloshed through the water and quickly turned the faucets to the off position, then planted his hands on his hips and surveyed the mess.

It wasn't a pretty sight. He stood in water two inches deep, at least in the bathroom. More water had begun to creep into the living room, and he cringed when he considered what might have leaked through to his landlord's apartment.

Dennis the monkey was responsible, of course.

A noise in the hall made him swing around, geared to let loose on the monkey. "Look, you little hair ball, I agree that you need a bath—" He swallowed the rest of his words when he realized it wasn't the monkey from hell standing in his living room, but Barry Fowler.

Zack also saw the monkey, clinging to the ceiling fan in his usual fashion and observing them with bright, curious eyes. Zack wondered how Barry would react should he decide to look up and see Dennis, or if Dennis decided to let go with one of his ear-splitting, murderous screams.

Barry, wearing the now-familiar smirk, gazed around him in feigned surprise. He *tsk-tsked*. "My, my. What have we here? Did you leave your bathwater running this morning, Mr. Wayne? Mr. Potter isn't going to be pleased about this, not at all."

"Who in the hell invited *you* in?" Zack snarled. He'd had just about enough of Fowler—*and* the monkey. When he risked another quick glance at Dennis, his heart nearly stopped. With his tail wrapped around the base of the fan to hold him secure and steady, the monkey's hands were free. In one of those hands he clutched a bar of soap that Zack had opened that morning; in the other hand he held a pewter dish that had been holding the soap.

Not good, considering the monkey's excellent aim.

He had to get Barry out of his apartment before he saw the monkey—and before Dennis decided to exercise his throwing arm. He didn't need the monkey's help in dealing with Fowler.

Justine's ex.

Zack felt water seeping into his sneakers. He tried not to think about how long it would take him to mop up the water, or what his landlord, Mr. Potter, was going to say about it when he found out. If the elderly widower discovered *who* or *what* was responsible, Zack figured he'd be booking himself into a motel for the night and apartment-hunting tomorrow.

If that happened, Barry would win, and Zack didn't like that idea at all.

"I think you'd better leave," Zack told him, his voice totally devoid of even the slightest friendliness. The civilized era was officially over. He'd tried his best to keep the peace—well, except for that one time when he'd left Barry dripping in the hall.

Barry, it seemed, wasn't inclined to leave.

"We didn't finish our discussion."

"I believe we did," Zack said in a steely soft voice that even a thick-skinned person like Barry should recognize and heed.

He didn't, unfortunately.

"Justine's just trying to make me jealous by hanging around you."

"I believe you mentioned that in the hall," Zack gritted out. A darted glance at Dennis showed Zack that the monkey was growing restless. He was eyeing the back of Barry's head almost thoughtfully, shooting Zack occasional glances as if he were waiting for his cue. "Now, I'm going to ask you one more time to get out of my sight—"

"And if I don't?"

Dennis decided to answer that question by throwing the bar of soap at Barry's head.

Thunk!

Zack winced at the sound. The monkey's aim was true, as it had been with the apple.

Barry's eyes widened in surprise, then rolled upwards before he slumped to his knees on the wet floor. Zack caught him before his face connected with the floor and eased him the rest of the way down.

He didn't know whether to laugh or cry. "You are in big trouble, my friend."

The monkey flashed his yellow teeth in a wide smile and chattered something at him. He pointed at Zack.

Zack shook his head. "No, I did *not* tell you to hit him with the soap, so don't try to pin this on me." He held up his hand to the monkey and sternly demanded, "Give me the soap dish. I don't relish joining Fowler on the floor." To his surprise, the monkey handed him the soap dish with only a moment's hesitation.

Now Zack had to figure out what to do with Fowler. If he waited until he regained consciousness, he suspected there would be hell to pay. He didn't doubt that Fowler would file assault charges, and if Zack told him the monkey was responsible, then Fowler would call the Animal Control Center.

The idea had its appeal, Zack thought, glaring at the monkey. "I should let him, you know. It would save me a lot of headaches."

Dennis laughed and shook his head, as if he were confident Zack would do no such thing.

He was right, too. Muttering every curse he could recall, then inventing a few, Zack grabbed Fowler's arms and began to drag him from the apartment. The man could stand to lose a few pounds, Zack discovered as he tugged and pulled him into the hall.

A quick search of Fowler's pockets produced a set of keys. With a satisfied grunt, Zack found the one he was searching for and unlocked the apartment door. Returning the keys, he pulled Fowler into the apartment and straight into Fowler's bedroom. The layout of the apartment was a duplicate of his own, he noted absently.

It wasn't easy lifting him onto the bed, and Zack was sweating and puffing by the time he got the man stretched out on the covers. There, that should do it. He stood back and looked at the unconscious man. When Fowler awakened to find himself in his own bed, there was a slight chance he would think he'd dreamed the entire episode.

It would be his word against Zack's.

Locking the door on his way out, Zack hurried into his own apartment and shut and locked the door. He didn't intend to answer it again until there wasn't a trace of evidence left.

He turned and stepped into something sticky. He glanced down, frowning at the pasty white substance. It hadn't been there a moment before, he was certain.

Slowly his gaze followed the trail of white until it reached a pair of white-coated bare feet. Long, ugly feet. He lifted his gaze, his jaw dropping at the sight of the white apparition standing in the middle of the floor.

While *he* was saving the monkey from an uncertain future, while *he* was literally saving the monkey's *hide*, the monkey had found the flour canister.

Mini could feel her husband shaking with laughter.

She stomped on his foot, shooting him a quelling glance. Holding the crystal ball aloft so that he couldn't see, she scolded him. "It's not funny. Poor Zack! If that creep Fowler decides to press charges, Zack could go to jail. He and Justine can hardly advance their relationship if he's behind bars!"

"Calm down, darling. If you want, I'll fly over there and help Fowler forget what happened."

"The spell won't stick once you fly out of range, remember?" Mini felt unusually irritable and anxious for reasons that eluded her. "And you nearly froze to death on the last trip."

"I did not!" Reuben argued. "A little ice never hurt anyone, and most certainly not a warlock. Besides, it's at least twenty degrees warmer now."

"Still below freezing. You also nearly got caught. You can't deny that."

Reuben opened his beak to object again, then apparently thought better of it. "So tell me, why won't Justine talk to Zack? She's been avoiding him all day, and you saw what she did with the roses—pitched them into the trash."

"Ah, but she took them back out later. And I suspect the reason she won't talk to him is because she's trying to forget what happened last night."

"Why, pray tell? As I recall, *she* was the one in a hurry."

"It takes two, darling. Especially in making love."

Reuben rubbed his wing over her breast, his eyelids drooping. "You can say *that* again," he murmured.

Mini pushed him away without thinking, surprised at her own actions. She *never* rejected Reuben's caress. What was wrong with her? To cover the awkward moment, she explained her theory. "I think Justine's deeply afraid she'll fall in love with Zack again."

"But you said she'd never stopped loving him."

"She didn't, but right now she's in denial. She *believes* she got over him. It was her way of dealing with the loss and getting on with her life."

"Hmm." It was obvious by his puzzled tone that Reuben didn't understand. "Do you think Zack will believe that nonsense about Justine being in love with Fowler and using him as a rebound?"

Mini clicked her beak in frustration as she remembered the scene between Zack and that blundering idiot, Barry. "If he's smart he won't, but I don't think Fowler helped matters."

"I wished he'd come into the store. I'd give him a rash or make his hair fall out, or *something,*" Reuben grumbled. "That mortal is a nuisance we can do without."

A giggle escaped Mini. "The monkey must have thought so, too."

With a deep chuckle, Reuben agreed. "The little creature reminds me of myself when I was a young warlock."

Mini cocked her head at his admiring tone. "You like the monkey, then?" It wasn't a cat, but . . .

"Not *that* much, so don't get any ideas about taking him home with us," Reuben said, guessing her thoughts. "Let's see how Justine and Jordan are doing, shall we? Zack will be cleaning for a while, I expect."

Producing her crystal ball again, Mini suspended it before them and waited. After a few seconds of concentrating on Justine and Jordan's image, they came into view.

"That looks delicious," Reuben declared, watching as the

young mortal Jordan took a huge bite from a slice of pizza.

"Darling." Mini nudged him.

"Hmm?"

"My feathers are getting wet."

"Pardon?"

"You're drooling all over my wing."

"Oh." Reuben produced a handkerchief and wiped the moisture from his beak. "Sorry, my dear. Say, you don't suppose—"

"No, we can't eat pizza."

She laughed at his crestfallen expression.

The monkey took one look at Zack's murderous expression and let out a shriek. He threw the canister in the air, scattering the remaining inch or so of flour, adding it to the rest that was settling on the wet floor. The tin container hit the floor with a crash, startling the monkey. With another squeal he plowed through the pasty mess and disappeared into Zack's bedroom—the only room that wasn't covered in water, flour, or both.

A second later the door slammed shut.

Zack slowly closed his mouth. Now he knew the meaning behind the saying, Truth Is Stranger Than Fiction. The monkey might be a little touched in the head, but he certainly wasn't stupid. He'd known how to turn on faucets, plug the drain, and he obviously recognized rage. Rage was a mild definition of what he felt, but he was too stunned to think of a word that *did* fit.

He wasn't sure there *was* one.

But standing in place wouldn't make the mess disappear. He needed to get it cleaned up before the landlord came home, before Fowler got to him and complained. Zack didn't doubt for a moment that he'd get a visit tonight from one or both. Fowler didn't really worry him; he'd just refuse to answer the door.

The landlord—Mr. Potter—had a duplicate key to his apartment. If the water from the bathroom *had* leaked through the floor into his bathroom, it would collaborate Fowler's story, and Mr. Potter would feel obligated to check out Fowler's claim.

They would find Dennis. He'd get a nice formal eviction notice, and Fowler would rub his pudgy hands together and smirk his little smirk. He'd get the hot water all to himself, not that Zack cared.

He felt sick. He knew it was his ego talking, but he just couldn't tolerate the thought of Fowler witnessing his humiliation, especially after what he'd said about Justine. True or not—and later he would *have* to consider it—it was unchivalrous of Fowler to talk about Justine as if she were nothing more than a . . . a slutty Goldilocks who couldn't decide which bed suited her.

There was only one thing to do—hide the monkey and get rid of every trace of evidence so that Fowler's incredible story wouldn't hold water. Ha. Ha. Zack didn't crack a smile, didn't have the slightest urge to laugh at his pun.

The water in the foyer would have to go first, and that meant he'd have to risk running into Fowler before he was finished. Unless . . . Zack's gaze narrowed speculatively on the south window. He walked across the room and lifted it, inspecting the fire escape. Yes, he could see a few dry patches in the ice. If he was careful, he could go down the fire escape, come in through the front door, and mop up the water in the foyer.

If he left the window open a bit, he could return the same way with Fowler none the wiser.

Zack grabbed an armful of towels and climbed through the window onto the fire escape. Leaving the window cracked, he tucked the towels under his arm and carefully placed his feet on the dry spots, avoiding the dangerous patches of ice.

He made it to the bottom of the slick metal stairs without mishap. After establishing that Mr. Potter's car was still absent from the garage, he rounded the corner of the house and entered the empty foyer. The cleanup took only moments, and once again he climbed the treacherous fire escape. This time the towels were wet and heavy. The left side of his sweatshirt was soaked and cold by the time he reached the window to his apartment.

It was closed.

Muttering a disbelieving curse, Zack dropped the wet towels and tugged on the window. It wasn't just closed, he realized, it was locked. There was only one explanation; the monkey had locked him out.

Zack peered through the glass, cursing when he spotted his keys lying on the hall table. It was a habit, and one he decided then and there to break. He'd never again take his keys from his pocket until he changed pants. Fat lot of good his resolution did him now, though.

He could break the window, but then he might attract unwanted attention with the noise. Another solution would be to wait for Mr. Potter's return and get his duplicate key.

But waiting would wreck his plans of getting rid of the evidence. He would get evicted, Fowler would gloat, the monkey would have to be returned to the store, and Justine would think him irresponsible.

Zack tapped his fingers against the glass as an outrageous idea came to him. It was a long shot, but what if Mr. Potter's window wasn't locked? He knew Cannon Bay's crime rate to be admirably low, and he himself rarely checked the locks on his windows. Zack's cold lips tilted in a humorless smile as he remembered the consequences of his indifference. Leaving his window unlocked had been an open invitation for *someone* to come in and snoop.

But he didn't want to snoop; he just wanted a key. It wouldn't exactly be breaking and entering, would it? He would be *borrowing* a key to his own apartment. In and out without anyone knowing. No harm done. Later, he could slip the key under Mr. Potter's door. It wasn't as if he was planning to steal anything valuable.

Zack shook his head, wondering if he'd gone crazy. He was sneaking around on fire escapes, thinking about slipping through his landlord's window, just to . . . what? Save his apartment? Protect his ego? Help a monkey who turned out to be much, much smarter than anyone anticipated? Oh, and he'd almost forgotten the assault charges Fowler was likely to bring against him.

The cold had begun to seep through his sweatshirt before Zack finally convinced himself there was no other way. The sun had sunk below a line of trees in the distance, reminding Zack that it would be dark soon. He had to do something.

With a bad feeling in his gut and a few choice curses directed at a certain clever monkey, he carefully descended again. The irony didn't escape Zack. His intelligence was superior to that of the monkey's, yet he was sneaking around in the cold while Dennis the Menace Monkey was safe and warm inside the apartment.

The realization did nothing for his bruised pride.

Evening shadows cast by the fire escape gave Zack a false sense of invisibility as he crept to Mr. Potter's window. With fingers raw and red from the cold, he gave the window a gentle tug.

It didn't budge.

Zack cupped his hands around his eyes and pressed his face to the glass. It was locked, but he saw that the latch was just a hair's breadth away from the edge of the frame. A quick jiggle or two might do the trick. It crossed his mind that just a few nights ago, someone might have been doing the same to *his* window, but Zack didn't think about it long.

He gripped the upper edges of the window and lifted up, then let go. Another peek. Yes, it looked as if that might work. He did it again and again. On the fourth jiggle, the lock slipped off the frame. The well-oiled window came up so fast it startled Zack.

But not as much as the voice that spoke directly behind him.

"Don't make any sudden moves, mister. Raise your arms real slow."

Since Zack already had his arms in the air, he simply left

them there. Something hard and cold pressed against his neck. It didn't feel like a gun, but it got the point across all the same.

"You have the right to remain silent."

Cold steel clicked over his left wrist.

"Anything you say can be used against you in a court of law," the faceless voice intoned.

Zack finally found his voice. "You're making a mistake."

"Is this your apartment?"

"Well, no, but—"

The handcuff clicked over his right wrist.

He tried a different tactic. "I'm Zachary Wayne, the substitute football couch—"

"I don't care if you're the pope. If I caught *him* breaking into someone's house, I'd arrest him, too."

Slowly Zack closed his eyes and leaned his head against the cold windowpane. Obviously the officer wasn't a football fan, or he would have recognized his name.

"Turn around, Mr. Wayne, nice and slow."

On second thought, Zack didn't think it would matter.

Fifteen

"I shouldn't have come here."

Justine said the words out loud as she waited for Zack to answer the door. She would step inside for just a moment—keep her coat on—and say what she came to say. He would nod. Perhaps his ego would suffer a slight stroke, but when he realized that she was serious he would have to accept that she wasn't the type to have casual affairs.

And absolutely no way was she going to believe him if he began to tell her it wasn't casual, that he cared. The cruise ship subject was out. Taboo. Long gone and over with.

She'd been that route once, had believed him once, and now she knew better. In fact, she wouldn't stick around to listen at all. He couldn't force her to listen, and he most certainly couldn't force her to believe. He'd see that she wasn't the same gullible fool she'd once been.

When Zachary Wayne left Cannon Bay, he wouldn't be leaving *her* broken heart behind.

Strengthened by her decisiveness, Justine knocked on the door again. Louder. She frowned, listening for the sound of footsteps or his voice calling out. Moments ticked by. She began to have doubts.

His Explorer was parked in the garage. She had seen a light shining through his window.

So why wasn't he answering the door?

"He won't answer."

She jumped and swung around, placing a hand over her clamoring heart. It was just Barry . . . holding an ice pack to the back his head. His suit was damp and wrinkled, and his hair was a mess. But there was an angry gleam in his eye, and his mouth was puckered in a pout.

He reminded Justine of the town bully who had finally met someone his own size. She immediately chided herself for her unkind thought and asked solicitously, "What happened to your head?"

"Ask your lover boy when you see him."

"*Zack* did that to you?" Justine saw a flicker of uncertainty in Barry's eyes before an ugly sneer took over.

"Don't look so surprised." He gingerly adjusted the ice pack. "And don't worry, he didn't stick his own neck out—he had someone else do the job."

"Do . . . the job?" Perhaps he had a concussion, Justine thought, because he certainly wasn't making any sense.

"He wants me out of the way now that he knows about us."

"Barry." Justine spoke gently, convinced now that he was talking out of his head. "There *is* no us. Not anymore. There hasn't been for a long time now." It shouldn't have been news to Barry; she reminded him at least once a week when he called to ask her out.

"But you agreed to go out with me. I thought—"

"I shouldn't have. It . . . it was a mistake." Justine felt her face heat in a shameful blush for leading him on. It was Zack's fault for coming to town and stirring up old feelings she thought she'd buried. Damn him. "Barry, I'm sorry."

"It's him, isn't it? He told me you were with him last night."

Justine froze. She figured someone could easily light a match on her face, it was so hot. *Barry* knew about last night? Zack had told him? Had bragged about it?

Of course he had. There was no other way Barry could know.

The realization settled like a cold hard stone in her belly. He'd turned a private moment into something nasty and public. She'd known he was a coldhearted man—anyone who broke hearts for kicks had to be—but she hadn't known he was *that* cold.

She asked another question, figuring she had nothing to lose. Better to be prepared than to be in the dark. "Did he tell you anything else?"

"Just that you fell in love with him on that stupid cruise."

He followed this with a scornful laugh that made Justine flinch and wonder for the hundredth time what she ever saw in him. He was a weak, mean-spirited person.

Justine clenched her hands inside her coat pockets. Her eyes burned, but there was no way in hell she was going to allow one single teardrop to fall with Barry watching.

"Zack was wrong," she lied without a qualm. "I *thought* I was in love with him, just like I *thought* I was in love with you." Her brittle smile nearly cracked her skin. "I was wrong on both counts. Guilty as charged."

She turned and walked away, gallantly fighting tears. When she reached the foyer, she slipped in a puddle of water and almost fell. She glared down at the water through a blur of tears.

If she had fallen, it would have been the last straw.

The close-up in the crystal ball of Justine's big, shimmering eyes was heartbreakingly clear. "Oh, dear," Mini whispered pityingly. "Poor Justine."

Reuben was too furious over what Barry had said to feel any sympathy for Justine. Mini was much better at it anyway. "Why, that lousy black-hearted—" He broke off, so incensed he was speechless for the first time in his long and checkered life.

"She believed him." Mini felt a spurt of silly tears spring

to her own eyes. "She believed him, and now things are worse. What are we going to do?"

"That obnoxious mortal twisted Zack's words!" Reuben raged. "When Zack tells Justine the truth—"

"I don't think she'll listen." Mini's heart sank at the thought. They'd made so much progress—or so she had believed.

"Let's see what Zack is doing. He should be finished cleaning by now." Reuben bent his head as Mini turned the crystal ball around. "I predict he'll get right on the phone the moment he finishes."

Her voice shaking, Mini said slowly, "I don't think so, dear husband. Look!"

Reuben blinked at the image in the crystal ball, stumbled back a step, and stared at Mini with his mouth agape. "He's behind bars!"

"Oh, Reuben! We've made such an awful mess!" Mini collapsed against his breast and began to sob as if her heart were breaking.

Stunned by her reaction, Reuben patted her back and made an awkward attempt to soothe her. "Now, now, dear. No need to get upset."

Mini cried harder.

Justine hated to cry. It made her eyelids swollen and red, and her face blotchy.

The bubble bath didn't seem to be helping. Each time she sniffed, more tears leaked out and ran down her blotchy cheeks. She couldn't even get the temperature of the water right. Maybe when she got out of the tub she'd write Calgon a nasty letter. She wiped at her cheeks and took a shuddering breath. Sue them for false advertisement. Yeah, that's what she'd do.

She cupped a handful of water and dribbled it onto Thor, who sat next to the tub waiting for her to do just that. Perched on the shelf above the tub, Rogue dozed off and on, jerking his head up each time he heard the water slosh.

Squeeze was nowhere to be found. Justine had made a quick search while the tub filled, but hadn't found her. She wasn't too concerned; she felt confident the snake couldn't have gotten out of the apartment. Justine hiccupped and slumped against the tub.

This was the pits, she thought. How had it happened? She'd been determined . . . strong. And stupid. Making love with Zack had been stupid, stupid, stupid.

The phone began to ring, but Justine made no move to answer it. That's what answering machines were—

Zack's voice interrupted her thoughts. Justine froze.

"Justine, it's Zack."

As if she didn't recognize his voice! It *did* sound strange, though, as if he spoke with his hand cupped around his mouth.

"I'm in jail. I need your help."

To the point, yet in a secretive tone totally unlike Zack.

I'm in jail. Justine sat up so quickly Thor got more than just a sprinkle. The iguana shook the water from its head and lumbered away as if insulted. She climbed from the tub and dried herself in record time.

Zack was in jail. She couldn't believe it . . . but it would explain why his Explorer had been parked in the garage when he apparently wasn't home. Had Barry pressed charges? she wondered, quickly rebraiding her hair. He hadn't mentioned it, which didn't exactly inspire comfort.

Zack needed her help.

In her bedroom, Justine grabbed a sweatshirt from her closet and yanked it over her head. She tugged on a pair of jeans, slipped on thick socks, and was halfway out the door before she realized she'd forgotten her shoes.

She took a deep breath and shut the door. Hysteria would not help Zack, she chided silently, pressing a fist against her racing heart. And where had she been going, anyway? To the jailhouse? To do what? They wouldn't just let him go because she insisted. She wasn't even sure *why* he was in jail!

But she could find out. Quickly she dialed the police station and asked for Mac. Mac would know. Mac would tell her.

A few moments later, more stunned than ever, Justine hung up the phone. According to Mac, Zack had been caught trying to break into someone's apartment. His bond was set at ten thousand dollars.

He would need bail money.

Justine slowly removed her coat, forcing herself to think rational thoughts. Her brother was a lawyer, so she knew a little more than some about what to do. She snapped her fingers, her small victory cry echoing in the quiet apartment. A bondsman! Zack would need a bondsman.

Clay would know who she should contact.

A quick glance at the kitchen clock told her it was past eight. Clay should be home, and if he wasn't, she would try his office.

Bea answered on the second ring. The sound of her voice momentarily froze Justine's vocal cords. Would her best friend and sister-in-law understand why she had to help Zack, the man responsible for her teenager's current depression?

Did *she* understand? No, she didn't, especially in light of what she'd learned tonight. But there wasn't time to consider her motives right now.

"Bea, I need to speak with Clay."

"Everything all right? You sound anxious."

Mildly put. "I'll explain later, I promise. Right now it's urgent that I talk to Clay." She crossed her fingers as Bea hesitated, suspecting her sister-in-law was debating whether she would let it go for now or pester her for more information.

"Okay. Hold on a moment."

Justine sagged against the wall. When she heard Clay's voice, she straightened again. Her mouth went dry at the thought of asking Clay to help the coach who had taken Jordan off the team. This was ridiculous! Zack possessed his faults, but he didn't deserve to be in jail. "Clay, I need a bondsman," she blurted out. Maybe he wouldn't ask—

"Are you in trouble?" he demanded.

Of course he would; he was her big brother. *Idiot.* "Not me. A friend."

"A friend." A telling silence followed.

He was waiting, Justine realized with a groan. Might as well come clean. "It's Zachary Wayne. He's . . . he's in jail."

This time the silence lasted a long time. Just when she thought he'd hung up, he spoke again.

"It might be difficult to get in touch with one tonight. Tomorrow—"

"I want him out tonight." Was that low, tense voice her own? Justine licked her lips, glad Clay couldn't see her fiery face. She refused to dwell on what he must be thinking. "It's . . . it's important to me."

"Don't you mean *he's* important to you?" Clay returned swiftly, putting on his lawyer's voice.

Justine swallowed a sharp retort. The last thing she wanted to do was get Clay riled. "Would that be so terrible?"

Clay lowered his voice. "Bea told me what happened between the two of you. I'm concerned for my sister, that's all."

"I can take care of myself." Justine closed her eyes and counted to ten. When she finished, she managed to hide her irritation. "Are you going to help me?"

"Let me make a few calls, see who I can find. I'll call you back."

"Thanks, Clay."

Justine returned the phone to the cradle. She was shaking, she realized, staring at her trembling hands. How could she care? How in the hell could she still care about Zack after all he'd done? Would she *always* care?

The possibility terrified her. Would she truly live out her entire life yearning for the one man she couldn't have? And she *couldn't* have him, she knew painfully, definitely. Zack played cruel games, and men who played games generally weren't thinking about white picket fences and bright-eyed children.

Maybe if she continued to sleep with him, the affair would last longer, but in the end Zack would leave Cannon Bay and she'd be back to nursing a broken heart. She respected herself too much to go into a no-win situation like that.

Yet knowing all of this didn't stop her from loving him from the depths of her very soul.

"Okay." Justine steadied her shaky legs and forced herself to walk to the counter to make coffee. "You've admitted it. What are you going to do about it?"

Rogue leaped onto the counter to investigate, but Justine absently shooed him away. She measured coffee into a filter and thrust the pot under the water faucet. "Nothing. You're going to do nothing about it." Her voice trailed into a miserable whisper. "Because you know Zack doesn't know the meaning of the word 'love.' "

The ringing phone startled her. With a gasp, she dived for it. It was Clay, and he'd found a bondsman willing to meet with her. She grabbed a used envelope from the island bar and found a pencil in the silverware drawer to write down his name and address. Clay not only sounded worried, but disapproving.

No more than she had expected.

"Do you need some money?" he asked abruptly.

Justine blessed him for asking, considering how he must feel about Zack. She calculated quickly in her head. She'd made a deposit into her checking account yesterday, but not enough to cover the 10 percent she knew most bail bond agents required. Writing a check tonight and transferring the amount from her savings first thing in the morning was her only option. With a little luck and prayer, the check wouldn't bounce.

"No, but thanks. Thanks a lot," she added gratefully. "Tell Bea that I'll call her tomorrow."

"Will do."

•   •   •

The holding pen at Cannon Bay's jailhouse reminded Zack of a very large cage. There was a small wooden bench, scarred and pitted, and a tiny window cut into the wire. A ledge protruded from the window. Officers milled about, shouting to one another and telling the occasional corny joke. They all ignored him as he sat on the bench and waited.

He was still having a difficult time believing he had been arrested. Arrested and *handcuffed*. A few minutes earlier, a female officer had ordered him to remove his socks and shoes, his jewelry, and empty his pockets. He'd placed these items on the ledge, wondering most of all why he'd had to take off his socks. The bare concrete floor was cold as ice.

She had written a description of the items on a form, then instructed him to sign his name.

It felt like a dream—a very *bad* dream.

"Zachary Wayne?"

Zack jerked his head up. It was a different officer, a short, stocky man who looked literally crammed into his uniform. The name tag on his shoulder read "Officer Woody Eller." There was nothing cold or informal about this officer; his blue eyes gleamed with curiosity and a touch of awe.

"*The* Zachary Wayne from the Miami Sharks?" Officer Eller questioned.

Relief flooded Zachary. Finally, someone who recognized him and realized that he wasn't the criminal type. Now all he had to do was explain to Officer Eller what happened. They would have a good laugh together, and then they'd let him go.

"Can I get your autograph when we finish getting your fingerprints? It's for my son. He's a big fan of yours. Or was." Officer Eller actually blushed. "Tough break, huh?"

But Zack wasn't paying much attention. He was still hooked on *fingerprints*. "Look, this has all been a mistake," he said, adding a rueful laugh for good measure. "You see, I was just trying to get my house key from Mr. Potter's apartment."

"Right."

Officer Eller nodded his head vigorously, but Zack had the sinking feeling he wasn't listening. Just when he thought he'd found an ally. . . .

The cage door swung open. Officer Eller beamed at him and waved his arm in a flourish. "If you'll come with me, we'll get those fingerprints."

As if I had a choice. Zack glared at the man's back as he padded barefoot after him. At least they had removed the handcuffs before putting him in the holding pen. Thank God for small favors, because it would be mighty hard to sign his name for Eller's kid with handcuffs.

When Officer Eller finished smearing his hands with ink, then cheerfully instructed him to sign his autograph on a blank ticket form, he led Zack to an empty jail cell.

Zack looked around at his new home, desperately seeking a glimmer of humor in his situation. But there was nothing humorous about the hard cot, the stained toilet, or the bars locking him inside.

Not a damned thing.

Sixteen

"Are you sure you want to do this?" Reuben asked Mini for the fourth time. They were perched on Justine's desk by the phone with the office shades drawn tight.

"Yes, I'm sure. It's our fault Zack is in this mess, so it's only fair that we help him out of it."

Reuben bristled at her slightly testy tone. "If I remember correctly, when I placed that spell on the monkey you called me a"—he pressed his wing tip against his lips and pretended to ponder—"genius, wasn't it? Yes, a genius. I'm sure of it. Now you've changed your mind."

"I haven't changed my mind," Mini snapped. Irritably she waved a wing over the phone. The receiver rose in the air and came down with a clatter on top of the desk. "We don't have time to fight. Call Jordan, quickly!"

Stabbing at the buttons with one of his four toes, Reuben dialed the number. He cleared his throat as it began to ring.

Bea answered. "Justine?"

Blasted Caller ID, Reuben mouthed silently to his wife. "No, this is Christopher Marshall, her assistant." He was pleased to note that he sounded *exactly* like Christopher. Zack's voice hadn't been so easy to mimic.

"Oh, Christopher! I thought you were house-sitting for your folks this week. Is something wrong?"

Reuben silently cursed the woman's infernal curiosity. "No, nothing's wrong. I was wondering if I might speak to Jordan."

"Jordan?"

"Yes. I stopped by the store to pick something up, and now my car won't start. Justine's not home, so I thought Jordan might give me a ride."

"Oh, of course. I'll get him."

Reuben covered the receiver with his wing. "Woman's got a memory like an elephant!" he whispered.

"Ssh! Jordan's on the phone."

"Christopher?"

"No," Reuben said, dropping the mimic. "This is Reuben. We need your help."

There followed a moment of shocked silence. Mini smiled, easily imagining Jordan's expression.

"Reuben . . . ? Is this some kind of joke?"

"You know it's not. You heard us talking yesterday. Mini's a witch, and I'm a warlock."

Another long pause. Finally Jordan spoke, his voice trembling with either fear or excitement—Reuben couldn't tell. Maybe both. A little fear might be useful.

"What do you want?"

"I thought you'd never ask." Reuben shaped his wing feathers into a victory sign for Mini. "We need a car . . . and a driver."

"You're nuts," Jordan whispered. "And if you're really who you say you are, then you'd know that I'm grounded."

"Oh, I am who I say I am, and I think your mother would allow you to help a friend. She thinks I'm Christopher and that I need a ride, so don't blow it. We'll be watching for you at the door."

Mini quickly waved her wing, replacing the phone in the middle of Jordan's squeaky protest. "Do you think he'll come?"

With a confident smile, Reuben nodded. "The young mortal takes after his mother. Curiosity will bring him to us."

"He's also very stubborn," Mini reminded him. "When he finds out where we want him to take us, he might refuse to help."

"Then we'll just have to persuade him."

She frowned, displeased with the idea of forcing Jordan. "Promise me that you'll only use witchcraft on Jordan as a last resort."

"I promise," Reuben grumbled reluctantly.

Exactly ten minutes later as they watched through the glass door, a mint-green older model Fairlane rumbled to a stop at the curb. A glance in Mini's crystal ball confirmed Jordan behind the wheel. Mini quickly unlocked the door, and she and Reuben waddled through the slight opening onto the sidewalk. With an absent wave of her wing, she shut the door and twitched the lock into place.

She should have thought to dim the streetlight before they exited, she fretted, shivering as the cold penetrated her feathers. If Mac happened by, she was determined that he would have no reason to become suspicious.

As they approached the car, the door swung open on the passenger's side. Mini nimbly hopped into the passenger seat. Reuben flapped his wings and joined her, gazing around him with appreciative male interest.

Jordan gawked at them, his eyes glazing over. Mini groaned. The poor mortal was in danger of going into shock! Perhaps he *wasn't* as strong as she believed.

"Killer car," Reuben praised, unaware of Jordan's reaction. He cocked his head and listened to the powerful rumble of the engine, finally letting go with an admiring whistle. "What have you got beneath the hood, anyway? A three-fifty?"

"Uh-huh." Jordan gulped. His Adam's apple did a crazy jig. He couldn't seem to drag his gaze away. "It's . . . it's my mom's car."

"I'll bet this baby can fly like a witch with her broom on fire."

Offended by his analogy, Mini poked him sharply.

He grunted. "Sorry, my dear."

"We really need to hurry, Jordan," Mini urged gently. "I know it's hard to believe that we're real, but the sooner you accept it, the quicker we can get going."

A tiny drop of drool slipped from the corner of Jordan's mouth. The hand he used to wipe it away shook noticeably. "Where are . . . are—"

"We going?" Mini finished with a sympathetic cluck of her tongue. She took a deep breath, exchanging a here-we-go glance with her husband. "We're going to Zack's apartment."

"C-coach Wayne?"

"I believe Zack and Coach Wayne are one and the same," Reuben observed dryly.

"No need to get smart." Mini glared at her husband before turning to Jordan again. His pale, shaken expression worried her. They should have given him more time to get used to the idea.

Only there hadn't *been* time.

"Jordan, are you okay to drive?"

"Of course he's—"

"Did I ask *you?*" Mini rounded on her husband. "He's clearly upset and possibly in shock."

"I'm telling you, he's fine!"

"He isn't. Look at him—he's as white as a ghost!"

"I'm not . . . in shock."

Startled, Mini and Reuben stared at Jordan.

"It's just that I'm . . . I'm finding this all hard to believe." He swallowed hard again. "You're *birds.*"

Mini shook her head. "But you see, we're not really birds."

"At least I wasn't until *she* turned me into one," Reuben added, his tone peevish.

With an outraged squawk, Mini flapped her wings. "You deserved it! Without consulting me, you invited that mealy-mouthed, obnoxious, prank-pulling warlock friend of yours to stay with us. You knew how I felt about him!"

"Jestark is an old friend of mine. What was I supposed to do? Tell him that my shrew of a wife can't stand the sight of him?"

"Yes, you—*what* did you call me?"

"Nothing."

"Yes you did!" Mini faced Jordan. "Did you hear what he said?" she demanded, so furious Jordan's silly grin hardly registered. "Now you know *why* I turned him into a bird. Although now I wish I had turned him into the *toad* that he resembles!"

"Well, you don't see me being rude to *your* friends," Reuben declared, ignoring her insult. "Take Xonia, for instance. She's so ugly I lose my appetite when I look at her, but do I mention it? No, I do not. And why? Because I am a gentleman."

"Xonia can't help being ugly! Jestark *chooses* to be insufferable."

"He's a warlock," Reuben informed her with a sarcastic tilt of his head. "That's his job."

"He can just perform his *job* elsewhere." Mini sniffed. "I won't have him in our home."

Reuben drew himself up, chest out, beak high. "Well, then, I refuse to eat another meal with Xonia."

"Fine. She says you have the table manners of a warthog anyway."

"Ha! At least I don't have to move my *nose* out of the way when I take a drink."

"Guys."

They ignored Jordan.

"She also says she doesn't understand why I put up with you."

"Is that so?"

"Guys! We're here. Why *are* we here, by the way?"

Again Jordan was ignored.

"Yes," Mini confirmed. "Sometimes I wonder myself." She blinked, determined not to start that silly crying again.

If she cried, Reuben would gloat. What in the stars above was wrong with her?

"I thought this was an emergency!" Jordan shouted.

A stunned silence followed his outburst. Mini swiveled around to stare at him. "You mean, we're at Zack's?" She hadn't even realized the car was moving!

"We're at Coach Wayne's apartment, and I'm *not* going in."

Well, he certainly had recovered from his initial shock, Mini noted wryly. "We need your help, Jordan. Our powers are diminished along with our size, and we can't do it alone. The monkey made a terrible mess."

Jordan turned off the engine and slid his arm along the seat, staring down at them as if he still wasn't quite convinced it wasn't a dream. "What happened?"

Briefly Mini explained about Barry, the monkey, and the arrest.

"So you see," Reuben finished, "we've got to put things back the way they were before Zack's landlord sees it."

A sulky look came over Jordan's face. "Why should I help *him?*"

"Because Zack *didn't* tell your parents what happened?" Mini suggested slyly. She felt a pang of remorse when Jordan's face turned red.

"How do you know about that?"

Reuben answered with his usual arrogance. "We know everything. Now, if you'll get out of the car, Mini and I will ride on your shoulder into the apartment."

Jordan hesitated, then finally opened the car door and stepped out. "Okay, I'll help, but I'm doing this for you guys, not for *him.*"

As the unlikely trio entered the foyer, Mini leaned close and whispered in her husband's ear, "What if we run into Barry?"

Reuben's eyes narrowed to threatening slits. "That would be Barry's extreme misfortune."

For the mortal's sake, Mini hoped he stayed out of Reuben's way.

Too much time to think wasn't always a good thing, Zack decided after an hour of staring at the peeling paint on the ceiling of his temporary housing. The cot had lived up to its image—hard, lumpy, and cold.

He'd spent the first half hour thinking about his dilemma, but he'd quickly grown tired of asking himself questions he couldn't answer. Either Mr. Potter believed his story or he didn't, and either Fowler would make a big fuss over the bump on his head, or he wouldn't.

He wouldn't know the answer to any of those questions until he got out of jail, and he couldn't get out of jail until the powers that be decided to allow him his one phone call. Not that he had made a decision on *who* he would call. There weren't a lot of choices: He hadn't been in Cannon Bay long enough to cultivate any close friendships, and because of the distance, calling Thomas would be his last resort.

Hell, it was probably his *only* resort.

There was Justine, but each time the idea slipped into his mind, heat crept into his face. His arrest was embarrassing enough without Justine finding out. If the newspapers got wind of it she would know anyway, but Zack would hold onto hope as long as he could.

His thoughts drifted to Fowler and his ugly insinuations about Justine. He found them hard to believe. The Justine he had known aboard the cruise ship had *not* been pretending to be in love with him. If it turned out that he was wrong, then he would definitely suggest she consider changing careers from being an entrepreneur to acting.

No, Fowler's actions had been that of a desperate, jealous ex-boyfriend, Zack decided, ignoring a lingering, niggling doubt that refused to be quiet. Justine *did* love him, and after last night he felt confident she would come around very soon. They were soul mates. They were *meant* for each other.

She had to see it, feel it, *know* it.

Officer Eller's disgustingly cheerful voice broke into his musings.

"Mr. Wayne?"

Zack unclasped his fingers from behind his neck and rose to a sitting position. He peered between the bars at Officer Eller, thinking it must be time to make that call. Not exactly good news, since he still hadn't decided *who* would be the first person to witness his humiliation.

Not Justine, though. He was pretty certain about that. She probably wouldn't believe his amazing story anyway.

"You're being released."

Zack wiggled his fingers in his ears, and stared at Officer Eller. Was this his idea of a sick joke? Nobody even knew he was here! "Pardon me?"

The lock clicked, the door swung open.

"You're being released," Officer Eller cheerfully repeated. "Someone's waiting for you up front. She's already posted your bail." He gave his head a quick, disbelieving shake. "Although where she found a bondsman this late . . ."

Frozen, Zack could only repeat the word over in his mind. She. She. She.

Justine?

It was the only *she* he knew who would post his bail. But how had she known?

"You plannin' on sitting there all night?"

"No, no. I'm coming." Zack hastily slid from the cot and followed the policeman from the cell. *Justine had bailed him out.* He was torn between embarrassment and triumph.

He hoped he was around when Fowler found out.

They stopped at a booth along the way and retrieved his belongings, and Zack quickly put on his socks and shoes as Officer Eller filled out his release form.

Ten minutes later they were standing before the heavy iron door. A buzzer sounded, and the door opened. Zack didn't realize just how tense he'd been until he stepped over the threshold to freedom.

His knees felt weak, and they got worse when he saw

Justine. Her eyes were red-rimmed and puffy, and her skin was blotchy.

She was the most heartwarming sight he'd ever seen.

"Thank you," he said softly, cursing the heat that returned to his face. "I know you're probably wondering how this happened—"

"It doesn't matter."

Her voice sounded cold and determined, so unexpected that Zack gave a start of surprise. "Of course it matters." He moved closer, frowning as he tipped her chin to study her face. "You've been crying," he observed.

She knocked his hand away, anger flaring briefly in her eyes. "Would you like for me to tell you why so that you can brag to Barry?" She marched to the door, flinging over her shoulder, "If you're riding with me, you'd better come on."

She was angry. Zack didn't know why, but she was. And what had she meant by that crack about bragging to Barry?

He followed her to the van. When they were cocooned inside its cozy interior, he stated the obvious. "You're angry about something."

"No. What you see is indifference."

It was an obvious lie. She ground the starter and spun the wheels on the slick parking lot. Zack prudently buckled his seat belt. "What happened? Were you worried about me? Is that why you're angry?"

"Don't flatter yourself."

Her laugh was so scorn-filled Zack's lips tightened.

"Look, you asked me for help, I came. Let's leave it at that."

If Zack had been confused before, he was completely muddled now. "I didn't call you."

She slanted him an incredulous look.

"I didn't," Zack insisted. "How did you find out I'd been arrested?"

She slammed on the brakes just as the stoplight turned

red. Zack felt the rear wheels slip sideways a few inches before the tread caught a dry patch of road.

"Cut the bullcrap, Zack. You called my apartment, told me you were in jail, and said you needed my help." Her furious expression didn't click with her casual, I-don't-care shrug. "I figured you didn't have anyone else to turn to."

"Wait a minute." The hairs on the back of Zack's neck rose. The conversation they were having sounded very familiar. "Do you have Caller ID?" He thought back, but couldn't remember seeing one.

"I've got one of those boxes sitting around somewhere." She paused as the light turned green. The van shot across the intersection. "But I haven't had time to hook it up."

"So you can't prove that I called."

"I don't have to prove it. I know what I heard, and I heard your voice."

He gave her a few seconds to realize what she'd said. "Doesn't this sound at all familiar, Justine? You believe that I called you. I know that I didn't."

"You're lying."

"Turn the van around."

"What?"

"Go back to the police station. They'll tell you that I never got to make my phone call."

Justine tried to convince herself that he was bluffing, but it would be easy enough to check out, and he knew it. Useless to lie. She let out a weary sigh and decided to give him the benefit of the doubt—against her better judgment—for the time being. "So we've got another X-file on our hands?"

Zack sounded grimly determined as he said, "Not if I can help it. We're going to find out who's behind this."

She thought about Barry and his ugly sneer. "Do you think it could be Barry?"

"Maybe."

His answer lacked conviction. She tightened her fingers around the wheel and forced herself to ask, "You still think it could be Jordan?"

"He's got a motive, but if it *is* Jordan, you'd think he'd be a lot happier leaving me in jail instead of pretending to be me and calling you."

A good point, Justine thought as she turned into the drive and parked behind his Explorer. Then, because she *was* curious, she said, "I've changed my mind. I *would* like to know how you happened to land in jail."

Zack gave a short, humorless laugh and ran a tired hand through his hair. "Come on in with me and I'll *show* you how it began." He paused with his hand on the door handle. "But I have to warn you, it isn't a pretty sight."

Justine had a sudden, awful premonition. "The monkey?"

"Good guess."

When he opened the apartment door a few moments later and ushered her inside, Justine found no sign of the disaster Zack had mentioned. Frowning, she turned to look at him. If this was an underhanded ploy to get her into his apartment, he would get an earful.

But Zack wasn't waiting to pounce; he wasn't even looking at her, she saw. He was staring at the meticulous apartment.

His jaw had dropped to his chest, and his eyes held an incredulous look too real to be faked. "You are never going to believe this," he finally muttered.

Seventeen

Stupefied, Zack gazed around the apartment, over the gleaming hardwood floors, the sparkling tile in the kitchen. He walked by Justine and into the bathroom, fearing his eyes were going to pop out of their sockets and roll across the *clean,* dry floor.

Unbelievable. Not a drop of water in sight. No dampness, no sign of flour, not a powdering of it anywhere. He hurried into the bedroom, smug in his belief that he would find the monkey's footprints mapping his path across the floor. It would be his proof that he wasn't going—

None. Not a trace.

"Crazy," Zack finished out loud. He returned to the living room to find Justine standing with her arms folded, regarding him with a mixture of concern and suspicion. Striding to the kitchen, he opened a cabinet door and brought out a bottle of whiskey. He poured himself a generous dose, downed it, then poured another shot. He raised it to his mouth as Justine spoke behind him.

"Zack? Are you okay?"

"Yes." But he didn't turn around. Her physical presence would remind him that he wasn't dreaming, and right now he wasn't sure he could handle the reality. "Do you want a drink?"

"No, thanks. I'm driving."

If he looked at her, he suspected her lips would be pursed primly. The thought almost made him smile—until he remembered why he was drinking in the first place. With a muffled oath, he slammed the glass onto the counter and capped the whiskey bottle. There was a reasonable explanation for this, he told himself.

All he had to do was think.

"Tell me about it," Justine urged, sounding less angry and more concerned. "Tell me what happened tonight."

Zack wasn't at all certain he preferred her concern, especially if it meant she thought he was going crazy. He turned abruptly and leaned against the counter, folding his arms.

She stood in the middle of the living room, still bundled against the cold, her eyelids red, her nose even redder. But the stunning gold of her eyes remained the same. He'd never forget those eyes, he realized. Not in a million years. He hoped he wouldn't have to.

In a voice that still echoed with disbelief, he started at the beginning when he walked into the foyer and ran into Barry. He left out a good portion of the conversation between them, focusing on the point when he noticed the water dripping from the ceiling onto Barry's head.

She gasped and smothered a spontaneous giggle when he got to the part about Dennis chucking the bar of soap at Barry. Her eyes widened when he told her how he dragged Barry across the hall and into his bed.

Those lips—so cherry red—parted in shock when he spoke of how the police officer cuffed him and read him his rights.

In the telling of his incredible story, Zack never lost sight of her face, following every reaction as if all his senses were magically heightened. And they were, he realized, adjusting his stance to try to hide his telltale arousal. She did this to him. But it wasn't lust, as she claimed.

It was much, much more.

He wanted to grow old with her, but first he wanted to have babies with her, to listen to her soft snore, to awaken each morning to the sight of her sleepy, tousled head lying on the pillow next to his own.

When he finished telling his bizarre story, she strolled around the room as if searching for clues, looking beneath the cushions, peering at the fire escape outside the window where he'd stood earlier, shivering and frustrated.

He shook his head, then realized she wasn't looking at him. "You won't find anything." He was somehow certain she wouldn't.

She glanced at him, her lips curved in a faint, wry smile. "So, you think that someone is trying to make us think that we're going crazy?"

"This didn't happen to you," he reminded her.

"Zack." She stuck her hands in her coat pockets and walked toward him. "Everything you've told me tonight could have happened to anyone. I admit that it's the strangest story I've ever heard, and it isn't *likely* to happen to someone else," she added with another one of her heart-stopping smiles. "But it's *possible.*"

"Except for the cleanup."

She nodded. "Except for the cleanup, which could also be explained."

"How?" He couldn't wait to hear her explanation.

"Your landlord could have cleaned up the mess while you were in jail."

"Mr. Potter wasn't here, and I doubt he would have had time." And there hadn't been an eviction notice on his door.

"He could have called a maid service," she pointed out.

"Doubtful."

"But *possible.*" She had reached the small dining table. Absently she drummed her fingers on the shiny veneer surface. "And then there's Barry."

To be fair, Zack tried to imagine the fastidious Barry pushing a mop. He suppressed a laugh. "You don't really believe that."

She shrugged. "No, not really, but I thought it was worth a shot."

"Tell me about Barry."

"There's not much to tell."

"Then it won't take long," Zack reasoned smoothly.

"We dated awhile." She hesitated, staring at her fingers drumming the table. "We discussed getting married."

"And then?" He could tell by her frown that her thoughts were not pleasant ones, but he had to admire her flippant tone.

"Barry is a real estate agent, and he'd hired this young girl fresh out of high school to man the phones when he wasn't there. She was very pretty."

When she looked up, her eyes were bright, but her voice was steady. Zack wished he'd gone ahead and crashed his fist into Barry's nose. "I think I get the picture."

She jammed her hands in her pockets again and changed the subject. "Well, at least now you won't get thrown out of here."

Zack was surprised to find himself chuckling. "Too bad I don't know who to thank."

"I know who you should thank," Barry said, stepping into sight.

Justine gasped.

Zack scowled. "Don't you know how to knock?" he growled, pushing away from the counter and putting himself between Fowler and Justine. He didn't want the creep ever to get close to her again.

Barry took a hasty step back from Zack's menacing presence. "Hey, the door was open. I heard voices so I came on in."

"What do you want?" When Fowler's gaze strayed to Justine, Zack clenched his fists. "On second thought, just get lost."

"Don't you want to know who cleaned up the mess?"

Barry asked with a friendly smile that didn't fool Zack.

"And you're going to tell me out of the kindness of your heart?" He was pleased when Justine gave a tiny snort of disbelief.

Barry's smile turned sly. "Well, there is one tiny favor you could do for *me* in return."

Zack sighed. "What is it?"

"I get first dibs on the hot water."

"You already do," Zack growled, wondering if Barry had ever talked to a shrink about his obsession with hot water.

"No, I mean *every* day," Barry clarified.

"All right. It's a deal. Now, tell me what you know." Then Zack would decide whether he was going to believe him.

Barry flicked another glance at Justine, hesitating. "She's not going to like it."

"*She* can speak for herself," Justine said, but Zack noted the tense set of her mouth, and the shadows flickering in her eyes.

Like her, he sensed something ugly in the air. He thought about throwing Barry out before he said whatever it was he was dying to say, but curiosity and the need to know—for his sanity's sake—won the brief battle. "Spit it out, Fowler. Then get out of my apartment."

Barry was watching Justine again, his eyes gleaming spitefully as he said, "It was Jordan Diamond, Justine's nephew."

Shock streaked through Justine like lightning. "You're lying!" she burst out, marching up to Barry and poking him in the chest. A red haze formed in front of her eyes, blurring Barry's features. "You're lying through your cheating, heartless teeth!"

She whirled to face Zack. "You know he's lying, don't you? He's mad because I won't go out with him, so he thought he'd . . . he'd make up this preposterous lie." She seethed, turning back to give Barry another blast.

He was gone.

"Of all the nerve," she spat out, staring at the closed door. She could feel Zack's gaze burning into her back. "Jordan didn't know—couldn't have known—anything about the monkey, and the water, or you going to jail." Slowly she turned to look at Zack, afraid of what she'd find but needing to know all the same.

She could tell nothing by his expression, which didn't make her feel better. If he had to hide his feelings, they couldn't be pleasant ones, she thought.

"You don't believe him?" *Please say you don't.*

"I don't see how it would be possible . . . unless . . ." He hesitated too long.

"Unless what?" she demanded.

"Unless he's been watching me," Zack finished quietly.

Did he think speaking softly would make his accusation hurt any less? she wondered bitterly. "You think Jordan's become so obsessed with getting even that he's *stalking* you?" She uttered a short, contemptuous laugh. "I guess you also think he trained the monkey to turn on faucets and lock windows. Or maybe you think Jordan was hiding in your apartment and did those things himself?"

"I didn't say—"

"You didn't say, but I know you're thinking it. Those are serious accusations, Zack. What I want to know is, how do you explain the rest of it?" She grabbed the bridge of her nose and shook her head as she drawled sarcastically, "Oh, I got it. Jordan called me to get you out of jail—sounding amazingly like you—and while I was running around town digging up a bail bond agent, my nephew decided to clean your apartment so that you wouldn't come home to a mess. Just what kind of obsession are we talking about here? Hate or hero worship?"

"That's enough," he commanded sharply.

But it wasn't enough, not yet. She wasn't quite finished showing him what a fool he was, and what a very nasty liar Barry was. "Because he *did* worship you before you ruined his life by taking him off the team. If he . . . he *is* responsible for any of this, it's your fault."

Suddenly she found herself almost nose-to-nose with a

very furious Zack, her arms gripped by strong, hurting fingers. She could feel his warm breath wash over her face in short bursts.

"You little hypocrite," he whispered roughly, but with an odd, underlying tenderness. "Wasn't it just last night you came running to me, believing Jordan was using drugs?"

Justine flinched. She couldn't argue, damn him!

"And yet I considered—only for a second, mind you—that Fowler might be telling the truth, and suddenly I'm a monster? What does that make you? The child shows a little imagination, and you think he's on drugs, yet *I* have an eyewitness who saw him come into my apartment!"

He released her, as if he realized he might be hurting her. With a four-letter curse, he presented his back and jammed his fingers into his hair.

"None of this makes sense," he said. "Of course Jordan didn't clean up this mess. You should have seen it—water and flour everywhere. It would take more than one teenage boy to—" He broke off suddenly, clamping his lips shut.

A moment ago, his brutal statements had forced Justine to take an honest look at herself; now her suspicions were aroused again. "What? What are you thinking?"

He cast a weary glance at her over his shoulder. "Nothing. It's nothing. This is crazy. Ever since my arrival, nothing has been normal or sane in my life."

The question was out before she could think. "Then why did you come here?" His smile, as weary and halfhearted as it was, made her heart trip. It was the kind of smile a man might flash at the woman he loved. *But it isn't real.*

"You can't be that naive, Justine. You know why I'm here. I'm a hopeless sap."

She didn't want to hear this. She had promised herself that she wouldn't listen. "Don't," she whispered.

He arched a brow, his hazel eyes soft, yet pained as they gazed at her. "Don't what? Don't tell you the truth? You know that eventually we'll have to talk about it . . . us. What are you afraid of?"

She backed toward the door with every intention of running. "I don't want to hear it. Last . . . last night was a mistake." There, she'd said what she'd came to say earlier. Why did it sound like a lie?

Her fingers closed around the knob. It turned easily in her hand. What *was* she afraid of? She was confident there was no way in hell she was going to believe anything he said, so—

"Last night was *not* a mistake. You call it lust, but it isn't. It wasn't then and it isn't now." He smiled faintly. "Not that I don't *lust* for you. Oh, yeah. I want you. Sometimes I want you so badly I can't sleep at night."

A thrill of that same lust coursed through her body as his voice deepened persuasively. He was good. She knew he was good. She also knew that it was a game. This time he would find that she wasn't so eager to play. Well, she was eager, but strong enough to resist. *Wasn't she?*

A muffled screech made her jump. It sounded close, and was quickly followed by a frantic thumping noise. Her startled gaze met Zack's, and she saw that he had heard it, too.

"Dennis," he said, striding to the hall closet. "I can't believe I didn't notice he was gone." He jerked open the door, and the monkey came lunging out, screeching and baring his teeth. Dennis loped past them and jumped onto a chair. From there he made an agile leap onto the ceiling fan, making it rock from the force of his landing. He wound his tail around the base and stared down at them with dark, accusing eyes.

While Zack was distracted by the monkey's antics, Justine slipped out the door.

In a burst of temper, Reuben struck the crystal ball with his wing and sent it skittering away. It fell to the cage floor and rolled into a corner. "I'm glad Jordan didn't stick around to see this," he ground out. "I should have finished that blasted mortal when I had the chance!"

"It's not our fault, darling. We had no idea Barry was watching when we went into Zack's apartment." Mini retrieved her crystal ball and prudently tucked it beneath her wing.

"We *should* have known he would be." Reuben wasn't ready to be pacified. "We should have stopped at *his* door first."

"What could we have done? The spell of forgetfulness would have been a waste of time. The moment we left the building he would have remembered."

Reuben snarled an oath and stomped to the birdseed holder. He pecked angrily at the seeds. "He's weak. We could have easily destroyed his mind by revealing ourselves."

Mini gasped, holding a wing to her breast. "Reuben! The witch's council would banish both our powers if we had done something so horrible."

"It would almost be worth it," he muttered, carelessly scattering seeds in his search for something with a little flavor.

He's beginning to care about the mortals, Mini thought, *but he's not yet ready to admit it.* Wisely hiding her delight over this discovery, Mini said, "We probably have nothing to worry about. Justine didn't believe Barry, and I don't think Zack did either."

"Maybe not, but it aroused Zack's suspicion. If he starts digging—"

"Zack doesn't want it to be Jordan any more than Justine does. Mortals are easily persuaded when it's to their advantage. Besides, what if Zack *does* find out it was Jordan? Jordan did him a favor."

Reuben cocked his head in her direction. "You're right. He did." He chuckled. "Imagine how confused Zack will be."

"Confusion seems to be the only thing we're accomplishing," Mini said with a dispirited sigh. "We're blundering, then scrambling around to fix our blunders."

"Mortals are more complicated than we thought."

"Some are, anyway," Mini agreed. "And just as stubborn as my warlock husband," she added beneath her breath.

"What's that?"

Mini cleared her throat. "They're stubborn, as well."

"Especially Justine."

Feathers bristling, Mini approached her husband at the feed cup. Sometimes her husband could so be insensitive! "I don't blame her for being cautious. Considering what she believes about Zack, I'd be wary, too, if I were her."

Reuben lifted his head, surprised by her attack. "Why can't she just give him another chance? She'd soon find out that she was wrong about him."

How many times did she have to explain before he'd get it through his thick bird skull? Mini wondered. "When Zack left the ship without a word—"

"She *thinks* he didn't leave word," Reuben corrected.

"Okay." Mini quickly counted to ten. "She *thinks* he didn't leave word. Not only that, but he waited a year to get in touch with her."

"Yes, but he has a perfectly reasonable explanation for waiting. She just won't let him explain."

"She will." Mini wished she felt as confident as she sounded. The way things were going between the two mortals, their sentence would be over before Justine and Zack came to their senses! "I think we're going to need Jordan's help again," she said.

"Don't you think we've caused him enough trouble?"

Mini couldn't resist teasing him. "Are you growing fond of the young mortal, darling?"

Reuben scowled, looking flustered. "Of course not. I just feel responsible for him. What did you have in mind?"

"I'll tell you over dinner." Mini twitched her wing tip and murmured a brief chant.

Eyes wide, Reuben stared at the table she'd conjured, then at the plates of food . . . or something. He was almost afraid to ask. "What's that?"

"A fruit feast. Dried crumbled bananas with raisins, chopped peanuts, and strawberry topping." Rubbing her wing tips in anticipation, Mini took a seat and buried her beak in the mixture. She groaned in ecstasy. Strawberry juice dripped from her red beak.

Reuben hopped closer, eyeing the concoction with lingering suspicion. "What are these green seeds sprinkled on top?"

"Dill seeds. I have a craving for them." She laughed at his horrified expression.

Eighteen

At noon on Sunday, Justine knew the moment she walked into her brother's house for the usual get-together feast that something was wrong.

It was too quiet.

"Where are the boys?" she asked as Bea took her coat and led her into the warm kitchen.

Dressed in jeans and a pullover sweater, Clay sat at the small dinette table drinking coffee and reading the *Wall Street Journal*. He glanced up and gave her a smile and a nod before quickly lowering his gaze to his paper again.

Justine wasn't fooled by his bland smile; she smelled a setup.

Bea handed Justine a roasted chicken on a platter. "They wanted pizza, so Clay sprung for it. Will you carry this into the dining room?"

"Wonder whose idea *that* was," Justine muttered, setting the platter on the table and returning for the peas and carrots. It was going to be a long dinner, and unless she misread the signs, the subject of her love life was going to stand in for the dessert.

The moment Bea removed their plates and returned with

coffee, Clay cleared his throat. Justine mentally and physically braced herself for the onslaught. That there would *be* one wasn't in doubt; how *fierce* was the question. More than ever, she wished her parents had not decided to move to Branson, Missouri, after retirement last year. Since the move, Clay seemed to have some silly idea that he should assume the role of her father.

At times it was damned irritating. She suspected this would be one of those times.

"Just how well do you know Zachary Wayne?"

"Well enough." So far so good. But Justine knew it wasn't over. *"You* should know him as well. He played pro football for the Miami Sharks until his knee injury."

Justine crossed her legs and settled in. She could tell by Clay's intense expression it was going to be a long chat. Bea fiddled with her coffee and remained silent. Justine didn't blame her for not wanting to get caught in the middle. *She'd* rather be mucking out cages.

"Do you have any idea why he came to Cannon Bay?" Clay asked.

A shaky question, but one Justine decided to answer honestly. "I really don't know." It was true. Zack had implied she was the reason, but of course she didn't believe him.

"You haven't considered that he might be dangerous?"

"Why would I?" she countered.

"He was arrested for attempted burglary."

"Breaking and entering," she corrected. "And it was a mistake. His landlord didn't press charges." She'd gotten the information about the dropped charges from Mac. She hadn't seen Zack since Tuesday night, and had decided against going to the game, but she'd gotten a check in the mail on Thursday for a thousand dollars. He'd wasted no time paying her back for the bond, and had apparently—Justine's heart gave a sharp twist at the thought—taken her at her word. "I would tell you what happened, but I don't think you would believe me."

"Try me."

With a doubtful shake of her head, Justine quickly related the bizarre story. She didn't, of course, mention Barry's accusations about Jordan, or the unsolved mystery of Zack's clean apartment. By the time she finished she realized the story was unbelievable enough without the addition.

Unamused, Clay simply nodded. Bea, on the other hand, shook with silent laughter. Justine smiled faintly. She might have also found it funny in the retelling if it hadn't been for that last little scene with Barry.

"So that's his story?"

"I have no reason to disbelieve it. Besides," Justine chided, "I don't know anyone with enough imagination to make up a story like that, do you?" Her brother was silent for a moment, as if debating something.

"You're not going to like what I'm going to tell you, Justine, but bear in mind that I did it because I love you and I'm worried about you."

Justine tensed. "What did you do?"

"I called in a few favors and had a friend run Zack's fingerprints through the FBI—"

"I could have saved you the trouble," Justine interrupted coldly. "If you've guessed that I'm in love with Zack, then you guessed right. What you don't know is that I won't give him the chance to hurt me again. He's not a threat."

"Don't you want to know what I found?"

Exasperated, Justine glared at him. "Didn't you hear a word I've said? I don't care what he did! You wasted your time."

"Clay, I don't think she wants to know," Bea said.

But Clay wore that stubborn look Justine recognized from childhood. He wouldn't rest until he said it, and he truly believed he was doing it for her own good. Sometimes big brothers were a pain in the ass, and this was one of those times, she decided.

"She needs to know."

"Go ahead." Justine slapped her hand on the table. "Tell me before you burst."

"He's been arrested before."

Justine waited for the punch line. When Clay remained silent, she realized he was waiting for her to react. With a lift of her brow, she prompted, "And? That's it?"

Clay frowned. "He was arrested for *burglary*."

He was serious, Justine thought. He honestly believed she'd go into a seizure to learn that Zack had been arrested before.

She asked because she knew he expected her to, not because she was curious. At least, that's what she told herself. "Was he convicted?"

"No. The charges were dropped."

She wondered if he knew how disappointed he sounded. "And how old was he when this happened?"

"Seventeen."

"Tell me, Clay." Justine leaned her elbows on the table. She loved her brother, but it was high time he realized she was a grown woman. "Would you be this interested in digging up dirt on Zack if he wasn't the coach who kicked your son off the football team?"

Clay flinched. *Bingo.*

"That was a low blow."

"Well?" Justine persisted, deciding she might as well forge ahead. "Isn't it true?"

"I'll get more coffee." Bea jumped up and disappeared into the kitchen, leaving Justine and Clay in the midst of a stare down.

It took a full sixty seconds of eye-burning contact before Clay looked away. Justine's victory felt hollow. She hadn't meant to hurt him, but to make him see that his interference wasn't necessary, and to force him to consider his motives.

Knowing she was on shaky ground, Justine tried to explain her feelings. "Clay, I knew Zack before he became Jordan's coach. Maybe he was wrong for taking Jordan off the team, but I think *he* believes he was right. I can't hate him for standing up for his beliefs." Oh, how much easier it would be on her heart if she could!

When Clay sighed, Justine knew the battle was over. She wasn't quite convinced she'd won, but she didn't think Clay had, either. Checkmate.

"I just don't want you to get hurt."

"As Jordan did?" she suggested gently. She flashed him a wan smile that quickly disappeared. "Believe me, I'm doing everything in my power to prevent that from happening." No need to add that she'd had a couple of close calls.

Bea came into the room with the coffeepot. She paused, looking from one to the other. "Is it over?"

Justine laughed at her hopeful expression. "Yes, it's over." She glanced at Clay. "Isn't it?"

Clay nodded, holding his cup in the air to give Bea easier access as she poured. "So, how did Jordan do at the store last week? His attitude seems to have improved."

"He did fine, and I know what you mean about his attitude changing. It is *definitely* better." Justine's relief matched her brother's in that regard.

"Oh," Bea said, snapping her fingers. "That reminds me. Jordan wanted me to ask you if he could work at the store a few afternoons a week, at least until the coach decides to let him back on the team. He wants to earn some extra money."

"I could definitely use him. Christopher is good with the customers and keeping up with our inventory, but Jordan has a special touch with the animals."

Bea set the empty coffeepot on the table and resumed her seat. "By the way, did Christopher get his car fixed?"

Completely clueless, Justine frowned. "I didn't know he was having car trouble. He didn't mention anything to me about it last Monday."

"This happened Tuesday night, not long after you called," Bea explained. "He called from Little House of Critters and asked Jordan to give him a ride home."

With a jolt of surprise, Justine leaned forward. "Christopher was at my store Tuesday *night?*"

"Yes." She shook her head and sighed. "Jordan was gone

so long I started to get worried that *he* had car trouble. I let him take my car, and you know how particular I am about it. He had to clean the floor mats afterwards—said he'd stepped in something. God knows what."

"She won't even let *me* drive it," Clay complained, "but she lets a teenager."

Bea shot him a tart look. "And why is that? I'll tell you why—because you drive like a maniac. We spent a fortune restoring that car, and I'm not about to let you ruin her."

Neither seemed to notice that Justine had grown very still, and she was glad. She suspected her face had drained of all color.

Jordan had been out Tuesday night.

"You leave me no choice," Zack informed a subdued Dennis after entering his apartment Monday evening. He leaned over and scooped up another huge ball of stuffing, adding it to the growing pile in his arms. "I wasn't particularly fond of that chair, but this is the last straw."

It took fifteen minutes to gather the rest of the stuffing scattered around the living room floor. There was even a pile of it in the fruit bowl—along with several mashed and mangled bananas. Zack tried shoving it back into the hole in the upholstery, but after a few seconds he realized it wasn't quite the same; it remained in one big lump instead of resuming its shape.

The monkey observed him from his secure position on the ceiling fan. Occasionally he shook his head and babbled a stream of nonsense, as if denying the charges.

Zack knew better. Dumping the pile of stuffing in the undamaged seat of the chair, he straightened. "This wasn't my chair, you know. The apartment came furnished." No doubt about it—he'd have to replace the chair.

Dennis screeched, then fell silent and watchful.

With grim determination, Zack brought the cage out of the bedroom closet and set it on the floor. He opened the cage door and pointed. "Get in there," he ordered.

The monkey, of course, didn't obey.

"Fine. I'll just call Melissa. She's got a big tranquilizer shot with *your* name on it." Zack was bluffing about calling the vet, but the monkey couldn't know. He seriously doubted the monkey understood him at all, but if there was one thing he'd learned this past week, it was that he should never underestimate the intelligence of a monkey.

Dennis in particular.

He strode determinedly to the phone. "You think I won't call her?" he challenged.

When he turned around, Dennis was in the cage. The door was closed and latched.

Zack's heart softened at the sight of his big brown eyes staring at him through the cage door. He walked to him and hunkered down. "I wouldn't have called her, you big dope." Sighing, he reached through the bars and scratched the monkey's head. "No offense, buddy, but I'm just not cut out for this monkey business. Besides, you probably belong to someone. I was just your temporary babysitter."

Feeling like the biggest heel in history, Zack hefted the cage and headed for the door. By the time he reached his vehicle, he was having serious second thoughts. What would happen to Dennis? What if the monkey missed him and refused to eat?

What would Justine think? Surely she would understand that he couldn't continue babysitting the monkey. Since the flooding, Zack had come home to a different disaster each evening; amazing what a monkey could do with a single black Magic Marker. It had taken him two hours to remove the scribbling from the pristine white walls.

On Thursday evening, it was toothpaste and shaving cream on the ceiling. Saturday morning, Zack's sleep was interrupted by the shrill beeping of the smoke alarm. He emerged from his bedroom to find Dennis racing madly around the room, shrieking and babbling, and the decorative stove-top coverings on the range rapidly turning black.

The monkey had switched on the electric stove burners.

Granted, none of these disasters matched the flooding—
well, the near fire was close—but they had been irritating all
the same.

Shaking his head at the memories, Zack put the cage in
the backseat and slid behind the wheel. He'd meant to give
Justine a little breathing space, hoping she'd come to miss
him, but he couldn't face another day with Dennis the Menace. His nerves were shot—not to mention his apartment.

He and the monkey just didn't *click*.

Justine would understand.

"Why are you so nervous?" Reuben whispered urgently the
moment Justine walked from the room. He knew she would
be back any second; the mortal had been in a frenzy of movement all day, distracted and edgy. She'd hardly given them
a glance.

Mini flashed him a startled look. "Me? Nervous?" she
squeaked out. "I'm not nervous."

"Yes, you are. You haven't taken your eyes off that door
since three o'clock."

"I'm just watching for Jordan. He's late." Her gaze returned to the door.

"Is there something you're not sharing with me?" Reuben
persisted, sidling closer. Like Justine, his wife had been edgy
and distracted. Now that he thought about it, she hadn't been
herself for a few days.

"What do you mean?"

"I'm talking about a plan. *Do* you have a plan that you're
not sharing with me?" No response. He had to nudge her
just to get her attention. "Mini?"

"Hmm?"

The blank look she gave him made his tiny heart flutter
in alarm. "What's wrong with you? You're acting strange."
That got her attention, he noted, watching her eyes widen.

"Strange? No, nothing strange going on." Her words came

too quickly. "I'm just worried about how things will turn out. With Justine and Zack, I mean."

"So you're watching for Jordan because you're worried about Zack and Justine?" he drawled sardonically. Before his wife could answer, Jordan came in, bringing with him the smell of impending snow.

He was whistling a jaunty tune.

Well, well, well, Reuben thought, *the young mortal appears to have gotten over his rotten spell.*

Mini leaned forward eagerly. "Did you find the book?"

Jordan glanced carefully around before approaching the cage. "Yes, I found it," he whispered.

"Put it on her desk, then. I'll look over it after Justine locks up for the night."

Reuben frowned. He had an uneasy feeling he was missing something. "Mini, what are you blathering about?"

"I asked Jordan to pick up a book from the library, darling," she said with an airy wave of her wing. "It's a book about birds. I think we should learn more about them since we're using their bodies."

"Not by choice," Reuben muttered, still suspicious. "That's all it is?"

Mini blinked innocently. "What else could it be?"

To Mini's great relief, the door opened to admit a customer.

Only it wasn't just any customer, she realized, eyes widening; it was Zack. She poked Reuben with her wing and whispered beneath her breath, "He's got the monkey with him! What are we going to do?"

"Leave it to me," Reuben mumbled.

Jordan turned to greet Zack, waving his hand as if he were greeting an old friend. Mini groaned. She smelled trouble—trouble the young mortal didn't need considering what Zack suspected about him.

But then, Jordan didn't know. She and Reuben had decided not to share the information with him unless it was absolutely necessary.

"Hey, Coach. Let me guess. Having a little monkey trouble?"

At the sound of his jeering laughter, Mini groaned and buried her head in her wing.

Nineteen

~

"Hello, Jordan."

At the sound of Zack's deep, knee-weakening voice, Justine stopped in her tracks. She edged back out of sight around the doorway to give herself time to gather her defenses.

Her heart beat heavily. It was longing, she forced herself to admit—reluctantly. She'd missed the sound of his sexy voice, the look of his heated, loving glances, the smell of his crisp, clean male scent. But most of all she missed the sight of his gorgeous, broad-shouldered frame and his intoxicating hazel eyes.

The memory of their frantic lovemaking filled her dreams—when she *did* sleep—and intruded on her waking moments as well. If only she could trust him. If only he loved her as she loved him. But sadly, she knew with Zachary, love was nothing more than glorified lust. Here today, gone tomorrow.

She thought—wisely knowing it was best—when she didn't hear from him after declaring their incredible lovemaking a mistake, he must have accepted her decision. So what was he doing here now? she wondered.

There was only one way to find out.

Taking a deep breath, she stepped into the room. Her gaze traveled quickly, hungrily over Zack, then fell to the cage he grasped in his hand. A pair of big brown eyes set in a snowy white face peered from between the bars.

The monkey. He was here to return the monkey. Now that she'd put an end to his games, he no longer felt the need to impress her by pretending to care for the monkey—"pretend" being the operative word.

Jordan had been right.

Disappointment swiftly turned to resentment. If she'd harbored any doubts about his sincerity, she didn't now.

She hid the hurt that had no business existing behind a mask of polite indifference. Inside she ached. This was the end, then. He was returning the monkey—cutting his losses. Never mind the feigned apology in his eyes. It wasn't real, just as his show of love had not been real. He had tried to lure her into his cruel clutches again, and he had failed. *She* had remained strong, so why didn't she feel exuberant?

Go figure.

"Coach is here with the monkey," Jordan explained, his knowing gaze as sharp and painful as an arrow through Justine's heart. "Since he can't get into your . . ."

His voice suddenly failed him. Justine watched his lips move, but no sound emerged. He rubbed his throat, casting a frightened glance at the lovebirds.

Frowning, Justine followed his line of vision. Reuben stared straight ahead, but Mini was glaring at her mate, her feathers bristling in a threatening manner. Justine supposed she should separate the two. Perhaps they were attempting to breed. She'd read that lovebirds could become quite hostile during the mating cycle.

Justine stepped forward, baffled. "Jordan, is something wrong? Are you choking?"

Jordan shook his head frantically, his eyes huge and fearful. "No," he croaked. "I'm fine."

"You don't sound fine."

"I am, I am." Again he darted a glance at the lovebirds.

With a bewildered shake of her head, she finally directed her attention to the reason for her current misery—Zachary Wayne, hunk extraordinaire, playboy, and heartbreaker.

The challenge slipped out uncensored. "Bored with him already?"

"What's that supposed to mean?"

Justine's eyes narrowed. For the moment she forgot they weren't alone—and forgot she didn't want him to know that she hurt. "Poor Dennis. I know how he feels."

"Why don't you enlighten *me,* then?" he demanded in a soft, angry voice. "Because I don't know what the hell you're talking about!"

"I'm talking about the monkey. You're bringing him back, aren't you?"

Zack finally began to comprehend her meaning and didn't much like it. "You think I'm bringing Dennis back because I'm *bored* with him?" He uttered an incredulous laugh. "This monkey is anything but boring, believe me. He's very artistic—with Magic Markers, toothpaste, and shaving cream. Want your chair reupholstered? He can do that, too. Or part of it, anyway. How about a cooking lesson?" Zack smiled with grim satisfaction as dismay replaced the chill in her eyes. "He can make a fine batch of burner covers—if you like them well done, that is. At least I know my smoke alarms work."

"He did all of that?" she asked.

"Oh, there's more. Dennis has aspirations to become a pitcher, too. I've been hit by so many apples, oranges, and pears that my head feels like a corny commercial for Fruit of the Loom." With great effort, he ignored Jordan's muffled snicker. His patience was just about at an end with the younger Diamond; and right now there was very little in reserve for the love of his life.

"Why didn't you keep him in the cage while you were gone?"

"Because I couldn't catch him." When she glanced at the cage where the monkey sat calmly regarding them, he added,

"I got him in there today by threatening to call Melissa over with a tranquilizer shot." Her arched brow made him flush. "Well, whether he understood or not, he got in the cage."

Jordan spoke up, his obvious enjoyment skittering across Zack's jumpy nerves like the sound of nails on a chalkboard.

"Uh, Coach Wayne? I don't think putting Dennis in his cage would have worked anyway."

Zack swung around with an impatient growl. "What . . ."

There wasn't any need to finish his question. Dennis launched himself into Zack's arms with enough force to make him stagger. The monkey chattered softly, as if greeting an old friend, winding his arms around Zack's neck and laying his head lovingly against his shoulder.

It was the first real contact with the monkey since the fateful day he'd come into the shop and Dennis leaped from the light fixture into his arms. Bewildered, Zack automatically closed his arms around the monkey.

This was bizarre.

Gone was the wild, hyperactive primate that had made his life a living hell these past seven days. The loving monkey was back, making him look like a whining, lying fool.

One glance at Justine's derisive face and he knew he was in trouble. Monkey trouble. She had folded her arms and was tapping her foot expectantly. Waiting for him to confess? he wondered. He glanced at Jordan, fully expecting the kid to be wearing a huge, smug grin.

He was grinning, but he wasn't looking at Zack and the monkey. Nor was he watching Justine; he was staring at the lovebirds.

Zack suddenly recalled Jordan's fantastic story about the lovebirds placing a spell on the monkey. If he didn't know better, he'd almost believe it. The monkey's abrupt personality change certainly demanded *some* type of explanation.

"I know this looks bad, but I swear this monkey hates me." Zack hated the desperate sound of his voice.

"Of course he does," Justine drawled scathingly. "No need

to convince *me*—I can see that he does. Besides, we both know that Dennis isn't your responsibility."

She met his eyes for a brief, chilly moment. Something flickered, something so brief and elusive Zack wasn't sure he hadn't imagined it.

It looked suspiciously like hurt.

"And we both know why you're bringing him back," she concluded.

Zack wished *he* knew. She obviously didn't believe his explanation. He ground his teeth in frustration. If he didn't have a monkey in his arms . . .

Without fear, she reached out and tugged on the monkey.

He refused to budge, whimpering pitifully.

Why was he not surprised? And why was she hurt because he wanted to return the monkey? Figuring he'd never understand the workings of a woman's mind, he let out a heavy sigh and said, "I don't think he's going to let go."

"I'll call Melissa," she said, stepping around him.

Dennis shrieked and tried to merge with Zack's coat. When the ringing in Zack's ear faded, he turned with the monkey in his arms, stopping Justine before she reached her office. "No, don't."

She paused. "Don't call her?"

Zack hesitated. He might have changed his mind again if it wasn't for that sweet, tiny note of hope he recognized in her voice.

Why was it so important to her that he keep the monkey? The answer continued to elude him, and until he knew he couldn't risk alienating her further.

Mentally calling himself a fool, he said, "I'll keep him awhile longer."

She remained paused with her back to him, her shoulders stiff and squared. "Are you certain?"

She wanted assurance? Zack asked himself, amazed. She expected him to sound *excited* about taking this hellion monkey home again? Hell, she was lucky he'd gotten the words out at all! Especially with the choke hold the monkey had on him.

He figured somewhere along the way he'd have to draw the line on just how far he'd go to win her back; he never in his wildest dreams—and he'd had plenty of those—figured a monkey would be the cause. "Have you tried to contact his owner?" he asked as he eased into a squatting position before the cage. Jordan jumped to his aid and opened the cage door, still grinning like a fool. Wary of his motives, Zack managed to mumble an ungracious thanks.

"I've left a message for Kewan at Bishops, but he hasn't returned my call."

Zack tugged on the monkey's arms. Dennis reluctantly eased his hold and allowed Zack to set him inside the cage. With a sigh of relief, Zack stood and faced Justine. She'd returned to the counter. "Bishops?"

"It's a delivery service. Kewan freelances for them."

"Can't you just tell the company about the mistake and ask them to send a truck?" He thought he'd done a terrific job hiding his dismay until he saw her frown. He tried a more diplomatic approach. "Surely someone is expecting Dennis somewhere?"

"Probably." She shrugged. "But that somewhere could be *anywhere*. Kewan delivers in several states. He's the only one who can straighten out this mess, so we'll have to wait until he calls."

Zack dreaded to ask. "How long do you think that will be?"

"I don't know. We have a truck due Wednesday, but it might not be Kewan."

It took a lot of effort, but Zack managed to contain his agonized groan until he reached his truck.

After Zack and the monkey left, Justine stood at the counter, tapping her nails and staring at the door. Was she being too hard on him? she wondered, suffering a spat of delayed guilt. If Dennis truly was the menace Zack claimed . . . On the

other hand, she had only his word, and why would she believe a man who had convinced her she was the only woman
in the world, only to abandon her?

Justine's face burned. He'd almost had her believing him
again. She knew better. *She damn well knew better.* Zack
wanted to shuck the monkey as heartlessly as he'd shucked
her, only he didn't want it to appear too obvious. Solution?
Invent imaginative horror stories, and good ole gullible Justine would believe them, feel sorry for poor, put-upon Zack.

Right.

To think that for a moment she had suspected Jordan. Not
only foolish of her, but insane. Jordan clearly disliked Zack,
and cleaning Zack's apartment was the last thing she would
find him doing. If not for Barry's dubious testimony, she
might believe the flooded, floured apartment was yet another
one of Zack's fabricated stories.

Like Zack's call for help.

She drummed her fingers harder on the counter, wishing
she'd called his bluff and turned the van around when he'd
made the suggestion. What would he have done if she had?
What lie would he have convinced her of if she'd gone back
to the jail and asked them if Zack made his call?

Of course Zack had made the call!

What was she doing, trusting such a devious man with a
frightened animal like Dennis? Justine's fingers slowed their
drumming, then stopped as an image of Zack and the monkey came to her mind. She knew, all right. She knew very
well. The monkey loved Zack, and although he tried to hide
the fact, Zack was fond of the monkey, too. She noticed the
way the hard planes of his face softened when he held the
monkey, and there wasn't a shred of doubt about Dennis's
feelings for Zack. Justine worked with animals, and she knew
they could sense when humans were nervous or disliked
them.

The monkey trusted Zack.

Justine frowned. It appeared Thor and Rogue had fallen
under his spell, as well. *She* had done so once upon a time,

and yes, she still loved him, but he wouldn't bewitch her again.

Jordan had retrieved a broom from the storage room and was sweeping the floor in front of the counter, head bent, apparently giving the chore his undivided attention. On impulse, Justine grabbed the moving broom handle.

Jordan jerked in surprise. "What—?"

"Barry said he saw you near Zack's apartment last Tuesday night," Justine blurted out quickly, deliberately changing the *in* to *near*. The *near* would probably induce scorn; the *in* would most likely make him explode.

Jordan looked at her in amazement. When he nearly collapsed against the broom handle, laughing, Justine let out a tiny sigh of relief. Of course Barry had lied, just as Zack had lied. She could easily understand Zack's motive, but what about Barry's?

Zack and Barry were clearly enemies.

"What a creep! Am I ever glad you wizened up about him." Still chuckling, Jordan paused to wipe his eyes before sending the broom into motion again. "What does he do, hover around with his door cracked, spying on Coach Wayne?"

The significance of his scornful remark might have escaped her notice if one of the lovebirds hadn't chosen that moment to make a harsh gasping sound, as if it were strangling.

With a suspicious eye trained on the birds and dread in her heart, Justine asked her nephew, "How did you know Zack and Barry were neighbors?" Both the birds were now preening themselves with frantic intent. *Just two birds doing what birds do, Justine. You know that although it's rare, lovebirds* are *capable of mimicking human sounds.*

"Well, I . . ."

For a terrifying moment, Jordan sounded flustered. Justine turned to look at him, praying for a miracle. When he spoke again, his voice sounded forced, deeper than normal, as if he were reciting lines for a part in the high school play. His face was flushed, but then, he'd been exerting himself by sweeping.

"Coach Wayne gave me a ride home after practice one day—before he suspended me—and he stopped by his apartment to check his messages. He said something about expecting a call from his brother, Thomas, I think." Jordan grimaced. "He mentioned something about a crabby neighbor, and I already knew that's where Barry lived. It wasn't hard to guess who he meant."

Justine might have questioned him further, but she knew Jordan couldn't have known about Zack's brother Thomas unless Zack told him. She had never mentioned Thomas to Bea or anyone. Besides, Jordan would know that it would only take a phone call to confirm his story.

"Hey, you didn't believe Barry the Creep, did you?"

Distracted, Justine shook her head. "No, no. I didn't believe him for a moment." It was true, too. Her suspicions had not been aroused until Bea had mentioned Jordan going out Tuesday night.

Which reminded her. "Did Chris mention his reason for coming to the store?"

Jordan looked at her blankly.

"Christopher? My assistant? You gave him a ride?"

"Oh! Oh, yeah." With a sheepish grin, Jordan said, "It wasn't Christopher who called. It was one of my friends. He didn't think Mom would let me out of the house if she knew who he was, so he pretended to be Christopher." He looked at her, half pleading, half defiant. "Are you going to rat on me?"

"I should, but I won't . . . this time." Justine put on her tough auntie face. "Just don't pull a stunt like that again."

"I won't." His gaze strayed to the lovebirds. "At least, I'll *try* not to."

Seeing what had captured his attention, Justine wondered if she should be concerned about Jordan's growing obsession with the birds. Perhaps they'd sell soon. They were quite a handsome pair, and if her suspicions proved true and they *were* attempting to mimic humans, they were more valuable than she first thought.

Time would tell.

"Why did you hurt Jordan?" Mini demanded the moment they were alone. Jordan had gone home, and Justine had closed shop. She had begun to think the day would never end. "You promised you wouldn't use witchcraft on the young mortal—"

"Unless it was necessary," Reuben concluded with a righteous sniff. "I felt it was necessary. You heard him—he was about to dig his own grave. *I* was merely helping him out."

"By choking him? Frightening him to death by taking over his voice?"

Reuben lifted his beak high. "I didn't *hurt* him, Mini. Besides, he's not a baby." Neatly turning the tables, he pinned her with an accusing glare. "What about you? Why did you refresh the love spell on the monkey? I thought we agreed Dennis was causing too much trouble for Zack!"

"Because . . ." Mini flapped her wing at him. "Oh, why do I bother? You wouldn't understand."

"Try me."

Mini hesitated. How could she explain women's intuition to a man? "The monkey isn't the real issue. He never has been." When her husband remained silent, she knew she had failed to make him understand. "In my opinion, Dennis represents Justine. If Zack dumps Dennis after showing Justine he cares about the monkey . . ."

Reuben's lower beak dropped open. "Then she'll continue believing he'll do the same to her if he gets the chance!"

"A *second* time," Mini reminded him.

"So she's testing Zack with the monkey."

Surprised and pleased with her husband's insight, Mini nodded. "Yes, I think she is."

Excited now that he understood, Reuben hopped around on the perch. "And if she believed Zack's stories about Dennis, she might be impressed with his—"

"Dedication? Determination? Heroism?" Mini smiled. "After what he's been through, I'd say there's something terribly wrong with her if she *doesn't* consider him heroic."

Reuben's excitement faded. "But how will she know Zack's telling the truth about Dennis the Menace?"

"I think, my dear, that in this instance *nature* will take its course."

"The monkey?" Reuben guessed astutely.

"The monkey."

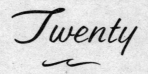

Twenty

Zack's gaze roamed slowly from one red, sweaty face to another. He and the team were gathered in the locker room for a heart-to-heart talk, and he wanted every ear listening.

Finally he was satisfied that he had their full attention.

He put all the conviction he could muster into his voice as he said, "You boys did great today, really great, and despite our recent losses, we're going to win the game Friday night."

There were a few head shakes, a doubtful murmur. A bold voice called out, "We will if you'll let Diamond back on the team!" Cheers of agreement erupted. As one, they stood and began to chant Diamond's name.

Zack's mouth tightened. He waved them down, disgusted to realize they truly believed they couldn't win without Jordan Diamond.

It was time to get brutal, time to produce his last ace.

"Would you follow Diamond to his death if he jumped from the Empire State Building?" he asked them, his voice edged with deliberate contempt. Overriding their murmurings, he continued. "How many of you ask Jordan's permission before you go to the bathroom? Do you take him along on your dates? Is he your *mama,* or a team player?"

Gradually the disgruntled murmurings died away. All eyes regarded the locker room floor as Zack's meaning sank in.

Zack stifled a surge of triumph; he wasn't finished. "When Diamond gets hurt and has to leave the game, do you give up like a bunch of sissy cheerleaders?"

"No!"

Finding the source of the defensive outburst, Zack focused on him. It was Avery Joebella, with the unlikely nickname of Belly. The kid was a passionate player and, with Jordan temporarily out of the game, their star quarterback. He was good, but according to his teammates, he couldn't hold a candle to Jordan. Zack suspected he was every bit as good, but lacked confidence. It wasn't hard to understand why; the players constantly measured him against the incomparable Diamond.

"Avery," Zack acknowledged, "do you have something to add to that?"

Nervously Avery rose from the bench. He turned his helmet around and around in his hands. "You don't understand, Coach. The Diamond is the best. He doesn't get hurt, because he doesn't get caught."

Zack lifted a disbelieving brow. "He's never been tackled?"

Avery flushed and glanced around him. "Well, a few times."

"Then he *is* human?" Zack drawled sarcastically. He was secretly impressed that a kid Jordan's age could command so much respect and awe. Making a mental note to talk to Jordan about a career in coaching, he folded his arms and played his last card. "Why doesn't he get caught?"

"Well, he's fast." The helmet made another turn in his hands.

"And?" Zack prompted softly. They were all listening intently, he noted. Good, because if his prediction proved right, he didn't want them to miss a word.

"We don't let him get caught."

"Repeat that, please. I'm not sure I heard you."

"We don't let him get caught."

"Again," Zack ordered. "Louder, please."

Casting an uncertain glance around him, the unsuspecting Avery raised his voice and repeated, "We make sure he doesn't get caught."

"Did you say, '*we* make sure *he* doesn't get caught'?"

Totally bewildered now, Belly nodded and stammered, "Y-yes, sir, that's what I said."

"You heard him, boys. Diamond doesn't get caught because of *you* guys. Not only because he's fast, and not only because he's slippery, but because you"—Zack stabbed a finger in the air at each blocker—"keep the other team away from him. I don't have a doubt in my mind that Diamond is good, but how many times could he make a successful throw or a touchdown if it wasn't for *you* guys clearing the way?"

A low murmur of agreement rose from the cluster of boys.

"My question is, why can't you do the same for Belly? Is he too slow? Too clumsy?"

"No! He's fast!"

"He ain't clumsy, neither!"

"We could do it!"

Zack got the desired reaction. "So what are we going to do Friday night?" he yelled.

"Kick butt!" they shouted back.

"Louder!" Zack demanded.

"Kick butt! Kick butt!"

Finally Zack allowed himself a triumphant smile.

"You should see this, Mini. They're shouting 'kick butt' at the top of their mortal lungs." Reuben chuckled gleefully. "And Zack's grinning like a warlock on Halloween."

"I don't have time for that now," Mini said shortly, using her beak to yank at the newspaper beneath his feet. "Move your scrawny legs—I've got to have this paper."

Reuben obediently moved from the paper, his gaze glued

to the crystal ball. "I think he might have a future in coaching, don't you?"

"Whatever."

"Do you think we could get Jordan to sneak us into the game Friday night?" Reuben asked hopefully. He yelped as Mini pulled a feather from his back.

"Sorry, but I need it."

She didn't sound the least bit sorry, Reuben realized, finally glancing over his shoulder at his wife. "What are you doing?"

"Shredding paper. Plucking feathers." She shot him an irritated glance. "What does it look like I'm doing?"

Puzzled, Reuben cocked his head as she carried the shredded paper and feathers to the far corner of the cage. She dumped it and began to stalk in his direction. He backed away from the purposeful gleam in her eyes. "W-what do you want now?"

"More feathers. You've got plenty, and feather-plucking is perfectly normal for lovebirds."

Reuben's mouth went dry. "Feather-plucking?" he squeaked as his back connected with the bars behind him. "Darling—"

Mini silenced him with a single glower. "Don't 'darling' me! *You're* the one who got us into this mess with your 'night to remember.' "

Mystified, Reuben watched as she drew closer. "I wish you would explain." He braced himself as she yanked several tender feathers from his breast. He was becoming rather fond of his feathers, finding them much easier to groom than his original shoulder-length black locks.

"Hmm, these are softer," she mumbled around a mouthful of feathers. "There's nothing to explain . . . yet." She stalked across the cage and dumped the feathers on top of the growing pile.

"If there's nothing to *explain*, why pluck my feathers?" He swallowed hard. "Maybe you shouldn't have read that book about birds. It's obviously gotten you upset." *Or driven you mad,* was Reuben's frightened thought.

"I'm glad I did. If I hadn't, I'd probably find you eating the eggs for breakfast before I knew what was happening."

Leaving him to contemplate her mysterious comment, Mini flew from the cage and disappeared into Justine's office.

She returned moments later with her beak full of facial tissue and, with an intensity that increased Reuben's fear, began to shred the tissue with her sharp toenails.

"Mini . . . what's all of this about?" Reuben asked cautiously.

For the next five minutes, Mini ignored him. She moved in a frenzy, scratching and shredding, shifting the feather and paper mass this way and that. Finally she stepped back to regard her creation.

Reuben's tiny heart began to flutter. "It . . . it looks like a bird's nest," he croaked.

"It is."

"B-but why?"

"I just felt this urge to build it." Mini swooped forward and adjusted a piece of paper with her beak. She gave it a loving pat with her wing.

"Then why didn't you use witchcraft?"

"Because . . ." Mini shrugged. "I don't know. It didn't seem right."

A startling premonition hit Reuben, nearly strangling him. He could barely speak above a whisper. "Mini . . . are you saying . . . are you saying . . ."

"Oh, for star's sake, can't you even say it?" Mini snarled. "Yes, I might be pregnant!"

Reuben swooned to the floor in a dead faint.

Restoring the team's confidence in their own ability was perhaps a small—and possibly premature—victory, but Zack decided to celebrate anyway. He stopped at the local market on the way home and purchased a bag of fresh fruit for Dennis and a six-pack of beer for himself.

They would order pizza, turn on the TV, and relax.

Zack paused as he hefted the sack of groceries from the backseat. He chuckled to himself when he realized he'd been thinking of the monkey like a roommate. Dennis probably either didn't like pizza or wasn't supposed to eat it. Well, that was okay, because he'd bought the monkey a smorgasbord of fruit from seedless grapes to tangerines. Surely there was *something* in the bag he would like.

Turning with his arms full, Zack nearly plowed into Mr. Potter. One look at the man's face and Zack's good mood turned as sour as his landlord's expression. Somehow, he knew Mr. Potter had not rushed out to help him with the groceries.

"Mr. Potter!" Zack managed a friendly smile. Mr. Potter, a short, thin man in his late sixties with gray hair and a neatly trimmed beard and mustache, didn't return his smile. He glowered at Zack over the rim of his spectacles.

"I need to speak to you, Mr. Wayne," he said, sounding slightly harassed. "Mr. Fowler has been a tenant here for five years, and he's rarely complained in the past."

Zack shifted the groceries to his other arm. "I take it he's complaining now? If it's about the hot water—"

"It's not about hot water. It's about the volume of your television set."

"My . . . television?" Zack frowned. "I'm afraid I don't understand what you're talking about."

"Can't you hear it, Mr. Wayne? I've been gone most of the day, but Mr. Fowler said it's been blaring since noon."

He *did* hear it then. How could he have missed it? He could even recognize the theme song to an old show he used to watch as a kid.

Dennis. God help them if the monkey ever learned to use the phone!

"I apologize. I . . . must have left it on when I left this morning." Zack moved around the irate man and hurried into the building.

Mr. Potter followed on his heels. "Mr. Fowler seems to

think you're harboring a woman in your apartment."

Zack froze in his tracks. His brows arching in disbelief, he turned to face Mr. Potter. "Fowler is mistaken. That basket case would like nothing better than to get me thrown out of my apartment."

"Then you won't mind if I have a look?" Mr. Potter's cheeks turned rosy as he added, "It's not that I mind you having . . . a woman in your apartment, Mr. Wayne, but I do like to know who's living under my roof. You can't be too careful these days."

Coldly Zack said, "You're the landlord. I can't stop you, can I?"

"I don't want to invade your privacy—"

"Then don't. I told you Fowler's wrong. I don't have a *woman* in my apartment." Just an insane, too-smart-for-everyone's-own-good monkey. Wouldn't Mr. Potter be shocked to learn he would rather have a dozen women? Oh, yes. Women, cats, dogs, or even a toe-biting iguana. Right now he'd trade *Squeeze* for Dennis. Gladly.

Mr. Potter remained persistent, much to Zack's grief.

"If I could just take a peek? I don't want to lose a good tenant like Mr. Fowler . . ."

"Like I said, I can't stop you, can I?" With a fatalistic shrug, Zack turned and stomped upstairs. He knew Mr. Potter followed and he suspected the outcome. The landlord would see Dennis and scream the house down. He'd be evicted, homeless.

Would Justine feel the slightest remorse? Zack wondered, jamming the key into the lock and giving it a vicious twist. Perhaps suffer a twinge of good, old-fashioned guilt for having taunted him into taking the monkey again? When he thought of the grief he'd suffered to woo her . . .

"Don't mind the mess," Zack growled, throwing the door wide. He sincerely hoped there was nothing wrong with Mr. Potter's heart.

Surprisingly there wasn't any mess to speak of, but Zack

could understand Fowler's complaint about the volume of the television; it made his ears ache.

Deliberately ignoring the landlord, Zack turned off the set, casually dropped his coat over the ruined chair, and went straight to the kitchen with the groceries. Feeling no special urge to watch the encounter, he stacked the fruit in the glass bowl as Mr. Potter nervously inspected the apartment.

When the landlord disappeared into the bedroom, Zack braced himself. Any second now, he'd spot the monkey and start shrieking bloody murder, which would in turn scare the living daylights out of Dennis, who would shriek right along with Mr. Potter.

As Zack all too easily envisioned the terrified man and the equally terrified monkey emerging from his bedroom, he actually grinned. He'd probably have *two* heart-attack victims on his hands.

He nearly had one himself when Mr. Potter strolled out of the bedroom, looking relieved and guilty. Zack popped a beer open and guzzled half of it, wishing he'd reached for the whiskey instead. He couldn't believe his good luck.

Mr. Potter had not found Dennis. Somehow, the monkey— wherever he was hiding—had managed to escape detection.

"I'm sorry for the intrusion, Mr. Wayne, but you have to understand my caution after that little mix-up with the police last week."

Dazed, Zack managed to nod. He supposed it *was* understandable, especially with that coward Fowler whining in his ear.

"Perhaps Mr. Fowler is still suffering from his head injury," Mr. Potter mused as he made for the door.

Startled, Zack nearly upset his beer. "Perhaps he is," he choked out. Apparently Fowler had decided not to tell the landlord *how* he got his head injury. The realization aroused Zack's suspicions about why Fowler had kept his mouth shut.

The moment the door shut on the landlord, Zack pushed thoughts of Fowler from his mind and began the search for

Dennis. The apartment was roomy but with a simple design, not exactly a maze with many hiding places. How could Mr. Potter have missed an eight-pound monkey? But then, Mr. Potter had been looking for a woman, not an animal. Animals could hide in places people couldn't.

After searching the kitchen—even beneath the sink—Zack stooped to look under the sofa and chair. No Dennis. He looked in the bathroom. Empty. The closet where Dennis had previously hidden revealed nothing.

The monkey had to be in the bedroom, Zack reasoned, heading in that direction.

Ten minutes later, when Zack had all but turned the mattress over in search of Dennis, he forced himself to admit he was not in the apartment. Somehow the monkey had gotten out.

His stomach did a sickening flip-flop, and with a grunt of surprise, Zack realized it was panic. Was this how parents felt when they lost sight of their child in a crowd? he wondered. But Dennis wasn't a child, he firmly reminded himself. He was a monkey.

A helpless little monkey with a bad attitude.

By the time Zack reached the phone, his panic had escalated. He tried to ignore it; he tried to laugh it away, but it refused to abate. He quickly dialed Justine's number, belatedly checking his watch as he listened for her voice. It was five-thirty. He knew the store closed at five, and unless she had to stay late—

"Hello?"

Relief washed over him. "Justine, I can't find Dennis," he blurted out. "I've looked everywhere." There was a tiny, shocked silence after his breathless announcement before her voice blasted over the line.

"What do you mean, you can't find him? How could he have gotten out?"

Zack's jaw clenched at her accusing tone. "I don't know. All I *do* know is that he's not here."

"That's unfortunate, because Kewan found his owner.

He's coming to get him tomorrow." There was another heavy pause that indicated disapproval. "I'll be right over."

The phone clicked in his ear.

With nothing to do but wait for Justine's arrival, Zack began a second search for Dennis.

Mumbling a curse under her breath, Justine turned off the boiling pasta, gave the clam sauce one last, wistful glance, and went to get her coat. Once again, she would miss dinner because of Zack.

She paused at the door and looked at Rogue, who lay dozing on the back of the couch.

"My clam sauce better be here when I get back, buddy," she warned. "All of it."

Rogue yawned and stretched his sleek body as if he'd never dream of eating her dinner. Justine gave a snort of disbelief.

She made the ride to Zack's apartment in just under ten minutes. He answered on the first knock, and she had to admit he *looked* genuinely concerned. His hair had been raked through with his fingers, giving him a wild, reckless look that made Justine's heart somersault. She realized she'd never seen him quite this . . . shaken before.

"Have any luck?" she asked as he closed the door behind her.

He shook his head. "I think he went out through the window."

"Was it open?"

"No. It was locked."

Justine lifted a skeptical brow. "You think he had the presence of mind to unlock the window, climb out, and close it again?"

Zack smiled grimly. "After everything he's done, you doubt he can unlock windows? He was watching *television* today. Fowler complained, and Mr. Potter came up to take a look around."

"Lucky for you Dennis wasn't here."

"Yeah, well." Zack raked his fingers through his hair again. "He's an aggravation, true, but that doesn't mean I want something to happen to him."

He cares, Justine thought, staring at his flushed face. *It isn't an act, he truly cares about the monkey.* The knowledge gave her a warm, cozy feeling in the pit of her stomach. "Well," she began in a brisk tone to hide her flustered state. "Let's start the search. We've got about half an hour before it gets dark."

"Where should we start looking?"

Justine's gaze drifted to the window as she speculated. "Isn't there a park near here?"

"A small one. I jog by it every morning."

His innocent statement evoked a vivid, arousing image of Zack in jogging pants and a lose sweatshirt, all sweaty, muscles pumping as he ran . . . Justine shook her head. What was she doing, fantasizing about Zack when they were in the middle of a crisis? Had she no shame?

"Do you have a flashlight?" she asked abruptly, glad Zack seemed too distracted to notice how oddly breathless she sounded.

"Good idea."

A knock at the door startled Justine. She frowned at the delay, watching as Zack strode to the door and jerked it open. A short, older man rushed into the room, clearly agitated— so agitated Justine didn't think he noticed her presence.

"I thought I should alert my tenants," he said in a rush. "This is just unbelievable!"

Zack stepped forward, his face tense. "What is?"

Mr. Potter paused to draw a breath and mop his face with a handkerchief he pulled from his jacket pocket. In a high, squeaky voice, he announced, "There's a *monkey* on the roof!"

Twenty-one

During the few seconds of silence following the man's announcement, Justine realized two things—the man was Zack's landlord, and Zack was in big trouble.

She had to do something, and fast.

"Oh, you found him!" She clutched her chest and let out a heartfelt sigh. She even managed to produce a few tears. "I thought I'd lost him for good." With a fraudulent smile, she grabbed the startled man's hand and gave it a hearty shake. "Thank you so much. Dennis is very precious to me."

"D-dennis?"

Justine blinked. "The monkey? You did say you found him?"

Mr. Potter gaped at her, his eyes nearly swallowing his face. "Th-the monkey belongs to *you?*" he stammered.

Blushing at Zack's admiring gaze, Justine laughed. "Oh, yes, he's mine. I've had posters out everywhere—haven't you seen them? There's a reward, as well. I think you deserve half of it, at least. I'm sure Mr. Wayne doesn't mind sharing." Still beaming happily, she reached for her purse.

"No, no, that's okay," Mr. Potter said hastily. "Just get your monkey." The look he trained on Zack held faint suspicion. "Do you know this woman?"

Before Zack could blow it, Justine gushed, "He called me earlier to tell me he'd spotted Dennis in the park during his morning run." She smiled brightly at Zack. "Isn't that right, Mr. Wayne?"

Zack nodded. "Yes . . . that's right. We'd better go get him before he decides to find another hiding place."

"Great Scot!" Mr. Potter exclaimed. "I left my door open!" He rushed from Zack's apartment, nearly stumbling in his haste.

Justine shared a warm, spontaneous laugh with Zack. Their gazes met. She was the first to look away from his compelling expression. Why did he have to be so damned irresistible?

"Thanks," he said.

"No need." She waved an airy hand. "I think we've established that Dennis isn't your responsibility anyway."

"He *is* my responsibility," Zack retorted, sounding angry.

"I didn't mean—oh, never mind." She really hadn't meant to make him angry. It *was* her fault. She had pushed him into taking Dennis. "We'd better go get him before he decides to jump."

Moments later she found herself wishing they had called the fire department instead. With her heart in her throat, she looked on as Zack balanced himself on the slick railing of the fire escape so that he could look onto the roof.

If he slipped . . . Justine shuddered and closed her eyes.

"I see him!"

Justine opened one eye, then quickly closed it again. *Please don't move, Zack!* "What's he doing?"

"Freezing," Zack answered cryptically. He raised his voice as he coaxed the monkey. "Come on, Dennis. We'll go inside and have a nice big bunch of grapes. I bought you a few tangerines, too."

She crossed her fingers and silently urged the monkey to respond. Heck, *she* had no trouble responding to his persuasive voice! He sounded so sincere. *Just like on the cruise, Justine,* a derisive voice chided. The voice was right; why should now be any different? Zack was a great actor. The best.

"Come on, little guy. I'm not mad at you." Glancing over his shoulder at her upturned face, he whispered, "He's coming!"

What happened next shaved ten years from Justine's life. One moment Zack was leaning forward against the roof shingles, and the next he was flying backwards.

"No!" she screamed, managing to snag a belt loop with her finger. Without a thought to her own pain, she jerked him in her direction—away from the railing and certain death.

One hundred and ninety pounds of muscle and sinew slammed into her, knocking the breath from her lungs and sending them crashing onto the icy metal landing. Justine's head banged painfully against the railing. Her finger remained hooked around his belt loop, and even now she couldn't bring herself to let go.

She was frozen at the horror she'd nearly witnessed. If she hadn't . . . Her teeth began to chatter, and the rest of her body shook. What if she hadn't caught him?

With an explicit curse, Zack rolled to his feet and swung around with the shrieking monkey firmly plastered to his chest. "Are you all right? Is anything broken? Hold on while I get an ambulance." He raised the window and pushed the frightened monkey through, then started after him.

"I'm all right," Justine assured him. But her voice shook, and her stomach quivered with lingering shock. "Really, I'm fine. Just give me a . . ."

He helped her to her feet and quickly ran his hands over her, frowning fiercely. "Where are you hurt? Did you hit your head? What were you *thinking*?"

Stung by his harsh tone, Justine brushed his hands away. "I was *thinking* about saving your hide. You could show a little gratitude instead of barking at me."

Zack's jaw worked as he fought for control. He wanted to pull her against him so that she could feel how hard his heart was slamming against his ribs. When he realized he'd landed on her! "I'm not exactly a lightweight—I could have crushed you!"

"*You* would have fallen to your death if I hadn't grabbed your belt loop!" She shoved her hands on her hips as she added, "And Dennis would have gone over the railing with you."

"Oh. So this is about Dennis." Zack swallowed a nasty ball of disappointment. For a moment there, he actually believed she'd been worried about *him*. If he was a lesser man, he might be jealous of the monkey.

Hell, he *was* jealous.

They stood facing each other, almost nose-to-nose, until Zack realized she was shaking. "You're cold. Let's go inside."

Her eyes flashed golden fire, and her tone was hostile as she snarled, "Fine with me." She pushed him aside and climbed through the window.

Zack followed and closed the window behind him. Now that his terror had subsided, he realized just how ungrateful he had sounded. Yes, she'd done a foolish, impulsive thing by saving him, but he knew he would have done the same for her.

In a heartbeat.

"I'm leaving. When the owner gets here tomorrow, I'll let you know." Flinging the curt words over her shoulder, she headed for the door.

Zack was fed up with her cowardly exits. He decided it was time he exercised a little "tough love." What did he have to lose?

Reaching her before she could grasp the doorknob, he turned her around and pinned her against the door with his lower body.

Her eyes flared wide with shock at the intimate contact.

"Running away again, Justine?" he taunted, his voice like silk over steel. Slowly he rotated his hips just enough to stir up a little friction. When she bit her bottom lip, he felt a savage, almost primitive surge of satisfaction. The ice princess wasn't as immune as she'd like him to believe.

Growing bolder, Zack shoved her coat aside and braced his arms against the door on either side of her head. He leaned forward, bringing the rest of his body flush with hers. His chest met her hardened nipples. There was a subtle change in her breathing, and as he watched, her pupils began to dilate slowly. Let her deny the attraction between them now.

"You don't play fair," she whispered.

"This isn't a game." Zack didn't think he could become any harder—until she shifted. He settled into her womanly cradle with a sigh. "I'm trying to apologize. You saved my life, and I was an ungrateful bastard."

She uttered a soft, shaky laugh. "If *this* is the thanks I get, then no thanks."

Zack moved his mouth closer to hers and dropped his gaze to her parted lips. In a husky whisper, he asked, "Then what *can* I do to make it up to you?"

Her slow, sexy smile weakened his knees.

"Do you really want to repay me?"

"Yes." Zack sucked in his breath as her tongue darted out and moistened her lips, the action too studied to be an accident. *This* was the siren he had known on the ship, seductive, provocative, so natural in her sensuality he'd fallen helplessly in love.

"Well . . . if you insist."

"I do," he agreed, mesmerized by her rosy, shapely mouth as her lips moved. *A kiss,* he thought, bending closer. *I can feel her trembling—she wants me to—*

"In return for saving your worthless life, you can help me find Squeeze. After all, I helped you find Dennis."

Reuben stared at the crystal ball in stunned silence.

Mini took one look at her husband's face and doubled over with laughter. She finally managed to gasp out, "You and Zack are wearing the same expressions!"

"I don't think it's funny." Reuben folded his wings and gave his head a haughty toss. "She's a tease."

"She's brilliant!" Mini argued, still chuckling over the scene. "And you have to admit, he had it coming!"

"I admit nothing. Whose side are you on, anyway? *This* could have been the reconciliation we've been waiting for, but no, Justine had to go and scr—"

"Watch your mouth, buster!"

"—mess things up," Reuben amended. "She loves him, so why can't she just admit it?"

"And lay her heart open for him again?" Mini snorted. "My girl's too smart for that."

"Mini, have you *completely* lost your mind?"

"What do you mean, 'completely'?" Her eyes narrowed. She tapped her toe, waiting for him to explain.

"Well, first you build a nest, and now you're talking as if—as if—"

"Yes?"

Reuben squirmed, but continued bravely on. "Now you're talking as if you agree with Justine."

Mini cocked her head. "And if I do?"

"But you *know* the real story!"

"Yes, I do, but that doesn't mean I don't understand Justine's motives for being cautious." With a flounce of her feathered tail, she strode to the nest and hopped inside, settling down with a contented sigh. Sitting in the nest felt so *right*.

"Besides," she continued, aware that Reuben's mouth had dropped open, "a woman never knows a man's true worth until a crisis strikes. Take Zack, for instance. Justine saved his life, but instead of thanking her, he shouted at her."

"But she could have been seriously hurt!"

Mini glanced at him sharply. "Is that how you would have reacted?"

"Well, I . . ." Reuben clearly sensed a trap. "I *might* have, out of fear for your safety," he added hastily.

"And instead of apologizing, would you have tried to seduce me?" she persisted, truly curious. Was this why their fights ended in lovemaking? Was lovemaking a male form of apologizing? Mini sniffed to herself, more inclined to believe it was a way to *avoid* apologizing.

"Well, that would depend on how angry you were." Reuben cleared his throat. "Mini, why are you sitting on the nest?"

"Because I'm going to lay an egg."

Mini froze. She hadn't realized until she said the words aloud that it was indeed true. With a gasp, her gaze flew to Reuben, who stood swaying on his scrawny legs. "No, darling. Please don't faint—"

He keeled over, breast and toes pointed skyward.

"—again," Mini finished. Exasperated, she rose from her comfortable nest and stalked across the cage to tend her husband.

When she'd pondered how Reuben would react in a crisis situation, she hadn't expected to get her answer so soon.

"I'm not sure it was a good idea to bring Dennis," Justine said, hanging her coat on the rack. "My critters have never seen a monkey." She turned as Zack began to unbutton his coat, revealing a wide-eyed Dennis snuggled warmly inside. There was no sign of Thor or Rogue. They had probably sensed the strange animal the moment Zack had come through the door, she mused.

"You saw Mr. Potter waiting in the foyer. Besides, I couldn't risk Dennis getting out again."

Justine lifted a skeptical brow. "You still think he unlocked the window and let himself out?"

"Do you have a better explanation?" Zack countered, shucking his coat and hanging it on the rack. He tried to pry the monkey loose, but finally gave up. "Guess there's no chance of putting him down," he muttered.

Her heart melted at the sight of Dennis nestled so trustingly against Zack's chest. She almost envied the little guy. Heck, she *did* envy him. "If you're the one who finds

Squeeze, you might get a break," she mused dryly.

His response was a deep chuckle. Her pulse quickened at the sound. Suddenly she was glad of the monkey's buffering presence.

What could she have been thinking when she invited Zack over? But she knew, oh, how she knew. She'd been so close to giving in, so close to compromising her sanity by forgetting how heartless he could be.

He'd once asked her if she believed in magic.

She had believed in magic on the ship with Zack, only to discover that it had all been a cruel illusion.

Giving herself a stern mental shake, Justine put space between them and began a thorough search of the cabinets. She couldn't imagine how the boa could have gotten inside, but the clever snake had to be *somewhere* in the apartment.

"I'll start in the bedroom," Zack told her.

"Okay." Justine clutched the cabinet doors and tried not to think about Zack in her bedroom. Her fingers trembled as she began removing canned goods from the shelves. Why hadn't she just told him a plain and straightforward "no"? *Because you couldn't say it, because you didn't want him to stop.*

"Yes, I did," Justine grumbled defensively beneath her breath. "Besides, there's nothing wrong with wanting him. It's the loving him I have to fight."

The cabinet was empty. No pretty rainbow boa in sight.

With a sigh, Justine began replacing the cans.

In the bedroom, Zack, with Dennis firmly attached, had completed a thorough search of the bed. He'd looked under the mattress, crawled on his back to inspect the springs beneath, and emptied the pillows of their casings.

But there was no sign of Squeeze.

"Looks like the closet is our next destination," Zack told Dennis. The monkey chattered something and tightened his arms around Zack's neck. Zack absently stroked the monkey's back as he opened the closet doors and began to push the hangers aside one by one. He paused when he came to a little black dress, his brow swooping upward. What he wouldn't give to see that on Justine! With a wistful sigh, he shoved the dress aside. His hand closed over a hanger draped with scarves in a rainbow of colors.

Something crackled beneath his fingers.

Zack jerked his hand away, frowning at the scarves. Cautiously he reached out and fingered the material. To his amazement, a portion of the scarf fell apart in his hands.

Either Justine had a serious moth infestation, or it wasn't a scarf after all. "Justine!" he bellowed, startling Dennis.

She came at a run, skidding to a stop in the doorway. "What is it?" she demanded breathlessly. "You scared the daylights out of me!"

"I think I've found something." He motioned her over, taking her hand and placing it on the scarf. Justine's eyes went wide.

"This is her skin! No wonder she's been hiding." She pulled the skin from her scarves and held the gruesome sight in the air as if it were a trophy.

Zack wasn't particularly intrigued. "Why did she hide?"

"Because for a bit—while the skin is sliding over their eyes—they're almost blind," Justine explained. "It frightens them when they can't see." With growing excitement, she began to flip through her clothes. "She's probably close by."

Trying to appear casual, Zack took a prudent step away from the closet. A tame snake was one thing; a frightened one was quite another. Besides, he didn't want to scare Dennis if Justine happened to pull a squirming snake from the closet.

When she came upon a garment bag, her fingers stilled. She slid it to the left, then to the right as if to test its weight. Smiling triumphantly, she lifted the bag from the rod and set it gently on the floor. Zack noted that the zipper running the length of the garment bag was partially open.

"This was empty, I'm sure of it. She probably crawled in and couldn't get back out."

Zack swallowed hard and tightened his arms around Dennis—to comfort the *monkey,* of course. "I'll bet she's hungry." To his surprise—and relief—Justine shook her head.

"Snakes can go for weeks without eating, and I fed her just before she disappeared." Gently she unzipped the bag and lifted the boa. Squeeze undulated in her hands, apparently anxious to stretch after her confinement. "My, you've got a shiny new skin, don't you, girl?"

Her crooning voice was like an aphrodisiac to Zack. He shifted and tried to steer his mind away from the seductive, compelling sound. They were in her bedroom, but she was holding a snake and he was holding a monkey. Any sane, *normal* guy would be thinking of how he could extract himself without losing face.

The bizarreness of the scene and his own acceptance made Zack laugh. Thomas would never believe him. Hell, *he* found it hard to believe.

"What's so funny?" Justine inquired.

She gave Squeeze her freedom. Zack watched as the snake made for the dark safety of the bed, effectively placing the bed off-limits. He shook his head, unwilling to share the nature of his amusement with Justine. He didn't think she would find it funny, and he didn't want her to think he was laughing at her expense. She owned a pet store, and days like today were probably ordinary for her.

For the first time, Zack realized that if he succeeded in winning Justine's heart again, his life would be peppered with bizarre days like today. Some perhaps even more bizarre.

Today they had rescued a monkey from a roof and a snake from a garment bag. Somewhere in the apartment lurked a giant lizard and a fierce cat, a part of Justine's misfit family that he hoped someday would be his own.

But at the heart of the jungle lived the woman he loved.

The knowledge made him smile.

"Are you hungry?"

Justine's query startled him from his pleasant fantasies. His mouth watered. Sliding a slow, deliberate gaze over her, he drawled softly, "Oh, yeah. I'm *definitely* hungry."

She blushed.

Twenty-two

It wasn't yet seven o'clock Wednesday morning when Zack heard a knock at his door. Since he'd just stepped out of the shower—a blissfully *hot* shower—he envisioned a glowering Fowler standing in the hall wearing his Henry VIII robe.

"You promised," Zack mimicked in a whiny, nasal voice as he opened the door. But it wasn't Fowler, it was Jordan Diamond.

"Surprised to see me?" Jordan queried with a cheeky grin.

Zack closed his mouth. "As a matter of fact, I didn't expect to see you until the last minute."

Jordan bounced by him, leaving Zack standing in the doorway wearing nothing but a damp towel. Zack slammed the door. "Come on in," he muttered sarcastically. "You'll have to excuse me while I get dressed."

"Don't let me stop you. Mind if I help myself to a glass of milk? I skipped breakfast so I'd have time to stop by here on the way to school."

"Help yourself, and pour me one while you're at it."

When Zack emerged from the bedroom a few moments later, the jug of milk was empty, and Jordan sported a thick, white mustache. He reminded Zack of those "Got Milk?" commercials.

Jordan handed a glass to Zack. "I saved you one. By the way, where's the monkey?"

He pointed to the ceiling fan above Jordan's head. "Asleep, so I'd appreciate it if you would keep your voice down." Zack tipped the glass and drained half the milk. He set the glass on the counter and folded his arms. "So, you've come to your senses?"

"I have. You didn't think I would?"

Zack shook his head. "I figured you would, but I didn't think you would this soon. The other guys have already contacted me."

Jordan made a face. "Yeah, well, those dudes don't have Clay Diamond for a dad. He'd *kill* me if he knew."

"Don't you mean he *will* kill you? That *is* part of the bargain, Jordan," Zack reminded him. "You have to tell your folks."

"Yeah, I know, I know." Jordan stuck his hands in his pockets and hung his head. "I just dread it. Dad's gonna hit the roof."

Zack was careful not to show his sympathy. "I think he'll be more disappointed about the fact that you lied to him."

"Yeah, and Mom, too." He fished a wad of bills from his pocket and handed them to Zack. "It's all there. Aunt Justine gave me an advance."

"There's another one who will be disappointed. You know that she blames me, don't you?"

Jordan flushed. "Yeah, that was pretty cool of you not to tell her." He darted a quick, sly glance at Zack. "Why don't you ask her to dinner and explain everything?"

For the second time in less than fifteen minutes, Zack's mouth fell open. "Are you *matchmaking*, Jordan? I thought you hated me."

"I did, but I don't anymore. Mini said—" He broke off, his face turning a darker shade of red.

Zack straightened, a quick flash of alarm skirting down his spine. "Mini, the lovebird? You're saying she *spoke* to you?" Maybe Justine *hadn't* been overreacting. Maybe the kid *was* experimenting with drugs. Despite what he'd told her, sixteen was a little too old for imaginary friends, wasn't it?

"Forget it. You wouldn't believe me anyway." Jordan scuffed his shoe across the floor, lowering his voice to a conspiratorial whisper. "I'm not sure *I* believe it sometimes."

"Why are you whispering?"

Jordan glanced around furtively, then leaned forward. "They watch you guys on Mini's crystal ball."

"Uh-huh. Right." Zack gulped the rest of his milk, deciding to go along with Jordan's strange behavior until he could talk to Justine. "About the game Friday night—"

"Yeah, I can't wait!" Jordan clamped his hand over his mouth and looked up at the sleeping monkey. He lowered his voice. "We're gonna stomp those Wildcats this time, aren't we?"

Zack hesitated, but he knew what he had to do. "I believe we'll beat the Wildcats, but I'm afraid *you* won't be playing Friday night."

"Aw, Coach! Why not? I gave you the money and I'm going to tell my folks tonight—"

"I'm sorry." Zack *was* sorry. The kid showed a lot of enthusiasm for the game, which was probably why each and every team member looked up to him. "But it wouldn't be fair to pull Avery from the game just because you decided to admit you were wrong."

For a moment he thought Jordan would continue to argue. He was immensely pleased when he didn't. Perhaps Jordan had learned his lesson.

"You're right again," Jordan admitted. "Belly's good, too. If I could pick someone to take my place, I'd pick Belly."

Hoping to ease the moment, Zack clapped him on the back. "Look on the bright side. You'll have more time to practice your apology." He walked him to the door. "And thanks for the tip about inviting Justine to dinner. I think I will."

Jordan smiled. "It wasn't my idea, but I'll give Mini the message. And don't worry about Aunt Justine finding out

from Mom first. My dad doesn't get home till late, and believe me, I don't want to tell the story twice."

"Good thinking."

"How do you think Aunt Justine will take it?" he asked,
hovering anxiously by the door.

"She might be disappointed at first, but I think she'll forgive you." Zack glanced at his watch and saw that he had
fifteen minutes to get dressed. He was due at the school for
a faculty meeting at seven forty-five, but Jordan still lingered.

"Don't you wish she'd forgive you, too?"

Zack stiffened. "What do you mean?"

"You know," Jordan chided, punching him playfully in the
arm and nearly knocking the empty glass from Zack's hand.
"For dumping her when you guys went on that cruise."

"I didn't *dump* her," Zack said, not sure of Jordan's meaning. "I left a message for her—along with my phone number.
She never called."

Jordan's youthful brows disappeared behind a lock of dark
hair. "That's not what she told Mom. She said you left the
ship without a word. Well, gotta go. Good luck tonight."

With a wink and a friendly wave, Jordan slipped out the
door, leaving Zack reeling with a stunning realization.

Justine never received his message.

The hostility, the mistrust . . . yes, even the fear he'd
glimpsed in her eyes. It all made sense to Zack now, and he
wondered why he hadn't considered the possibility.

Justine believed he'd wooed her into his bed, convinced
her that he loved her, and then walked away without a word.

Yes, it all made perfect sense.

She probably believed he'd come to Cannon Bay to tram-
ple her heart a second time. No wonder she fought him at
every turn. No wonder she shied when he mentioned the
cruise. No wonder she didn't believe a single solitary word
he said.

Jordan's innocent remark opened Zack's eyes, but it also
gladdened his heart. Justine *must* love him, or she wouldn't
be so angry.

Zack prayed he was right.

• • •

Justine was late opening the shop, but she had a good reason; her bottom was black and blue, and there was a tender lump on the back of her head where she had hit the railing yesterday.

She didn't notice the bumps and bruises until she had gotten out of bed that morning. Stiff and sore, she'd literally crawled into the shower. The jet stream of hot water had helped, but the stairs leading to the street might as well have been a gauntlet.

After making coffee in her office, Justine emerged with a cup of the strong brew. She stopped so suddenly the hot coffee sloshed onto her hand, adding to her aches and pains.

There was a note taped to the outside of the birdcage on the counter.

Slowly she approached the covered cage, chilled to the bone when she recognized Jordan's bold scrawl. *Aunt Justine: I stopped by this morning to check on the lovebirds and noticed Mini had built a nest. The book says they need a nesting box and a quiet place to raise their young. I found a nesting box in the storage room, but they still need to be in a quiet place. Love, Jordan.*

Dazed, Justine read the P.S. at the bottom of the note. *Don't worry, I didn't bust in. Mini was kind enough to open the door.*

Justine quickly turned the paper over, praying she would find *Ha-ha* written on the back. Just one of Jordan's practical jokes.

The page was blank.

Her stomach did a sickening flip-flop. She dropped the note and pulled aside one-half of the birdcage cover. Reuben squawked and flapped his wings as if to protest her intrusion. Justine could see the bold white ring around Mini's eye as the bird peered at her through a small hole in the nesting box.

Jordan was right about one thing; Mini was nesting.

In the next hour, as Justine fed and watered her critters,

her concern continued to edge into the panic zone. She kept thinking about the note and its ramifications. Her instincts urged her to move the birds so Jordan could not continue his dangerous fantasy.

After all, the lovebirds *did* need peace and quiet.

Kneeling on the floor, Justine cuddled a beautiful black-and-white kitten, finding comfort in its soft fur and rumbling purr as she searched for a solution. She couldn't take them up to her apartment. Rogue, Thor, and Squeeze could not be trusted around the lovebirds, and their presence would agitate the nesting female.

What to do? She had to get them out of the store—away from Jordan—which meant her brother's house was also out of the question.

She let the puppies out of their kennels for their daily exercise, automatically mopping up puddles and steering them out of trouble while her mind remained focused on the problem. The storeroom might do temporarily, but she hated to put them in such a dark, dreary place, and while it might solve the problem of the lovebirds' privacy, it wouldn't keep them away from Jordan.

Christopher . . . Christopher lived in a small apartment and owned two rambunctious German shepherds he'd purchased from her last year.

Jennifer, the beautician, was an avid cat lover.

No, the birds needed a place completely free of other animals, a place where they would be left alone for the most part. A place where Jordan couldn't reach them.

The ringing phone put Justine's frenzied plotting on hold. With a pain-filled groan, she gathered the puppies and returned them to their kennels before answering the phone. "Little Shop of Critters, Justine speaking."

"You're in pain," Zack guessed immediately.

The sound of his voice triggered an idea and made her forget his shrewd observation. Justine nearly whooped with joy. Zack's apartment would be a perfect place for the lovebirds. It would take some skillful persuading, but surely he knew birds were far less trouble than a monkey?

"Justine?"

"Just a little sore," she said. "Nothing to worry about."

"Are you certain?"

"I'm certain. Any particular reason you called?"

"I just wanted to tell you thanks for dinner last night."

Justine laughed—gently. "You're thanking me for sticky pasta and lumpy clam sauce?" She hardly remembered eating, but she would never forget his good-night kiss. Thank God she'd managed to retain enough sanity to break away before things had become too hot! Not that Dennis had allowed too much contact, much to her relief *and* chagrin.

"I'll admit, I wasn't paying much attention to the food," he said huskily, echoing her thoughts. "Any word from Dennis's owner?"

"Not yet, but I'm expecting him anytime. Where can I reach you when he arrives?"

He gave her his beeper number and instructed her simply to punch in the word "Dennis." "Another reason I'm calling is to see if you'll let me cook dinner for you tonight. I owe you."

Justine stopped breathing. Finally the words tumbled out in a rush. "I don't think that would be a good idea." When the silence grew, she had to bite her lip to keep from changing her mind. He had been on his very best behavior last night, but they'd had the monkey.

Tonight they wouldn't have the monkey.

"I need to talk to you about Jordan."

Her earlier chill returned. He sounded very serious, and considering what she had learned this morning, she didn't think it was a coincidence; Zack must have information about Jordan.

"Okay."

"About seven-thirty? My place?"

"No funny stuff," she warned him.

"I can't make any promises, but I'll try. You're hard to resist."

Justine's hand shook as she hung up the phone.

She knew exactly how he felt.

Dennis's owner arrived shortly after noon. Late fifties, tall, well-dressed, and sporting an enchanting Australian accent, he was nothing like she imagined.

"I left my organ-grinder in the car," he teased, apparently recognizing her surprise.

Justine immediately liked him. She smiled into his twinkling eyes. "I confess I was expecting a short, rotund man with an organ-grinder slung over his shoulder." She blushed when he threw back his head and laughed at her candid comment.

"You wouldn't be the first. Actually I'm Banjo's agent, Reno Web."

"Justine Diamond." She took his proffered, well-manicured hand, blushing when he brushed a light kiss across her knuckles. He might have thought twice about his flirtatious move if he'd known what she'd been handling before he arrived, Justine thought, hiding a smile as she tugged her hand away.

"His owner fell sick, and Banjo was under contract for a new movie, so the owner sent him on ahead. When he didn't arrive on schedule, I assumed Bernard decided to wait until he was out of the hospital so that he could accompany Banjo."

"So, our little stray monkey is a star. We knew he was something special." A definite understatement.

It also explained a lot about his behavior—at least, the intelligent part. Dennis was not only intelligent, but also *trained*. Not Dennis, she amended, but Banjo. She decided the name suited him.

Zack probably wouldn't agree.

"Yes, his last movie was *Monkey Fever*. He received tons of fan mail from children, and adults as well." Reno checked his Rolex and looked beyond her. "Where is he, by the way?"

Justine quickly told Reno the story of the monkey's arrival

and his attachment to Zack. "We didn't know anything about Banjo," she concluded. "So when he refused to let go, Zack offered to take him home until we found his owner." No need to purge her conscience by telling Reno *she* had persuaded Zack to take the monkey.

Reno was frowning by the time she finished. "That's strange. He's usually very calm as long as he has Cocoa with him, and I know that Bernard wouldn't have sent Banjo along without Cocoa."

"Cocoa?" Justine repeated blankly.

"Cocoa was Banjo's twin."

Justine's heart stopped. "There was *another* monkey?"

"No, no. The Cocoa I'm talking about is a *stuffed* monkey—a toy. When Banjo and Cocoa were separated, Banjo refused to be consoled. He wouldn't eat, wouldn't sleep, and became wild and uncontrollable. Bernard tried everything, and nothing worked until he found a stuffed monkey that resembled Cocoa. He presented the monkey, and *voila*— Banjo became calm." Reno shook his head at the memory. "Heaven help anyone who tries to take Cocoa from Banjo."

His explanation was almost as shocking. Justine gulped. Everything Zack had told her about the monkey must have been true. Granted, it didn't explain the mystery of why the monkey became calm when Zack was in the store, but she knew she couldn't use the enigma as an excuse for her mistrust.

She had a lot of apologizing to do.

Inwardly cringing, Justine excused herself and went to her office to leave a message on Zack's beeper to let him know Reno had arrived. When she came out, Reno was disappearing into the next room where the birds were housed, giving Justine the perfect opportunity to slip into the storage room.

She found the empty crate beneath a stack of boxes, and inside the crate she found Cocoa, a white-faced replica of Banjo.

"Zack's going to kill me," she whispered. "And *I'm* going to kill Christopher."

But after a short deliberation, she knew this wasn't Christopher's fault or her own. Who would have thought a monkey would have his own stuffed toy? No one, that's who. It was all a terrible mix-up, with the exception of her unforgivable behavior regarding Zack and Dennis.

Banjo, the movie star.

Who would have *thought?*

Shaking her head, Justine clutched the stuffed monkey against her chest and went to find Reno.

The moment Zack opened his apartment door, Dennis leaped from the ceiling fan into his arms. Zack held him for a moment, both surprised and moved by the unusual greeting. He rarely ventured from the ceiling fan unless Zack was either gone from the apartment or asleep.

"So, now that it's time to leave, you've decided you like me, huh?"

Dennis pulled back to stare solemnly at Zack. He reached out with his finger and stretched Zack's bottom lip downward. The huge grin that split his face made Zack laugh.

"You're a mess," Zack said. "And I may be crazy, but I think I'm actually going to miss you." Dennis seemed to be listening intently, and not for the first time, Zack sensed the monkey understood. "After having you around, a kitten or a turtle is going to seem mighty boring."

The monkey chattered and shook his head so fast it made Zack dizzy. Then he twined his arms around Zack's neck and laid his head on his shoulder. His legs were wrapped firmly around Zack's waist. If it wasn't for the hair covering his entire body, Zack could almost imagine he held a toddler in need of comfort.

He swallowed the lump in his throat. Ridiculous, really, feeling this way after all the trouble the monkey had caused.

Behind him in the open doorway, a nasty, familiar voice drawled, "Well, well, well. I can't wait until Mr. Potter hears about this. The great has-been and a monkey. What's the matter, Wayne, can't get any women?"

Zack turned with Dennis in his arms, surprised and pleased to discover Fowler had lost the power to anger him. His smile was genuine. "How's your head, Fowler? Dennis here has a great arm on him, don't you think? You should be thankful he was holding an apple instead of a baseball."

Barry's eyes narrowed. "You expect me to believe this little . . . *ape* was the one who knocked me out?"

Zack shrugged and walked with Dennis over to the bowl of fruit. "If you don't believe me, I'm sure Dennis would be glad to give you another demonstration." He glanced down at the monkey in his arms. "How about it, sport? Want to show him how it's done?"

Eagerly Dennis grabbed an apple from the bowl.

When Zack turned around, the hallway was empty.

Twenty-three

When Zack entered the shop with Dennis, he ran into the green-eyed monster of jealousy.

It was Justine who prompted the unfamiliar emotion with her spontaneous, husky laughter, and before Zack could truly focus on the man standing before Justine at the counter, he developed a keen dislike for him.

The suave-looking older man in a three-piece suit spotted Zack standing by the door. With a friendly smile Zack didn't return, he strode to him and thrust out his hand, introducing himself.

"Reno Web. You must be Zachary Wayne. Justine tells me you've been taking excellent care of little Banjo here."

The devil in Zack prompted him to ignore the outstretched hand. He knew he was being churlish, but Justine's laughter—laughter *this* man had evoked—still rang in his ears. Besides, he had a perfect excuse; he was holding the monkey. "I call him Dennis." To Zack's satisfaction, Dennis lifted his head from Zack's shoulder at the sound of his name.

Reno's smile slipped at Zack's aggressive tone. He dropped his hand. "Well, Banjo and I need to get going, so if you'll just hand him over . . ."

Zack tugged at the monkey, perversely reluctant to give him up now that the moment had come. Dennis seemed equally reluctant; he screeched and clung to Zack. Trying not to look *too* smug, Zack closed his arms around Dennis and said, "I don't think he wants to let go."

With a mysterious smile, Reno turned to Justine. "Miss Diamond? May I have Cocoa?"

Frowning, Zack watched Justine give Reno what appeared to be a stuffed black-and-white monkey. When he shot her a questioning glance, she shrugged. *I'll explain later,* she mouthed silently.

Reno held the toy monkey out. "Look, Banjo. It's your old pal Cocoa."

Banjo slowly turned his head. He stared for a long moment at Reno before looking at the monkey Reno held. Finally he swung his gaze to Zack, then back to the toy. Zack felt the monkey's grip loosen and knew he'd made his choice.

He should have been relieved but he wasn't.

Ridiculous to feel hurt, but he did.

Dennis—*Banjo*—Zack corrected, curled an arm around Reno's neck and grabbed the stuffed monkey with the other. The transfer was complete, and Zack was left feeling lost and abandoned.

"Miss Diamond, Mr. Wayne." Reno nodded to each in turn. "I can't thank you enough for taking care of Banjo."

"Yeah, well, I'll send you a bill for the damages," Zack muttered, hoping they didn't notice the slight, unmanly crack in his voice. He reached out and patted Banjo on the back. "Take care, little guy, and stay off the roof."

"Beg your pardon?"

"He's joking," Justine said hastily. She flashed a warning glance at Zack. "Have a safe trip!"

The moment they were out the door, Justine turned on Zack, regarding him from beneath half-lowered lids. "You're going to miss him," she stated.

"Miss *Dennis?*" Zack forced a disbelieving laugh. "Not on your life. I'm glad that fruit-throwing, roof-climbing, chef wanna-be is gone. Now I can relax in the comfort of my home without worrying about flying objects, and I can come and go as I please without fear of the building catching fire while I'm gone. Furthermore, he was eating me out of house and home. Do you have any idea how much off-season fruit costs these days?"

Justine folded her arms, a knowing smile playing about her full lips. There was no need for words.

Zack snorted, dismayed to feel his face warming up. He'd never developed a great talent for lying. "You're crazy. That monkey is a walking disaster. Anyone with an ounce of sense would be *glad* he was gone."

"But you're not," Justine observed softly.

She wasn't going to give up, Zack thought with an inward sigh. "Maybe I did get a *little* attached to him." When she rewarded him with a brilliant smile, Zack decided the embarrassment was worth it.

"Now, that wasn't so bad, was it?" she asked teasingly. "I guess your apartment will feel empty with Dennis gone."

"Yeah, it will." Quiet, empty, and lonely.

"Zack, I was wondering . . ."

"Yes?" Zack prompted cautiously. She lowered her gaze to study her nails, an evasive action Zack noted with rising suspicion. A dark curtain of hair fell forward, hiding her expression.

"Do you remember Mini and Reuben?" She nodded at the covered cage on the counter.

How could Zack forget? Just this morning Jordan had claimed the birds talked to him.

"The lovebirds are nesting, and it's important they have a quiet place until the eggs hatch. Birds are nothing like monkeys," she added quickly. "You hardly notice they're around most of the time."

"I've got a bad feeling there's a point to this nature lesson," Zack drawled. "So why don't we just cut to the chase?"

She took a deep breath and looked up. The liquid gold of her gaze was compelling—and, in Zack's case, irresistible.

At that moment, if Justine had asked him to harbor an alligator in his bathtub, he would have agreed.

"I was wondering if you would let the lovebirds stay at your place for a while. You wouldn't have to do anything. I could come over each day and feed them after I closed the shop."

Zack quirked a wicked brow. "Now *there's* an offer I can't refuse."

She rushed on as if she hadn't heard him. "I know you had a bad time with Dennis—Banjo—so I wouldn't blame you if you said no."

"I said *yes.*"

"And of course there would be no hard—" Her eyes widened as his words sank in. "Did you just say yes?"

Smiling, Zack nodded. "After Dennis, lovebirds will be a piece of cake. Besides, I think it might be a good idea to separate them from Jordan."

A chill swept over Justine at his words. "That . . . that was my second reason for wanting you to take them. Is there something you're not telling me?"

"We'll talk about it tonight over dinner. Do you want me to take them now?"

Justine hesitated, hating to inconvenience Zack more than she already had. But Jordan was scheduled to work today, and she didn't want him around the lovebirds another moment. Maybe without their influence Jordan would snap out of his fantasies.

If he didn't . . . Justine shuddered at the terrifying thought. He had to.

"Yes, please take them now. I'll bring food and clean newspapers tonight." She carefully lifted the covered birdcage from the counter and handed it to Zack. Their fingers brushed. A tremor shot through her at the brief contact, reminding her she was playing with fire by continuing to find excuses to keep Zack in her life.

Was this what she was doing? she wondered, quickly moving her hand away and scolding her undisciplined body.

When she chanced a look at Zack, she saw that his eyes had darkened, indicating she wasn't the only one disturbed by the contact.

"Is the living room okay?"

Justine blinked. "The living room?"

Zack lifted the cage. "Is it okay to put them in the living room? Or should I settle them in my bedroom?"

"Living room," Justine answered quickly. Just the thought of having to go into Zack's bedroom each evening to feed and care for the lovebirds made her weak all over. She was hopeless!

"I'll have an extra key made in case I'm gone when you come over."

Justine flushed at his faintly amused tone, assuring herself that he couldn't read her mind. She darted a nervous tongue over her lips, her eyes flaring wide when he sucked in a sharp breath.

"Don't do that," he whispered roughly. "You don't know what that does to me."

Oh, she had a good idea . . . if it was *anything* compared to what his rough voice did to *her*. Deciding it was best to pretend as if he hadn't spoken, Justine stepped ahead of him to open the door. "If you have any problems, just call."

Zack paused at the door. Their eyes met. Undeniable tension crackled between them. Justine wanted to look away from the intensity of his gaze, but she couldn't.

"I'll see you at seven-thirty?"

"Yes."

Justine didn't realize she was holding her breath until the door closed on Zack and the lovebirds. Pressing her forehead against the cold glass, she exhaled slowly, frosting the pane with her breath. She had less than seven hours to build her resistance against Zack's considerable charm.

Right now it seemed an impossible task.

Why did she bother? Justine was shocked that she could ask herself such a question. She bothered because of soaked pillows and sleepless nights. She bothered because she didn't want to suffer through another broken heart.

She bothered because when Zachary Wayne decided to walk back out of her life, she wanted to be able to smile and wave as if it didn't matter.

Too late for that, of course. Her heart had already surrendered. But this time—*this* time was different. This time her eyes were wide open. There would be no humiliating surprises in the end.

Justine gave a start as a customer pushed on the door. She moved away, pasting a professional smile on her face as she greeted the newcomer.

Seven hours. Plenty of time to prepare herself for what she suspected would turn out to be a test of her willpower. It was obvious Zack wanted them to become lovers, and just as obvious her body eagerly agreed. But her heart wasn't strong enough for a sexual relationship with Zack; she loved him too much.

Tonight she would show Zack they could be friends without muddling the relationship with insincere—and painful—pledges of love.

Reuben felt ridiculous talking to Mini through a small hole in a box. "You should come out here and see what he's doing," he whispered urgently. "No candles, no flowers, and he's making some kind of foul-smelling soup!"

"I'm . . . I'm feeling kind of dizzy, darling. I don't think it would be safe to go hopping around a cage. And truthfully, I think we've done enough meddling. It gets us nowhere."

Her calm reaction disturbed Reuben. If he wasn't afraid they'd declare her insane and take her away, he'd consult the witch's counsel about Mini's strange obsession with the bird's nest. "Mini, if nothing has happened, why are you sitting on the nest?"

"Well . . . I'm resting."

Reuben propped a wing against the nesting box, frowning. She was keeping something from him, but he knew her well enough to know she wouldn't tell him until she was good and ready. "All right, I'll buy that excuse. Meanwhile . . . what are we going to do about Zack and Justine? He's ruining everything!" The silence lasted so long he thought she'd fallen asleep.

"I see you're not going to take my advice about the mortals," Mini grumbled. "While Zack was gone earlier, you took a look around the apartment, didn't you?"

"Yes, I did." Reuben tapped his foot and waited for her to explain. Mini poked her head through the hole, startling him.

"This is what I think we should do . . ."

As Reuben listened to her plan, he began to grin.

Zack wished the lovebirds would chirp or sing, anything to break the silence. He twisted around and eyed his stereo with longing. Probably not a good idea, he decided, transferring his gaze to the elaborately covered birdcage he'd placed on top of the entertainment center. Justine had been specific about the lovebirds not being disturbed.

He missed Dennis.

With a sigh he turned his attention back to the special dinner he was making for Justine. He hoped she liked her chili spicy. Chuckling, he imagined her expression when she arrived to find not the seduction scene he was sure she was expecting—he'd recognized the look on her face—but a simple feast with a simple guy. Not that he wouldn't be averse to making love with the woman he loved . . .

But tonight he was going to concentrate on earning her trust again. After what he'd discovered today from Jordan he suspected it wouldn't be an easy task. If he could get his hands around that steward's neck he'd throttle him.

He tasted the chili, frowned, and searched the cabinet above him for the ground red pepper. Unscrewing the cap, he tapped a little into the bubbling chili. Maybe a tad more—

The sound of breaking glass startled him. His hand jerked, spilling a considerable amount of red pepper into the chili.

With a curse, Zack grabbed a spoon and tried to scoop it out, but the bubbling mixture sucked it under.

"Damn!" Throwing the spoon aside, Zack lowered the fire beneath the pot and went in search of the noise. If he didn't absolutely *know* better, he'd think Dennis was back. Breaking glass? He was alone in the apartment with the exception of the lovebirds—who were securely locked in a cage.

On impulse, he backtracked and peeped between the satin covering. One of the lovebirds stared back at him from the perch; he glimpsed the white-ringed eye of the female looking through the hole in the nesting box.

Laughing at his silly thoughts, Zack continued to the bathroom. It was probably nothing more than a drinking glass he'd left on the sink. Vibrations from the ancient heating system had most likely sent it crashing to the hard tile floor.

Zack stopped abruptly in the doorway, his brain registering the shock of finding not a shattered drinking glass, but pieces of the large mirror that had hung over the sink. Did they have earthquakes in Nebraska? he wondered. And if there had been an earthquake, wouldn't he have felt it?

Puzzled, he shook his head, squatting to pick up the larger pieces and placing them in the bathroom trash can. The task took him several moments, for the shards were razor-sharp and he had to move slowly. When he'd picked up as much as he could by hand, he went to get the broom and a dustpan. As he was returning, another unexpected noise stopped him in his tracks.

It was the annoying sound of a phone left off the hook.

Zack slowly turned his head, staring at the phone. He walked to it and gently tapped the receiver. There was a little click as it settled into the cradle, and the noise stopped. Well, that explained it, Zack decided, relieved. They'd experienced a small tremor and he'd been so preoccupied, he hadn't noticed it.

Despite the logical explanation, Zack picked up the receiver and pushed redial. The last person he'd called had been—

"Hello, Diamond residence."

—Justine's shop. *Not* Clay and Bea Diamond.

"Hello?"

"Yes." What would he say? What *could* he say that wouldn't sound crazy? *Hey, I think someone called your number, but I'm the only one here?* Zack closed his eyes, using the only excuse he could think of that wouldn't alarm the woman. "This is Coach Wayne. Could I speak to Jordan?"

"I'm sorry . . . he left a few moments ago with some friends." There was a chilly, expectant pause, then: "Can I take a message?"

"No thanks. I'll call back later."

Zack hung up before Bea could respond. He tapped his fingers against the phone. "And the plot thickens," he murmured aloud, his gaze straying to the covered cage.

Clothes lay scattered on the bed, the chair, the dresser, and the floor. Justine kicked a skirt aside and walked into the living room for the tenth time. She pivoted in a slow circle, giving her silent audience plenty of time to form an opinion.

"Well, what do you think? Too frumpy? Too obvious? Remember, I don't want him to think I'm deliberately trying to look unappealing." Justine smoothed her hands along the thigh-length hunter-green sweater with matching wool slacks.

Rogue dutifully opened his sleepy eyes, yawned hugely, then closed them again. Squeeze took one glance at her and slid under the couch. Thor, evidently, was tired of the fashion show; he never opened his eyes.

"You guys are no help," Justine muttered, stalking back into her bedroom to stand before her closet. There was one garment left, a simple black dress that was neither fancy or alluring. In fact, she'd once worn it to a funeral. Her mother had talked her into buying the dress, declaring no wardrobe was complete without a simple black dress.

No, not a dress, she thought. She'd wear the outfit she

now had on, and to hell with what Zack believed. If his ego was so enlarged he'd think she dressed simply for him, well, then, that was *his* problem.

With a sigh, she brushed and braided her hair, then twisted it until it lay thick and heavy against the back of her neck. She was striving for severe, somber . . . *cool*. It was a casual date between two friends, whether Zack knew it or not.

A quick stroke of lipstick, a dab of mascara, and she was almost ready to go. She took a deep breath and went to get her coat, checking her purse to make sure she'd put the video inside. The care package she'd fixed for the lovebirds sat waiting by the door.

Five minutes later, she was back in the apartment, exasperated and cold. Her van had not responded to her repeated attempts to start it. Rubbing her frozen hands together, she moved to the phone to call Zack.

He answered on the third ring. "Zack, it's Justine."

"Something wrong?" he asked sharply.

"Nothing serious." She bit her bottom lip, wondering if she should cancel the date altogether. Perhaps it was an omen. "My van won't start."

"I'll be there in ten minutes. Wait for me inside where it's warm."

Justine stared at the disconnected phone with a wry smile. So much for her thoughts of canceling. Zack had made sure she didn't get the opportunity.

For the next fifteen minutes, she waited with her coat on. Finally she took it off and began to pace, having serious second thoughts about agreeing to this date.

After another fifteen minutes, she moved to the bedroom and quickly changed into jeans and a comfortable sweatshirt with Cannon Bay Indians emblazoned in red letters across the front, adding the green sweater and wool pants to the pile of clothes on her bed.

What was she thinking when she picked that sweater? Come to think of it, what was she thinking when she agreed to have dinner with him?

Jordan. Justine took a deep breath and concentrated on her nephew. Zack had said he needed to talk to her about Jordan. Perhaps asking her to have dinner had merely been a polite formality. They had to talk, so why not talk over dinner? They had to eat, didn't they?

Forty-five long minutes after the call, Justine opened her apartment door to a grim-faced Zack. His cheeks were red with cold, and the look in his eyes had her backing up a step.

"I was about a mile from my apartment when I noticed my back tire was going flat."

Justine waved him inside and shut the door, shivering. "Bad day to have to change a tire."

"I didn't change it, because my spare was also flat."

She attempted a rueful smile. It wasn't easy, considering how murderous he looked. "Seems we're both having bad luck tonight."

"I don't think it's bad luck. The gas station attendant found nothing wrong with either of the tires."

Justine gasped. "You think someone let the air out?"

"I do. Come on, let's go. I don't want to leave the truck out on the street any longer than I have to."

"I don't blame you," she murmured, following him out the door. She wondered if Zack's flat tires had anything to do with her van not starting. It was almost as if someone was determined to keep them apart.

They made the trip in silence, each preoccupied with their own thoughts. In fact, Justine was beginning to think he'd forgotten her presence until they reached his apartment door. He stopped and turned to her, grasping her chin and tilting it upward.

"Before we go inside, I want you to know that I'm not planning on seducing you, so you can relax."

"I didn't—"

"Yes, you did," he chided softly. "And considering the way I've been acting, I can't really blame you for thinking it." His thumb moved back and forth across her chin, almost absently. "I want us to spend time together, to talk about things we never got the chance to talk about before."

"Jordan—"

"Yes, we need to talk about Jordan, too."

He dropped his hand and turned to unlock the door. Justine bumped into him as he stopped abruptly, blocking her view of the apartment.

"Ah, wait here."

"Zack?" Alarmed at his shocked expression, Justine tried to look over his shoulder.

"I'll just be a moment. *Wait here!*"

He quickly pushed her into the hall and slammed the door in her face.

Twenty-four

Soft music, candlelight, and roses.

Zack swallowed to ease the dryness in his throat and forced himself to take another look around the apartment—if it *was* his apartment. It certainly wasn't the apartment he had left an hour ago.

Frank Sinatra, an old favorite of his mother's, crooned a love ballad over *his* stereo. Tall, white candles flickered softly on the table. Roses, red and vibrant, jutted from a sparkling crystal vase.

The table itself, apparently moved by *someone* from the kitchen to the living room area, had been covered with a snowy white tablecloth. A silver-covered platter served as the centerpiece, offset by the candles and the rose. Two place settings with delicate amber-tinted wineglasses graced the table.

Soft music, candlelight, roses and . . . wine.

It could have been an advertisement for *How to Seduce a Woman*, Zack thought, gulping again. He gave a start as Justine knocked on the door.

"Zack? Is something wrong?"

Oh, was it ever! He cleared his throat, hoping his total

confoundment would allow him to speak. "It's . . . it's the mess," he croaked. "I forgot to clean up the mess."

And he *had* left a mess purposely to relax Justine, to convince her he wasn't just another playboy after a few tumbles.

Where was his kettle of chili? The stovetop was bare, the almond-colored range wiped clean of the chili splattering he knew he'd left. Nor was there any sign of the cutting board with the fragrant remains of the onion and garlic he'd chopped to add to the chili. The counter was clean . . . empty with the exception of an ice bucket and a bottle of wine.

Zack forced his paralyzed limbs to move into the kitchen. He opened the refrigerator door, his knees nearly buckling with relief at the sight of his battered old chili pot sitting on the near-empty shelf. It was proof that he hadn't fallen into a rabbit hole.

"Zack?"

Justine's muffled voice made him pause.

"Are you finished? I've seen messes before, you know!"

He couldn't let Justine see *this* particular mess. Oh, no. She would take one look at the setting and run screeching from the building. He would never convince her that he'd had nothing to do with it.

So he had to get rid of the evidence before he opened the door. Zack grabbed the kettle of chili and set it on the stove. He turned the burner on beneath the pan, shoved the ice bucket and wine out of sight beneath the counter, and raced into the living room.

Blowing the candles out, he took the ends of the tablecloth and whipped them together, not the least bit curious about what was beneath the covered platter. He winced at the sound of shattering glass and clinking metal as he hefted his bundle and headed for the bathroom at a brisk trot.

"Zack? Are you hurt? I heard something breaking!"

He ignored the pounding on the door. Sweat beaded his brow and upper lip. She was beginning to sound angry, and he suspected it wouldn't be long before she'd tire of waiting.

Emerging from the bathroom after dumping the bundle in

the bathtub, Zack raced back into the living room, turned off the stereo, and started flicking every light switch he could find until the apartment resembled a hospital operating room.

He was ready. Wiping his brow, he headed for the door.

Halfway there he spotted an unfamiliar object protruding from the fruit bowl. He snatched it up and gave it a cursory glance as his hand reached for the doorknob.

He froze, his gaze widening on the package in his hand.

It was a pack of condoms. Neon colors. Super sensitive.

With a smothered curse, Zack shoved the condoms into his pocket and opened the door.

"Something's wrong, isn't it?" Looking worried and agitated, Justine moved by him into the apartment. She glanced around, then looked at Zack again. "What is it? What did you break?"

"A couple of glasses. Nothing important." As he shut the door, he felt a moment of grim satisfaction in thinking *someone* might have thought so.

"You're not going to tell me, are you?"

Zack hesitated. He hated to lie, but in this instance, he thought she might prefer it to the truth. "There's nothing to tell. I knocked a few glasses from the shelf looking for . . . the red pepper."

"Red pepper?" She cocked her head, her gaze narrowed with suspicion.

"Red pepper," Zack repeated. "For the chili. It was a surprise."

"Don't you mean 'chili' pepper?"

"No. It's an old family recipe." He held out his hand. "Here, let me take your coat." Removing his own, he hung them in the hall closet. He took the care package for the birds and placed it on the counter.

He's jumpy about something, Justine decided, and she didn't think it had anything to do with red pepper or a family recipe of chili. She inhaled, recognizing the familiar aroma of garlic and onions. Beneath those scents, however, she identified the faint smell of burning wax and the sweet perfume of roses.

She didn't believe for a moment that Zack was telling her the truth. "Is there anything I can help you with?" she asked as he moved to the stove and began stirring the bubbling soup.

"Yeah, you can pour the milk."

Warmth flooded Justine. "You remembered."

He turned to her, looking surprised. "That you like milk? Of course. It was only one of *many* things we had in common."

When he stretched his arm to remove two bowls from the cabinet above his head, Justine's mouth watered at the sight of his flexing muscles. Flustered and furious with herself, she tore her gaze away and grabbed two glasses from the same cabinet. She poured the milk and carried them to the table in the living room.

"Crackers or French bread?" Zack called over his shoulder.

"Crackers are fine." The smell of wax was stronger here, she thought, setting the glasses on the table. Deciding to shake him up, Justine asked casually, "Zack, did you know that it's dangerous to burn candles while you're out of the house?"

He whirled around. The bowls of chili wavered in his hands. "What? Oh, the candles."

Justine lifted a questioning brow. "Yes, the candles."

"It . . . it smelled like a monkey in here, so I lit a couple of those scented candles." He approached the table, making a face. "I love the little guy, but his hygiene habits left a lot to be desired." With an indulgent smile, he added, "Don't worry, the candles were the safeguard kind."

"Oh." Justine took a seat as he retreated into the kitchen. She didn't know why he was lying about something so insignificant, but she knew instinctively that he was. It would be amusing to see how far he'd carry the lie, and interesting to find out why. "So, where are they?"

Zack returned, smacking a box of crackers in the middle of the table with a little more force than Justine thought was necessary. She was getting to him, she thought. Good.

When he pitched her a spoon, she caught it, flashing him an innocent smile as she waited for his answer.

"Why?" he demanded, his frustration finally bleeding through.

Justine shrugged, reaching for the crackers. She doubted she would have to crush them after the landing they'd received. "I thought maybe we'd light them again. I've always had a fondness for candles."

"If I had known that, I would have left the damned things lit," Zack muttered. "You never told me that you liked candles."

"Oh, yes." Justine smiled sweetly as he shoved a spoonful of chili into his mouth. Even the way he ate made her squirm. Wisely lowering her gaze, she stirred the crushed crackers into her chili and took a cautious bite. It was good. "Hmm. Spicy."

"Too spicy?"

She shook her head. "No, I like it."

For the next several moments, they ate in silence. Finally Justine scraped the last bite into her mouth and put down her spoon. She sipped her milk and waited for him to finish before she asked evenly, "Are you going to tell me what happened tonight?"

"Don't you want to know the *true* reason why I suspended Jordan from the team?" he countered.

"Yes." She hesitated. "But why are you telling me now?"

Zack considered her question, deciding he might as well tell the truth. He hoped he'd used his quota of lies tonight. "Because Jordan suggested I tell you . . . over dinner." Her stunned gasp came as no surprise. Zack knew exactly how she felt.

"Are we talking about the same Jordan? I was under the impression he didn't approve of our—our—"

"Relationship?" Zack supplied helpfully . . . hopefully.

She licked her lips. "We *had* a relationship. Now we're friends. Anyway"—she waved her napkin in the air in a gesture of bewilderment—"I can't imagine Jordan suggesting you ask me to dinner—"

"I'll get to that in a bit," Zack interrupted. "First, let me start at the beginning. The true reason I suspended Jordan from the team, along with a few others, was because of their unsportsmanlike conduct. We were scheduled to play the Panthers from Scott Plains—"

"I've heard rumors about that team," Justine said. "They've got a reputation for rough play."

Zack nodded. "So I've heard, but that doesn't excuse the prank pulled by Jordan and a few of his teammates. They sneaked into the visitor's locker room and painted the benches just before the Panthers arrived." Her gasp of dismay fell neatly into his pause. "They painted the seats red. Their uniform pants are white."

"Good grief!" Justine looked stricken. "What happened?"

He sighed and leaned back in his chair. "What choice did I have? I forfeited the game and suspended those responsible."

"How . . . how did you know who they were?"

An understandable question, Zack thought, and thankfully one he could answer with remembered pride. "I asked. One by one, they came forward."

Justine looked shell-shocked. "I just can't imagine Jordan doing something so . . . so unsportsmanlike. Clay will be furious, and Bea will be so disappointed." She blinked her teary eyes as she added, "*I'm* disappointed."

At the sight of her crying, Zack wanted to gather her into his arms and nuzzle her tear-streaked eyes. He refrained, but only because he feared she would reject his comfort or think it was a plot to get her into bed. "I think he's learned his lesson. They not only lost the game before it started, they had to pay for the other team's uniforms *and* tell their parents the whole story before next Monday, or they were permanently suspended." He gentled his voice. "Jordan came to me this morning with the money, and he's telling his parents right now."

"He led us to believe *you* were the bad guy." Justine sniffed and swiped at her eyes, looking mad and hurt at the same time. "And I foolishly took his side."

"He's family," Zack pointed out, letting her know that he understood. "I would have done the same."

"What do you think made him change his mind?"

Ah, now they were getting to the tough part. Zack chose his words carefully. "I'm not exactly sure. I'd like to think he made the choice without outside influence."

Justine jumped up and gathered the bowls, heading into the kitchen. He made no move to help her, suspecting she needed the distraction and the time alone to get a handle on her emotions.

"Why do you think he changed his mind about *you?*"

Zack froze at her question. Before tonight he'd planned on telling her about his worrisome conversation with Jordan and share his concerns about Jordan's fantasies.

Now . . . he wasn't so certain they were fantasies.

He remained silent so long she popped her head around the corner, her questioning gaze assuring him she wasn't going to let it drop. Deciding a counterattack was in order, Zack said, "I haven't a clue. Why do *you* think he changed his mind about me?" There was silence from the kitchen. Finally he heard her soft footsteps coming in his direction. She leaned against the wall and folded her arms, looking so wary Zack stifled the urge to laugh.

"Maybe . . . he realized you weren't such a bad guy," she began slowly, as if she had to force the words out. "What Jordan did was reprehensible. I'm not sure if I would have been as understanding, had I been you."

A warmth bloomed in Zack's heart at her praise. He moved his shoulders in a careless shrug to cover his sappy reaction. "They all paid the price."

"Yes, but in a way that allowed them to make up for what they did. You're a wonderful coach, and I think you deserve a—" She broke off, excitement flaring in her golden eyes. "As a matter of fact, I *do* have a reward for you! Actually, it's a surprise, but since you deserve a reward, we'll call it one."

Intrigued, Zack watched as she dug something out of her purse. It was a video, he saw when she held the object in the air as if it were indeed a trophy. He could think of much more interesting rewards, but he kept them to himself. *Earn her trust before you jump her bones, idiot.*

"May I use your VCR?" Before he could answer, she motioned him to the couch. "Come on, have a seat. It's show time."

With an indulgent smile, he moved to the couch, watching as she slipped the tape into the VCR and turned on the TV. He held his breath when she sat next to him. They weren't touching, but her show of trust was more than he could have hoped for.

As the tape started, the lights went out.

"What happened?" Justine asked with a girlish giggle that gladdened Zack's heart.

She was opening up to him, trusting him. He could hardly contain his excitement. *Now don't blow it,* a wise voice cautioned.

"I don't know." Zack didn't care, either, but he kept *that* little secret to himself, as well. But . . . just to show his sincerity, he reached over and tested the lamp.

It clicked on, its low wattage bathing the room in soft, romantic light. *Like the candlelight earlier,* was his startled thought. A magical force was definitely at work, but as long as it worked *with* him, he wasn't fighting it.

The screen on the TV, an older model Zack figured was a castoff from the landlord, finally came to life. They watched a series of previews—some he recognized, some he didn't—before the movie came on.

The camera panned a dusty field, the clear formation of the sandbags indicating a baseball diamond. Two small figures began to grow bigger and bigger as the camera zoomed slowly in. Sounds became louder. Zack heard the steady *clack* of the ball hitting a glove just as a monkey dressed in a red-and-white-striped baseball uniform filled the screen. He was pitching to a young boy dressed in a similar uniform.

The monkey's face was white, and when it split into a wide grin, shock slammed into Zack. He leaned forward. "He looks like Dennis!"

Smiling at his reaction, Justine said, "It *is* Dennis, or Banjo, rather. He's a movie star."

Still finding it incredible, Zack shook his head. His gaze kept returning to the screen. "I find that hard to believe. Dennis was *not* movie-star material. The monkey I knew would destroy a movie set—"

"Ah, I think I can clear that one up." Justine plucked at the couch. "You see, Dennis came with this little stuffed monkey named Cocoa—"

"The one you gave to that Reno guy?"

She nodded without glancing up. "I found it today. Christopher must have overlooked it when Dennis jumped out of the crate."

Zack rubbed his jaw, aching to kiss her senseless. Sitting this near without touching her was a struggle. "I take it Dennis was fond of this Cocoa?" he asked softly.

"Very. He was a twin, and when they separated them, he was heartbroken. Cocoa looks like his twin."

"Poor guy," Zack muttered.

Her lashes made an upward sweep; her gaze locked onto his with a solemn intensity that stole Zack's breath. He'd never loved her more than he did at that moment.

"I'm sorry for not believing you about Dennis . . . and Jordan."

With her gazing at him like that, there was only one thing Zack could think of to say. "It's water under the bridge."

It was an effort, but he managed to drag his gaze away from her upturned face and back to the movie. Inside, he was a quivering mass of jubilation. She'd admitted that she'd been wrong about him on *two* occasions. When he felt secure that he'd earned her trust, he would explain to her what had *really* happened on the cruise.

Now, if he could just keep his hands to himself in the meantime . . .

Mini peered at her husband through the hole in the nesting box. He stood frozen on the perch, watching the mortals on the couch through a window he'd created in the covering. She knew the signs; rigid spine, beak held high, eyes glistening and fixed. His breast rose and fell in swift, sharp movements.

Reuben was furious, and a furious warlock was a dangerous warlock. She had to do something before he exploded in a riot of colorful feathers and did something he'd regret. After all, she had purposely misled him.

Gently she stood, peeking between her legs at the single egg she'd been keeping warm for the past eight hours. According to the bird book, it was likely she'd lay three more, one every other day. She ached with all her heart to share the miracle with Reuben, but she didn't think she'd make it through another fainting spell without throttling him. She needed him—conscious and alert.

Plucking feathers systematically from her body, Mini covered the egg with feathers to keep it warm. She would be away no more than a few moments but she didn't want to take any chances.

The idea of using magic to keep the egg warm strangely repulsed her. Reuben wouldn't understand.

With one last, worried glance at the nest, Mini hopped through the larger hole carved into the back of the nesting box and joined her husband on the perch.

Even her unexpected presence failed to distract him from his fury. "Reuben, talk to me," she whispered, staring at his magnificent profile. "What's going on?"

In a low, vicious voice, he snarled, "The crazy mortal swept our hard work into the bathtub, that's what's wrong.

And he broke Bea's anniversary glasses—the ones Jordan 'borrowed.' "

"Oh." Mini didn't know what to say. *She* had known intuitively that setting the scene would put Justine on alert, possibly send her running, and she had deliberately instructed Reuben to go ahead with his plans.

Her decision to stall Justine and Zack's reunion hadn't been an easy one; but she knew deep down it was the *right* one. If the mortals resolved their differences now, their assignment would be over. There would be no reason to stay, but Mini knew she couldn't leave the nest, and she feared she would not be able to make Reuben understand *why*.

Underhanded tactics seemed her only alternative at this point. When the time came, she would confess all and beg Reuben's forgiveness. She would then do everything in her power to make it right between Zack and Justine, even if she had to break the golden rule and use magic on one or both.

Looking at the mortals, Mini said, "They look like they're doing fine, Reuben." Maybe *too* fine? she wondered, casting a worried glance at the nesting box.

Reuben snorted. "Look at him—he hasn't made a move in thirty minutes. The man's a fool! I turned out the lights, and what does *he* do? He turns the lamp on !" With an angry curse, he thrust his wing out. The lamp flickered off.

Mini cocked her head, listening to the conversation that erupted between the couple. If she wasn't careful, Reuben would succeed, and they would be free to leave.

"The lamp must have a short," Zack muttered.

"Yes, it must."

Justine's profile, illuminated by the light of the television, turned in Zack's direction just as Zack looked at her. They froze, staring into each other's eyes.

Mini panicked. With a crafty twitch of her wing—the one her husband couldn't see—she created a diversion.

Twenty-five

Zack was going to kiss her, and she was going to let him.

Why shouldn't she? Justine asked herself. Tonight she'd discovered just how wrong she'd been about Zack. He hadn't pressured her, hadn't pulled the seduction scene she'd fully expected. He wasn't the monster she had thought, and he hadn't lied about Dennis.

Maybe she should trust him . . . give *them* another chance.

Her lips parted in anticipation as his mouth edged closer. She inhaled his clean male scent, and the acrid smell of smoke—

Smoke!

Justine's eyes flew open. "Zack, I smell smoke."

"What?" he croaked. Then *his* eyes flew wide. His nostrils flared. He leaped from the couch just as the smoke alarm began to beep its strident warning.

She followed his headlong rush into the bathroom, coughing as a thick cloud of smoke rushed to meet her. Through the haze, she saw Zack bending over the bathtub, heard him curse as he twisted the faucets.

"Should I call the fire department?" she gasped out.

"No, I think I've got it."

Water sizzled, and steam rose to smother the smoke. When the air cleared, Justine stepped forward and looked down at the soggy mess in the bathtub. The roses were crushed but recognizable. A silver dome lay on its side, revealing two charred Cornish hens surrounded by a fancy green garnish. She spotted a broken stem from a wineglass, and the melted remains of a white candle.

Roses, candles . . . wineglasses. She realized now why he'd shut her out of the apartment when they first arrived. He had apparently decided to change his game plan at the last moment.

Justine clenched her fists. Her heart filled with disappointment.

It had almost worked. She'd been trembling with anticipation, thinking, wanting desperately to believe she was wrong about Zack.

She pivoted and walked from the room.

"Justine, this isn't what you think," Zack called after her, sounding frustrated and angry.

Of course he was angry—at being discovered as the sly, sneaky heartbreaker that he was!

"I can explain!"

Well, now, that would be a new one. Zack explaining instead of disappearing. Justine grabbed her coat from the hall closet, ignoring Zack as he reached her. Her foot bumped against something on the floor. She reached down and grasped the object, sucking in a furious breath.

"Justine, will you at least let me explain?"

"Can you explain *this*, Zack?" Justine held the packaged condom between her fingers and waved it in front of his face. She threw it at his chest, viewing his startled expression through a blur of tears. "I was beginning to think . . . it doesn't matter. Please call me a cab."

"I'll take you home."

Stiffly she said, "That won't be necessary." The thought of listening to his *explanations* made her physically ill. "I just want to go home and forget this night ever happened."

His voice was harsh, his fingers none too gentle as he grabbed her arm. "Like you forgot about those four nights on the ship?"

The gall of the man! She jerked her arm from his grip, her scornful gaze raking him from head to toe. Inside she was shaking. "Look who's talking! You forgot for an entire year!" She cocked her head. "What did you do, Zack, wake up one morning and think to yourself, 'Hey, she was a pretty good lay. Maybe I should give her a call?' "

His mouth tightened. "This—*we*—are not about sex. The candles, the wine—it wasn't *my* idea!"

Justine laughed in his face. "Oh, yeah? And just whose idea was it?" She looked around as if searching the room. Her gaze landed on the caged lovebirds, and with unmistakable sarcasm, she drawled, "Was it *their* idea, Zack? Did Mini and Reuben conjure the wine and the roses?" She snapped her fingers as if a brilliant idea had suddenly occurred to her. "And the lights! I'll bet they turned out the lights, as well."

"As a matter of fact, I think they did."

She was too astonished to respond immediately. Finally she managed through clenched teeth, "Call me a cab!"

"Gladly!"

"Fine!"

Yanking the door open, Justine stepped into the hall and slammed it shut behind her. Just as she lifted her irate gaze, the door across the hall clicked shut.

Barry. For two cents she'd beat on his door and ask him if he'd like to take a picture! A tad ashamed of her childish thoughts, Justine descended the stairs and waited in the foyer for the cab.

She hoped the driver was a female!

The receptionist who answered the phone at Carl's Grab-A-Cab responded to Zack's barked order with gum-popping cheerfulness. After Zack replaced the receiver, he moved to

the window facing the street and propped a shoulder against
the wall.

For ten minutes he stood watch. A light snow had begun
to fall, coating the ground with a fine white powder. To oc-
cupy himself, Zack followed a few flakes as they spiraled
past the window on their lazy way to the ground.

The cab finally arrived, and he watched the dark shadow
of Justine's bundled form as she dashed out to meet it. Only
then did he allow himself to think.

She believed he was a heartless bastard, a lecher, and now
a lunatic. Or perhaps a compulsive liar. One thing was clear;
she hadn't believed in his innocence for a second. And why
should she? he asked himself. He had yet to tell her the truth
about what had happened on the ship with the forgetful steward. He clenched his jaw when he recalled how close he'd
been.

If the tablecloth hadn't caught on fire . . .

With a grim smile, Zack flung himself away from the window. It was time to get to the bottom of the recent pranks
and obvious meddling, and he had a gut feeling just where
he should start.

Striding to the birdcage, Zack grasped the top of the cover
and pulled it up and away. He cast it carelessly behind him.

The male lovebird—whom Zack remembered Justine calling Reuben—fluttered his wings and squawked at the sudden
intrusion. Zack stared at him for a moment, then transferred
his wrathful gaze to the nesting box. He could see the white-
ringed eye of the female as she gawked at him through a
small hole in the box. If it was possible for a bird to look
alarmed, this one did.

Folding his arms, Zack demanded, "What the hell is going
on? I thought you two were supposed to be on *my* side. At
least, that's what Jordan claims."

Reuben froze on the perch with one wrinkled foot in the
air; Zack heard a distinct feminine gasp from inside the nesting box.

"Surprised, Mini? Did you think I wouldn't make the connection after *that* little stunt?"

Silence.

Zack wasn't deterred. He knew he wasn't crazy, and he wasn't moving until he proved it. "You might as well speak up. I'm not going to leave you alone until I hear an explanation *and* an apology."

Reuben made a noise that sounded suspiciously like an outraged snort. Zack's eyebrow shot upward at the sound. Perhaps he was finally getting somewhere, which was a good thing, because he was beginning to feel very foolish.

Deliberately taunting, he focused on Reuben as he asked, "You don't think you owe me an apology? You and your chick not only wrecked my date, but also you've ruined my chances with Jus—"

"Why, you insufferable mortal!" Reuben screeched at him, his feathers bristling ominously. "*We* didn't ruin your chances, you blundering dimwit! *You* did that when you destroyed our hard work."

Zack gaped at the talking bird. He shouldn't have been surprised—he had suspected they weren't ordinary birds, hadn't he? After the bizarre happenings he'd witnessed tonight, he had little choice but to believe.

But the reality far suppressed his imaginings. Reuben's strident, furious voice was definitely not the voice of a parroting bird.

"Then you had yet another golden opportunity on the couch, but no, you had to sit there like a scared little boy on his first date!"

The insult registered, but Zack remained speechless. His mouth was dry, his heart was racing, yet his brain was slower to agree with his eyes and his ears.

It *was* true; the birds were magical.

Darting a glance at the nesting female, he amended his thought. *One* bird was magical; Mini had yet to speak.

"Why didn't you tell her about the steward?" Reuben demanded, pointing an accusing wing at him. "Are you completely brain-dead?"

A strange blue light shot from his wing to Zack's chest. Startled, Zack staggered backwards, brushing at his singed sweater. The attack snapped him out of his daze. "Stop that!"

"Well, he *can* talk!" Reuben jeered.

Frowning at the hole in his sweater, Zack decided it was time he put an end to the bird's abuse. "Try that again, and I'll—"

"No!" Mini shrieked, hopping from the box and skittering along the perch to stand beside Reuben. "Never, ever challenge a warlock!"

"A warlock?" Zack repeated skeptically. He had come to terms with the fact that they were magical, but . . . warlocks?

"Oh, dear," Mini said, staring at her mate with a wing clutched to her breast. "It's too late."

Puzzled, Zack followed her gaze. Reuben had straightened majestically on the perch, his wings folded across his breasts, his eyes closed. He seemed to be muttering something beneath his breath. Zack had an ugly suspicion Reuben's chanting and the pitying look Mini shot him were somehow linked.

"You shouldn't have challenged him."

Zack uttered a short laugh. It would be a cold day in hell when he cowered at the sight of a mealy-mouthed little—

"It sounds like a turning spell," Mini informed him, her look so grave it raised the hair along Zack's arms. "But our powers are diminished because we're birds, so it's possible it won't work."

His ears were ringing . . . and itching. Zack refrained from scratching, fearing what he would find. "Can't you stop him?" he demanded. He clasped his hands together to keep them from his ears.

Mini suddenly flapped her wings. "I've got an idea!" She leaned close and whispered something in Reuben's ear. His eyes flew wide.

Before Zack's astounded gaze, the bird fell backwards

from his perch, landing on his back with his toes stuck comically in the air. "What happened to him?"

"He fainted." She clapped a wing to her beak and giggled. "But I had to tell him sooner or later. Might as well be sooner."

Cautiously Zack stepped closer to the cage and inspected the prone lovebird. He almost felt sorry for the arrogant warlock. "What *did* you tell him?"

"I told him that he's going to be a father."

Zack glanced at the nest. "Didn't he already know?"

Mini shrugged. "I told him a few days ago, but he didn't believe me. That was before I laid the first egg."

Reuben's foot twitched, and Zack took an involuntary step away from the cage. He flushed when Mini flashed him a knowing glance.

"He may be a bird, but he's also a warlock. You might keep that in mind when he awakens."

Zack did a perfect imitation of Reuben's earlier snort. "He doesn't scare me."

"He should," she informed him in a tone too serious to ignore. "Reuben's always had a powerful temper. When he was a warlock he—" She broke off, casting a nervous glance at the unconscious bird.

"So, he's not a warlock?"

"He is, but he isn't."

"I'm confused."

"When he married me, he gave up his warlock ways—or most of them. He's still incredibly stubborn, horrendously hot-tempered, and totally insensitive."

Zack arched a brow at her descriptive, heartfelt words. "How did you become lovebirds?"

Mini groaned and rubbed a wing over her back. "Mortals and their curiosity! It's a long story, so you'd better pull up a chair. I've got to return to the egg before it becomes cold."

When Reuben let out a moan and began to stir, she quickly chanted a spell over his body. Intrigued, Zack watched as

Reuben's beak parted. Soft snores erupted from his open mouth.

"I conjured a little sleeping spell to give him time to cool off and give *us* time to have a nice long chat without interruption. Meanwhile, you'd better be working on your apology."

"Apology?" She thought *he* should apologize to *Reuben?* Zack laughed, shaking his head. "Now I think *you're* confused. I'm the victim. I'm not apologizing to anyone."

"Okay. If you want to wear those donkey ears forever, that's your business." She made the rings around her eyes wiggle suggestively. "*I* think they're kinda cute, but what will Justine think?"

As her meaning sank in, Zack felt the blood drain from his face, leaving him numb. He slowly lifted his hands to his ears and felt around.

Hair tickled his palms.

He moved his hands up, and found more ears covered with rough, bristly hair. Miles of ears . . .

They ended above his head in a hairy point.

When he opened his mouth to curse a blue streak, a braying sound emerged. To think he had actually believed taking care of a pair of innocent little lovebirds would be a piece of cake compared to Dennis!

Her cabdriver was definitely not female. He was thirtyish, with shaggy blond hair and a potbelly that his too-short jacket did not cover. He not only reeked of garlic and cigar smoke, but also he obviously didn't believe in car heaters, as her frozen toes could attest to.

Nevertheless, he'd gotten her home, and for that Justine thanked him and paid her fare without complaint.

Her van was parked at the curb, and acting on impulse, Justine climbed inside and turned the key. It would be embarrassing to call a towing service only to discover it was nothing more than a loose or corroded battery cable.

The van purred to life without a hitch.

She turned the engine off and tried again. It started instantly.

Justine frowned, tapping her fingers against the wheel. Her mind jumped from one possibility to another. Cold weather? Bad cables? Weak battery? Her knowledge about cars was limited, but in her opinion none of these possibilities fit the bill. Before her date with Zack, she had tried starting the van for five long, cold minutes. Not a single click or rumble did she hear.

What was going on?

She rubbed her frozen nose and stepped out onto the snow-crusted road, belatedly realizing she could be warm and cozy while she contemplated the mystery of her van. Besides, she needed a cup of hot chocolate to ease the ache in her throat, an ache that had continued to build during the cab ride.

The answering machine was blinking when she entered the apartment. By this time she figured Zack would have perfected his sorry story and wanted another shot at convincing her, so she ignored the blinking light and took her time boiling hot water for instant cocoa.

When the cocoa was ready, she braced herself and pressed the button on her answering machine. She felt a quick, illogical stab of disappointment as Jordan's boyish voice rose from the speaker.

"Aunt Justine, this is Jordan. Mom thought—well, *I* thought so, too," he amended, sounding sheepish, "I should call you and apologize to you personally. I know Zack's probably already told you, and I know you're probably disappointed in me."

Justine's anger at him began to melt at his sincere tone. Deep down she knew Jordan was a good kid. He'd learned his lesson, and had acted responsibly in paying the price.

His voice picked up, sounding excited. "I hope you had fun on your date with Zack. He's a pretty cool guy. I mean, any guy who would go to the trouble he did tonight—"

The machine beeped, ending the unfinished message and leaving Justine's curiosity highly aroused. She would have

given just about anything to hear the rest of his sentence.
Trouble? Chili, crackers, and milk. Granted, the chili had
probably taken a bit of preparation, but she wouldn't exactly
call it *trouble.*

Thinking the message over, Justine turned away with
every intention of finishing her chocolate and crawling into
bed. She needed a good, cleansing cry.

Melissa Copeland's voice stopped her in her tracks.

"Justine, you won't *believe* what happened today! Mrs.
Winberry came in with her cat, and she's claiming the goldfish you gave her attacked him! Can you imagine? A goldfish
attacking a cat?" Melissa's disbelieving laugh rippled from
the speaker. "His paw was mangled, so I'm guessing he tangled with a dog."

Justine swayed and grabbed the island counter for support,
remembering big, impossible teeth grinning at her through a
plastic sack the day she replaced Mrs. Winberry's fish.

"Anyway, just thought I would alert you. The old lady
said something about calling her lawyer. She thinks *you*
should pay her vet bill."

Hot chocolate soaked through Justine's jeans. She let out
a sharp cry and dropped the cup, staring at the shattered
pieces with burning, stunned eyes.

Her heart thundered. Slowly she reached out and pressed
the button on her machine, replaying the message.

Twenty-six

Beneath her mask of black feathers, Mini could feel the guilt-induced flush burning her skin. Throughout her entire story, Zack had listened patiently, interrupting only to ask a question or to correct a flaw in the telling.

Reuben still slept.

"So you see, Zack, tonight's fiasco was my fault. I suspected Justine's hackles would rise if she believed you were setting her up just to . . . to . . ."

"Jump her bones?" Zack supplied.

Mini cleared her throat, uncomfortable with the subject. If Reuben should hear her talking sex with another man, Zack would have more to scratch than just his ridiculously large donkey ears. "Yes. I was afraid tonight would be the night, and our assignment would be finished."

"And you believe Reuben would insist you leave the egg." Thoughtfully Zack rubbed his chin. "Sounds to me like you and Justine have the same problem."

"Problem?" Mini frowned. "I'm not following you."

"Well, Justine doesn't trust me to not love her and leave her again, and you won't give Reuben the benefit of the doubt that he might understand your mothering instincts."

Sorrow welled in Mini's breast. "He thinks I'm crazy for making a nest. He'll think I'm even crazier for laying eggs and staying with them. I'm a witch, not a bird."

"Ah, but right now you're both," Zack pointed out. "And so is he. He hasn't seen the egg, right?"

Mini shook her head. A single tear rolled from her eye and soaked the feathers on her breast. "No. I was afraid to show him. He's going to laugh—"

"Maybe not. Maybe he won't laugh. Maybe *he'll* get that same feeling *you've* got and want to take care of the eggs until you can safely leave them."

Despair thickened her voice. "But what if he *doesn't* have that reaction? What if he makes me leave the eggs?"

"That's where trust comes in, Mini."

A shuddering sigh lifted the feathers on her breast. "Okay, so let's say he does agree to stay until they hatch. What then? What if I can't bring myself to leave the babies?" Her obsession over bird eggs had ceased to amaze her. Now it just seemed natural. She supposed the thought should have frightened her, but it didn't.

Zack pulled absently at his ear. "Do you think I took good care of Dennis?"

"Yes. Yes, I do." She bobbed her beak. "I was proud of you. I'm not sure I would have been so patient with the little squirt."

"Well, there's your answer. Justine has experience, and she'll have me to help."

"And Jordan," Mini added thoughtfully.

"And Jordan. Three people you trust. We'd take good care of them for you—*if* it so happens you have to leave after they hatch. I'm putting my money on Reuben, though."

Reluctantly Mini consented. "All right, and thanks, Zack. I realize you have problems of your own—"

"Which reminds me." Zack crossed his ankles, his hip propped against the couch. "I think I'm going to lay all my cards on the table and let the chips fall where they may."

Mini struggled to translate. "Tell Justine everything?"

Zack nodded. "Yep. After tonight, what have I got to lose?"

His solemn expression tugged at Mini's heartstrings and deepened her guilt. "Trust her, Zack. It's all about trust anyway, isn't it? If she's going to be your life mate, she has to learn to trust you now." She paused to let that sink in before she added, "But, Zack, don't expect her to believe you about *us*. When you and Justine were on the cruise ship, she was so happy I think she would have believed in anything—even magic."

"But now?" Zack asked softly.

"Now she's more cautious. Her mind has put up safeguards, and I'm afraid they won't be easy to get around."

A knock at the door startled a shriek out of Mini. "Zack! Your ears! Get something and cover them up, and I'll wake Reuben. Maybe I can convince him to reverse the spell."

Zack scowled. "*Maybe?* He'll reverse it, or I'll—"

"Zack!" Mini's voice rose as she glanced into her crystal ball. "We don't have time to argue. It's Justine!"

The urgency in Mini's voice moved Zack to action. With a string of curses spilling from his mouth, he raced to his bedroom closet and pawed through the clutter on the top shelf. Talk about amazing animal stories! He couldn't believe he was looking for a hat to cover his donkey ears! Zack shook his head at the absurd thought, shoving a football helmet onto the floor in his mad search.

With a triumphant shout, he pulled out a battered baseball cap and clamped it over his ears. It was a tight fit, but it would have to do.

Justine nearly fell into the room when he opened the door, giving Zack the impression that she might have had her ear to the wood. He caught her against him, relishing the contact and inhaling the cold, clean scent of her hair. "Gee, when you fall for a guy, you really fall hard," he teased gruffly. Had it only been an hour since he'd last seen her? It felt like a lifetime.

"I have to talk to you about Jordan," she said breathlessly. She pulled away from his arms and brushed her hair from her eyes. "I think he might have been in your apartment tonight."

Zack shut the door and braced his shoulder against it. "What gave you that idea?" He knew from Mini that Jordan had helped set the romantic scene waiting for them, of course, but he was extremely curious to discover how *she* knew.

"It all makes sense. You were surprised, weren't you? You didn't just change your plans from Cornish hens to chili, did you?"

"Are you asking, or making a statement?"

Justine drew in an agitated breath, her eyes flashing him a warning. "Look, I'm trying to put this puzzle together, and you're not helping by mocking me. I realize I didn't give you a chance to explain and I'm sorry."

"But now you're willing to listen," Zack observed. He wanted to shout with joy. Justine had come to *him*. She was saving him from having to kidnap, bind, and gag her. Instead of shouting, however, he held out his hand for her coat. "You'd better get comfortable. This might take a while."

She fumbled with her coat buttons until Zack gently pushed her hands away and finished the job. When he'd removed her coat, he gently led her to the table and pushed her into a seat. He pulled a chair around and straddled it so that he was facing her.

"My father suffered a stroke," he announced abruptly.

Her face washed clean of color. Tears sprang to her eyes. "Oh, Zack," she whispered, "I'm sorry! How—how is he?"

"He died."

"God! Why didn't you tell me?"

"I haven't had a chance."

"When did it happen?"

"Which one?" Zack queried softly.

"Both! Oh, darling . . ." Stricken, she glanced away from his intent gaze. "I'm sorry. That just slipped out."

Zack let it go for now. In a moment he was pretty certain she'd forget all about being embarrassed over calling him darling, and with any luck, she'd be calling him darling the rest of his life.

Bracing himself, he said, "He suffered his first stroke the day I left the cruise ship. Six months later, he suffered his second stroke. Eight months after the first, he died."

She became so still and pale Zack feared she'd faint.

Her voice was a hoarse whisper. "Why didn't you tell me?"

Here came the tricky part. Zack was suddenly seized with a terrible fear that she wouldn't believe him. As he hesitated, Mini's soft, encouraging voice filled his head with startling clarity. *"Trust her, Zack."*

"I left a message with one of the stewards," Zack said, looking straight into her beautiful golden eyes. For a long moment their gazes remained locked. He knew she was looking for the truth, but he couldn't tell if she'd found it. "The message contained my address and phone number and the reason I had to go."

"I didn't get it." Her neutral tone revealed nothing. "Why didn't you call?"

"We never exchanged phone numbers, remember? We both thought we had plenty of time. At first when you didn't call, I thought you were maybe just busy. My father was so ill I didn't have much time to think about it. After a month, I tried to find your number, but there was no listing for a Justine Diamond."

"It's unlisted." Justine felt a rising horror as the pieces of the puzzle began to fall into place. With Barry's betrayal fresh in her mind at the time, she hadn't wanted to talk about the past or anything personal, with the exception of her family. She hadn't wanted anything to mar the wonderful magic she'd discovered when she met Zack.

"So I gathered. After a few months, I forced myself to face the truth; that you'd changed your mind about us."

"But I . . ." Justine tried to say the words, but fear locked her throat tight. Zack's understanding nod made her blush guiltily.

"I still couldn't get you out of my mind. Then Dad had his second stroke. I was running the business, so between working and taking care of him, I couldn't pull away to come looking for you." His voice dropped. "By that time I knew I couldn't get on with my life until I won you back, or heard from your own lips that what we have isn't real."

Have. Justine hugged the word to herself, afraid, so terribly afraid to believe. Even more afraid not to. Inch by inch, she stretched her hand across the table until her fingers touched his. "You—you came to Cannon Bay for me?"

He smiled crookedly. "No, I came to Cannon Bay for the nice weather. Of course I came for you." His smile dropped abruptly, and a cold, hard light entered his eyes. "If I ever run into that steward again, I'm afraid I might do a little damage to his kneecaps."

Justine let a trickle of joy seep into her heart. She grinned. "And I'll stand guard."

His fingers captured hers. He brought her hand to his mouth and brushed his lips tenderly across her skin. She shivered and closed her eyes.

This time there was a flood of joy, and no resistance.

"I love you, Justine," he said roughly, pulling her onto his lap. "These past thirteen months have been hell."

"Yes," she agreed, winding her arms around his neck. The bill of his cap struck her squarely in the nose. She grabbed it with every intention of removing it.

"No!"

His frantic shout startled her. She jerked away with the cap in her hand, her alarmed gaze on his equally alarmed expression. "Zack? What is it?" Bewildered, she looked on as he felt his ears.

She heard a tiny, muffled cackle from the direction of the birdcage.

"Nothing. It's nothing *now.*"

He sounded adorably disgruntled and relieved. Justine

smiled and linked her arms around his neck again. She pressed her breasts against his face and held him tight. "I love you," she whispered.

Tugging at her arms, Zack pulled her face to his and claimed her mouth in a long, lingering kiss that left her breathless and aching. She broke the kiss reluctantly. "Take me to bed," she ordered.

"Yes, ma'am!"

She laughed as he stood and lifted her in his arms. When they drew even with the birdcage, Justine winked and waved at Mini and Reuben. "I'll talk to *you* guys later."

Zack froze in place, staring into her smiling face. "You *know* about them?"

She nodded, giggling at his expression. "Oh, yeah, and I have a bone to pick with Reuben about a goldfish with big teeth."

His brow shot upward as he whispered, "Just be careful. He doesn't take criticism very well."

"Zack?"

"Hmm?"

"I love you."

"I love you, too." He found the hollow in her neck and nuzzled with his lips. "Do you mind if I show you how much?"

"Hmm. Not at all."

He stepped across the threshold with Justine in his arms.

When the door closed on the reunited couple, Mini said in a small voice, "I guess this means we can go home."

Reuben looked at her in surprise. "You don't sound happy about the prospect. I thought that's what you wanted."

This is it, Mini thought. She took her husband's wing and tugged him around to the back of the nesting box. "Come here. I want to show you something." She hopped in and gestured for him to follow. When he was inside, she brushed the feathers away to reveal the egg.

Reuben gasped and swayed on his skinny legs.

"If you faint and crack this egg, I'll never speak to you again," Mini warned.

Amazingly, Reuben straightened at her threat. He looked at the egg for a long, long time.

He didn't laugh, as Mini expected. She slowly exhaled, wishing she knew what he was thinking. "I'm going to have three more, I think. After that, it will take a couple of weeks for all of them to hatch. Zack said he and Justine, with Jordan's help, would care for them after they hatch." *She* wanted to care for them herself, but she knew she didn't dare hope—

"If you think," Reuben began so fiercely that Mini stumbled back a step, "that I'm going to let those bumbling mortals take care of our babies, then you are most certainly out of your mind!"

His voice ended in a roar.

Mini tottered. The box began to spin around her. She drooped forward, and her last amazed thought before she fainted was that she was going to crack her own egg.

Reuben caught his wife before she could damage the precious egg. He held her in his wings, his tiny heart swelling with love. "Foolish witch," he murmured tenderly. "Married two hundred years and you *still* don't know me."

With his wings occupied, he used his toes to cover the exposed egg with the loose feathers. He could have used magic with a twitch of his wing tip, but he didn't.

For some strange reason, it didn't feel right.

TIME PASSAGES